BALTIC COMMANDO

BALTIC COMMANDO

Peter Leslie

This first world edition published in Great Britain 1997 by
SEVERN HOUSE PUBLISHERS LTD of
9–15 High Street, Sutton, Surrey SM1 1DF.
First published in the U.S.A. 1997 by
SEVERN HOUSE PUBLISHERS INC., of
595 Madison Avenue, New York, NY 10022.

British Library Cataloguing in Publication Data

Leslie, Peter
        Baltic commando
        1.   World War, 1939-1945 - Campaigns - Atlantic Ocean - Fiction
        2.   War stories
        I. Title
        823.9'14 [F]

        ISBN 0-7278-5208 6

Typeset by Palimpsest Book Production Limited,
Polmont, Stirlingshire, Scotland.
Printed and bound in Great Britain by
Hartnolls Ltd, Bodmin, Cornwall.

This one is for Ken Smiley, companion of many nocturnal adventures, who was kind enough, one Blitz night in 1943, to introduce me to the original on whom the character of Charles G. Fortune is based.

The original 'Major Webster' was a flight-lieutenant in the Royal Air Force when I met him. He was reputed to have been the only pilot ever to loop a Handley-Page Heyford bomber. The machine was subsequently taken out of service.

Prologue

The Snow Queen

The walls of the Palace were formed of driven snow, its doors and windows of the cutting winds; no sounds of mirth ever resounded through these dreary spaces; no cheerful scene refreshed the eye.

The hunted man leaped over the gunwale and splashed ashore through the shallows as his dinghy grounded on fine shingle. The pursuers couldn't be far behind: already he could hear the steady beat of the motor-boat engine on the far side of the long, low spit of land hiding the inlet from the open sea. If only he could make the shelter of the dunes before they rounded the point he might have a chance. It would be no more than a slim chance, but it would be better than nothing.

The back-breaking row across the sound had exhausted him. His breath creaked in his lungs as he staggered up the steeply shelving pebble beach. The put-put-put of the motor-boat was much louder now. It would be clear of the promontory at any moment. Frantically, he glanced over his shoulder, feet scrabbling among the shifting stones. The desolate, steel-grey waters of the creek were still empty.

With a sob of relief, the fugitive clambered up the final ridge of shingle. Beyond this was a stretch of soft sand that dragged agonisingly at his waterlogged shoes, slowing him down, slowing him down. But at last he was among the tall dune grasses, stumbling like a drunken man to pitch forward and lie face down on the damp ground, fighting back the panic threatening to choke him.

But he dared not rest for an instant. Panting, he hauled himself up onto his hands and knees, and peered back through the reeds. They were at the mouth of the creek now. He could see the gleam of steel helmets over field-grey uniforms as the small craft surged towards the shore. An officer in a peaked cap and a long greatcoat stood up in the stern, shouting a command over the noise of the engine. They had seen his boat.

Painfully, the hammering of his heart tightening an iron band around his chest, the hunted man rolled down the far side of the sandy slope and got to his feet. There was no escape for him now, he knew; it was just a question of whether or not he could stall them off long enough for him to get to the radio and send the message. He stared desperately around him. Under a sullen sky, the flat island landscape spread away on either side, featureless in the gathering dusk. A long way to the north, the domed tower of Bagenkop church rose above a line of trees, but otherwise there was no sign of life. Between the dunes and the road to the town, ploughed fields lay awash, the ridges of sandy earth barely surfacing above the water in the furrows. It would be useless trying to make it that way: the sodden ground would be harder going than the sand, and he'd be a sitting duck as soon as the pursuers breasted the rise behind him. There was no alternative: he would have to run through the dunes and head for the village, three-quarters of a mile to the south.

They would know he must have gone that way, of course. If he wasn't crossing the fields, there was no other way he could go. He could only hope that one man, running light, exhausted as he was, could outdistance uniformed soldiers carrying guns and equipment. In any case, the undulations of the sand-hills following the shore should give him a certain amount of cover.

He set off at a lumbering trot, the breath rasping in his throat.

He had gone less than a hundred yards, keeping to the firmer sand at the foot of the dunes, when the engine of the pursuers' boat was cut as it ran ashore. In the sudden silence, the barking of the officer's orders, the clink of equipment and the splash of wading men sounded frighteningly close. Eyes staring, nostrils flared, the hunted man willed his failing legs to carry him faster.

A low murmur of wind stirred the grasses on the slope above his head, and a squall of rain blew past him like a cloud of smoke. Seconds later a persistent drizzle began to fall from the darkening sky. It rolled up behind him from the north and east, soaking the shoulders of his thin jacket, plastering the hair to his skull and striking cold against the sea-wet legs of his trousers.

He ran doggedly on, heedless of the shouts behind as the

4

soldiers spilled over the lip of the dunes and sighted him, ignoring the crack of rifles and the whine of bullets over his hunched, zigzagging figure. He could hear nothing now but the thudding of his own feet, the pounding of blood in his ears and the anguished whistle of his breath. His mind was empty of everything but the three stages of that goal he must at all costs achieve: *the village, the radio, the message . . .*

The white walls and slate mansards of the village had disappeared in the murk. Sea and sky formed a single dun backdrop, and the ripples flowing across the Kieler Bucht from the Danish mainland were breaking into tumbles of dirty grey foam.

The soldiers spread out through the dunes in pursuit of their quarry.

Erik Bergstrom heard the clatter of running feet on the cobbles of the village street as he stowed away his nets. Frowning, he hurried out onto the slipway and crouched behind his upturned boat. The rain had already silvered the slate roofs of the houses and polished the granite quay.

Bergstrom recognised the wild figure of the hunted man as soon as he erupted around the corner of the fish-loft. "Hanson!" he called, rising quickly to his feet. "What the devil . . . ? We were expecting you yesterday!"

Hanson collapsed across the curving belly of the boat, arms outflung, thin hair falling damply over his face while he gulped air into his labouring lungs. "Quick!" he choked. "Bastards after me . . . couple of hundred yards behind . . ."

"Krauts?"

Hanson nodded, barely able to speak. "Nothing doing at Marstal . . . Telder's blown. I almost walked into the swine . . . Managed to get away but they saw me rowing out past the jetty . . . Thank God the only craft afloat was that old tub of Halborg's: I was halfway across the sound before they could get her started! But they damned near caught me just the same . . . I had to run ashore at the creek."

"But you have the message?"

Again the exhausted man nodded, his wet face livid in the gloom. "Must send . . . right away," he gasped. "Could you, maybe . . . draw them off . . . while I . . . send?"

5

"Of course." Bergstrom helped Hanson to his feet. They could hear the pounding of jackboots now, at the far end of the village. "You know where it is," he murmured. "And . . . good luck, Olaf!"

"Good luck, Erik!"

For an instant they clasped hands, then Hanson lurched into the darkness of the boathouse at the head of the slip. Bergstrom swung shut the double doors, waited until he heard the heavy locking bolts slotted into place on the far side, and then ran noisily away along the hard.

Half the German patrol followed him, sweeping on along the narrow street; the remainder wheeled around the boathouse to cut off the waterfront.

Inside the building, Hanson felt his way up a ladder to the fish-loft. The radio transmitter was concealed under a loose floorboard beneath the window. Squatting down to grope inside the recess, he peered through the grimed glass at the quay. Far away along the cobbles, someone – curious perhaps about the sudden burst of noise – opened a door in one of the waterfront houses. Light streamed across the wet stones to fragment in the ripples lapping the jetty.

"Put out that damned light!" an angry voice shouted in German.

At the same time Bergstrom's sprinting figure jerked sharply into silhouette as he ran through the slanting beam of illumination.

For a hundredth of a second, Hanson saw the façades of the nearer buildings etched luridly against the dusk as rifles and machine-pistols spat flame in a shattering volley. Then Bergstrom, caught in a hail of fire like a puppet in a shooting gallery, was slammed against a mooring post to crumple sideways and slide from the dock into the sea.

Hanson uttered a cry of despair. He drew the blackout curtain across the window with trembling fingers. There was still a roaring in his ears, and his vision was dimmed at the edges. It could only be a matter of minutes now. Bergstrom had been a much taller man, and he was wearing a fisherman's jersey and sea boots. As soon as they dragged him out of the water they would realise they had made a mistake. After that, they would simply block off the street and start a house-to-house search from the scene of the killing back to the entrance to the village.

He took a box of matches from his pocket and lit an oil lamp. It was only at the fourth attempt that the phosphor head, damp from its immersion in his sodden jacket, spat into flame.

Carefully, he set up the clandestine transmitter. His own control would not be listening now, but he had been given a frequency that was monitored twenty-four hours a day. He would beam it out on that – and he would have to send the message in clear because there wasn't time to turn it into cipher groups or tap out Morse. Thank God he had memorised the right code-names, for the transmission would naturally be picked up by German monitors too. But it wouldn't mean a thing unless they had the wit to realise that there were map coordinates buried in the text. And even then . . . Hanson sighed. There was nothing else he could do anyway.

The loft smelled of fish and weathered rope and tar. It was very cold in the wavering light cast by the lamp. Hanson watched his shadow advance and recede across the wooden wall, twirling dials as he settled the headset over his ears. He shivered, plugging in the microphone. The earphones screeched. Somewhere outside, harsh voices called. Further away, they were already hammering on doors.

Now he had it right! The signal had been acknowledged. He pressed a key. Fighting to still the chattering of his teeth, he began to speak slowly in English.

"Operation Andersen . . . Operation Andersen," he called in a low voice. "Here is Hans transmitting with a Number One priority from Fairyland. Message begins. The tale can – repeat can – be told. The Snow Queen is alone in her Palace—"

He broke off with a gasp. Gun butts were pounding violently on the boathouse doors.

"The Palace," he went on desperately, "is fourteen – one four – point seven two three miles from the Giant's Castle . . . the Queen can see the fairies coming and going . . ."

The knocking had increased in volume. Now it stopped. There was a fusillade of shots, and then a louder hammering that shook the walls. The doors had no lock that could be shot out, but the old timber bolts wouldn't stand up to that kind of punishment for long. He had better finish it as quickly as he

7

could. With a shaking hand, he swivelled the heel of one shoe aside and took a twist of paper from the cavity it revealed.

"The Queen's treasure chest is buried within the Palace walls," Hanson said hoarsely. "Guess how many jewels there are inside. Yes, children, there are no less than one seven four nine . . ." Smoothing out the paper, he read off the string of figures scrawled beneath the juvenile metaphors he had made up and learned by heart.

There was a splintering of wood from below. "That is all," he said. "The wind is blowing. Message ends."

Glass shattered somewhere overhead and tinkled to the floor.

Aghast, Hanson looked up from the transmitter. He had forgotten to draw the blackout across the skylight in the steep, sloping roof. It would be visible from the quay.

The grenade which had dropped through rolled across the floor and came to rest against his foot.

In the split second of time that remained to him, Hanson's mind worked clearly. Bergstrom was dead. He himself was finished and they had taken Telder. That meant that it was only a matter of hours before they laid hands on the rest of the cell, because Telder would crack. They would get Nils and Bengt and Helga too. There was nothing he could do for them now. But at least he had got the message through: Operation Andersen would proceed as planned. They couldn't take that away from him.

The only thing that remained was to make sure – absolutely, positively, one hundred per cent certain – that there was no way they could find out what his mission had been.

Bergstrom had been the only one to know the details and he couldn't talk now. Hanson's eyes registered the tell-tale scrap of paper beside the radio. How could he be certain that it was destroyed?

Burn it? There wasn't time.

Swallow it? Helmut had tried that and they ripped open his stomach while he was still alive and recovered the paper before the writing was totally obliterated. No, there was only one foolproof way, for the effects of nearby explosions could be capricious . . .

Leaning swiftly down, he wrapped the paper around the deadly little bomb and then clutched it to his belly.

8

Part One

The Wild Swans

Tonight when I was among the reeds where the quagmire will scarcely bear me, I saw three swans flying past, and there was something about their flight which said to me, "Beware! Watch them: they are not real swans! They are only in swans' plumage."

Chapter One

The fight wasn't really the fault of the commandos. It started the way pub fights usually did in wartime – too much drink and not enough women. The Scottish Highland battalion quartered in the village had by now got used to the commandos, a tough-looking group of about twenty men who kept very much to themselves. But tonight there were strangers in the bar. About nine o'clock two corporals from some southern infantry regiment lounged in. A little later it was a Cockney sergeant with a big-breasted blonde wearing the light-blue uniform of the Woman's Auxiliary Air Force. The moment he saw her, the barman knew there would be trouble.

She moved her ample body inside the shapeless jacket and skirt like a practised whore, and her wide violet eyes roved from man to man in the smoky, crowded saloon as though she were weighing them up to decide which one was fit to share her bed. Every soldier in the place was aware of her by the time the burly sergeant had shouldered his way through to the counter and ordered their first drinks.

The barman sighed as he turned the taps beneath the upended bottles of whisky and gin, flicking his eyes sideways to check that the sand-filled sock was in its accustomed place on the ledge to the right of the beer engine. The blonde was already staring in a calculated way at two tall commandos leaning over their tankards a little way along the bar. For the hundredth time he wondered what the hell the unit was doing in this God-forsaken hole anyway. The village was ten miles from Wick, on the north-eastern tip of Scotland, and there was no combined-ops base within fifty miles. The Highlanders, most of them raw conscripts from Glasgow and Greenock, were always out on manoeuvres, playing war games over the barren, rolling country inland, but the commandos, who were

11

billeted in an abandoned manse overlooking the cold wastes of the North Sea, never seemed to do anything. There were hardly enough of them to make up a platoon, anyway!

Not that they ever caused trouble in the pub, although there were expected grumbles from the few locals who hadn't been drafted into the army or the munitions factories: their allowances were too generous . . . they had too much time on their hands . . . they bribed the village girls with extra rations . . . they had no idea of discipline.

There had been poachers nevertheless on the grouse moors behind the village. Colonel Campbell swore that he'd seen three of them – in uniform! – netting salmon on his estate. And a Bedford 10-cwt van loaded with cartons of cigarettes for the NAAFI at the Highlanders' camp had disappeared one night from the car park beside the church . . . just vanished into thin air!

That didn't have to be the commandos, of course (the barman mused as he drew two more pints of dark ale for the English corporals). There'd been a lot of criticism about the calibre of these Lowland conscripts pushed into a crack Highland regiment. It was funny, just the same, all these things happening in a remote and placid village so soon after the arrival of the hard men with the green berets. As for the local girls – thought the barman, who came from Northern Ireland – the strangers were welcome to them! Probably they couldn't care less anyway: there were rumours that a coachload of women arrived at the old house once a week from Inverness.

This blonde WAAF with the big tits, though – she was a bit of all right! Several of the young Highlanders were eyeing her covertly over their beer, and the commandos, most of whom had been drinking steadily since opening-time nearly four hours ago, were openly discussing how good she might be in bed. The few village girls in the bar were talking very fast and very earnestly to their companions, pretending they hadn't seen her at all.

The Cockney sergeant drained his double Scotch and threaded his way through the boisterous crowd towards a cigarette machine standing beside the blackout curtains masking one of the pub's mullioned windows. Beyond the window, doors labelled *Lads* and *Lassies* bore identical kilted silhouettes. The

12

machine, which was empty, carried a small placard reading: *Don't you know there's a war on?* Banging it angrily with his fist, the sergeant disappeared through the first door.

The blonde finished her drink and turned around, leaning back with her elbows on the bar so that the breasts tilted provocatively upwards. Coolly, she surveyed the drinkers once more, and then she caught the eye of the tall, rangy commando with the Canada shoulder flash who was standing next to her. The Canadian grinned.

"Hi, soldier!" the girl said. "What brings you so far north?" The voice was husky, unmistakably southern, with a touch of Mayfair drawl.

He frowned. "Business," he replied tersely. "Didn't they tell you about security at your finishing school?" He jerked his head at a framed notice above the bar announcing: *Careless Talk Costs Lives.*

The blonde was unrepentant. "Sorry. I was only trying to be friendly," she smiled. "You know – extend a welcoming hand to our gallant allies."

"Now you're talking!" the Canadian exclaimed. "Baby, I could sure go a bundle on friendship with you, hand or no hand! You know what I mean?"

The man next to him guffawed. "Would you listen to that!" he said. "Are you after runnin' a private club there, or can a person join in at all?"

"I'll make you a founder member, Barry," the Canadian said. "I reckon there's enough here for more than one, at that!" His eyes roamed over the out-thrust curves of the blue uniform. "We was – uh – talking about international friendship."

The girl picked up her empty glass. "I'm thirsty," she said. "If you really want to be friendly, you could buy me a drink."

"No sooner asked than done, lady. What'll it be?"

"A gin and lime, actually. That's very kind of you."

"My pleasure. Hey, lemme introduce myself. Name of Renard. I mean like foxy, you dig? From Montreal" – he pronounced it in the French way: Mon-ray-all. "And this here's my buddy, Barry Reilly, who hails from the wilds of Cork." He turned to the barman. "Pat, you lazy bum: a large gin and lime for the lady."

13

By the time the sergeant returned from the men's room, the girl was in the centre of a vivacious group of commandos, her violet eyes switching from face to flushed face as they flirted and joked and kidded her along. There was a half-finished drink in her hand, and two more lined up on the bar beside her elbow.

The Cockney glanced sharply at the group, went back to his place and ordered another large Scotch. "Jill!" he called. "I thought you was supposed to be with me?"

Either the blonde didn't hear him, or she affected not to, for she continued smiling and talking to the men around her. The sergeant's eyes were slitted and there were beads of perspiration dewing his forehead. Breathing heavily, he slid his glass along the bar and shifted nearer to them. "Jill!" he rapped more loudly. "Come back here!"

The barman's hand was hovering close by the sap hidden below the counter. Still the WAAF paid no attention to the angry sergeant. "Oh, you!" she laughed up into Renard's face. "Americans, Canadians, you're all alike: a girl never knows when to take you seriously! Anyway, it's no good my giving you my number now: I've just been posted."

Abruptly, the sergeant levered himself upright off the bar. Shoving Renard roughly aside, he reached in and snatched the glass from the girl's hand, banging it down on the counter beside the other two.

"Hey, who the hell d'you think you're pushing?" the tall Canadian glowered.

The Cockney ignored him. "When I take a skirt out on a date," he said thickly to the blonde, "I don't expect her to piss off with the first bleedin' Yank to flash his wallet at her."

There was a sudden silence in the saloon. Laughter and shouts and conversation ceased as though an unseen hand had turned off a switch. The WAAF swung slowly around towards her escort. She raised her eyebrows. "*What* did you say?"

"You heard."

She compressed her lips. "Ronnie," she said, "just for once, do *try* and behave like a little *tiny* gentleman!"

"Gentleman, is it?" the sergeant shouted, flushing with rage. "You call it the act of a gentleman to worm your bloody way

14

in and try to pinch a bloke's girl the minute his fuckin' back's turned? Is that the kind of behaviour—"

"Just a minute, buster," Renard interrupted, placing himself in front of the blonde. "Number One, there's no Americans in this bar. Number Two, nobody's tryin' to horn in on anybody. The lady spoke to us first, as it happens: she *asked us* to buy her a drink. It's still a free country, no? Or d'you wanna make something of it?"

"Mind your own bloody business," the sergeant yelled. "Nobody asked your opinion, you loud-mouthed cunt. This is between me and her. You keep your damned nose out of it."

And then suddenly everyone was shouting at the same time.

"Gentlemen, please!"

"Pack it in, mates, for Pete's sake!"

"I'm sick and tired of you bloody Yanks—"

"It was the girl's fault."

"No Limey sonofabitch is gonna call me—"

"Ronnie, for God's sake!"

"Who does he think he is – fucking Montgomery?"

"Just another drunk from the wrong side of the border . . ."

"Aye, ye can expect neether yon nor the ither to behave in a civilised fashion."

"I reckon I know when some fucker's tryin' to pinch my girl!" the sergeant cried furiously. "Bloody *bastards!*" Without warning, without looking, he swept an arm backwards along the polished top of the counter. Bottles and glasses smashed to the floor. A soda siphon toppled, rolled over the edge and exploded against the brass rail below. Water splashed from an overturned jug.

The barman grabbed the offending arm and reached for the sap with his free hand. "What d'ye think ye're doin'?" he demanded. "Sure, ye can't carry on like that in here. Come on now, away out of it!"

Before he could produce the sap, the Cockney danced out of range. "There's one or two of our gallant bloody allies need to be taught a lesson," he roared. Ducking down swiftly, he picked up the broken top of the siphon, still bristling with shards of glass, and advanced menacingly on the angry commandos.

15

"Now come on, come on," the bartender shouted. "That's quite enough of that. Outside, you!"

He raised the flap of the counter and hurled himself through, closely followed by the landlord, who had hurried in from the private bar at the sound of raised voices. The sand-filled sock rose and fell, numbing the sergeant's arm so that the wicked improvised weapon fell from his nerveless fingers. Then they grabbed him by the elbows and ran him towards the door.

He heaved, dragging them from side to side in a series of frenzied lurches. The three of them cannoned into a group of locals at the far end of the bar. "Och, look out what ye're doin' there!" one cried out wrathfully, dabbing spilled beer from his jacket.

"Throw him out!" yelled another.

"The *language* of him!"

"Will you look at that, now!"

The Englishman was swearing viciously as he fought. Together with his two captors, he crashed into a table. For a moment there was a tangle of limbs threshing on the floor, then they rolled into the men around the bar again, bringing down two Scots and a commando. And the next minute – nobody quite knew how it happened: somebody pushed someone, somebody tripped, a voice called out an insult, a man was too ready with the back of a hand – there was a free-for-all raging all along the bar. Soldiers swore, chairs and tables overturned, fists flew.

The civilians crowded back towards the toilet doors. Some of the girls screamed. The sergeant was on his feet again, swapping punches with Renard and Reilly. The two English corporals were fighting off three more commandos who had tried to come to the aid of their friends, and the rest of the green berets were embroiled with a group of Highlanders further along the bar. Somebody had knocked out the barman with his own cosh. The landlord was in the back room, calling the Military Police.

Renard stumbled back under the impact of a vicious left hook carrying all the sergeant's weight behind it, fell over a broken chair and sprawled to the floor. At the same time Reilly rabbit-punched the Cockney and, as the man doubled over, brought up a knee to smash sickeningly into his adversary's face.

16

The sergeant was tough. Shaking his head, he came up with blood streaming from his nose to swing a murderous back-hander at the Irishman's throat with the flat of his hand. Reilly rode with the blow and came back off the bar with a judo lock on the sergeant's arm. The sergeant blocked it and threw Reilly over his shoulder. Behind them, a huge commando as tall as Renard and two stone heavier broke another chair over the head of a Highlander.

By now Renard was on his feet again. He slammed a long, looping left to the side of the sergeant's head, whirled sideways to take a savage kick to the groin on one thigh, then punched the Englishman low in the belly. As the winded man folded forward, he whipped a sharpened pencil from his pocket and aimed the point at one of the sergeant's bulging eyes.

"What the devil's going on here? Reilly, Renard, Hunter, Crisp – stop that this instant!"

The voice cut through the uproar like a whiplash, its steely tones commanding immediate obedience. At once the fighting stopped and all eyes turned towards the doorway leading from the private bar. A lean man in the uniform of an infantry major was standing there, his eyes glittering and his lined, hawklike face flushed with anger. "Zygmund," he barked, "get up at once! Hewitt, put down that blasted chair!" Sheepishly, the huge commando lowered the splintered wreckage to his feet.

"You men are a disgrace to your uniform," the major grated. "You will report back here to repair as much of the damage as you can tomorrow morning. The rest will be docked from your pay. In the meantime this bar is out of bounds to all of you until further notice. Now get the hell out of here before I lose my temper."

Silently, the battered commandos trooped from the bar. The officer turned to stare coldly at the others. "I have no authority over you people," he said evenly. "But if you don't clear out of here in two minutes flat, the whole damned lot of you, I'll see to it personally that every man in this bar's on a charge before midnight!"

The place cleared as if by magic. It was only when the locals had recovered their drinks and begun excitedly to discuss the brawl that they realised the blonde who had been the cause of all the trouble was nowhere to be seen.

17

Outside the pub, the bloodied sergeant and the two English corporals behaved in a curious fashion. Waiting until the last of the Highlanders had vanished along the dark road leading to their camp, they crossed the street and climbed into a Humber staff car that was parked without lights by the kerb. The blonde was already behind the wheel. As soon as the door closed she switched on the hooded headlamps, started the engine and drove rapidly away towards Wick. Forty minutes later, the four of them were 5,000 feet above the Cairngorms, sitting in the cabin of a Dakota transport flying south to London.

The two corporals were in civilian clothes, the blonde was wearing the uniform of a Commandant in the ATS and the sergeant now sported the crown and green tabs of a major in the Intelligence Corps. "You played that beautifully, Jill," he said, his accent no longer Cockney at all. "You were smashing, just great!"

"So long as you found out what we came for," the girl said.

"Absolutely. They're tough. They know all the tricks. But under their own CO their discipline is one hundred per cent. That's what the old man wanted to know."

"They're certainly tough," one of the corporals grinned, fingering a swelling on his jaw and eyeing the other's battered face. "But what's so special about this particular commando unit? And what exactly was the aim of the operation? I mean, okay, start a fight. But why?"

"Don't ask me, Hugo," the major said. "They're wearing commando duds, but I fancy it's some specialised cloak-and-dagger show. You know how keen the old man is on private armies. I imagine he has a top-secret job in mind for them, and he wanted to find out first how they ticked, that's all."

"Christ," the other corporal said, "I wouldn't want that bloody major for *my* CO, and that's a fact! Did you get those gimlet eyes?"

"Very impressive," the first corporal agreed. "Who is he, anyway?"

The intelligence officer shrugged. "Funny thing is," he replied, "that the chap has the reputation himself of being something of a playboy! Bloke by the name of Webster."

Chapter Two

"Ian Lindsay Webster," the red-tabbed general read aloud from the cover of the buff top-secret folder on his desk. "War Substantive Major. I should have thought he'd've got further than that if he was any good, what!"

The tall, thin naval officer at his side frowned. As a regular himself, Commander Lang knew better than most that the undercover battlefields of the cloak-and-dagger business were not the most rewarding for those in search of promotion. "Webster's collected a DSO and bar as well as an MC in the past fourteen months, sir," he said mildly. "He hasn't had too much time for the spit-and-polish and the saluting that – if you'll excuse me – boost you up the ladder in his particular regiment."

The general grunted. He opened the folder and began to read the sheets of typescript it contained, each of them with the same top-secret seal in its upper right-hand corner. Lang walked across the big second-floor room and looked out through the latticework of anti-blast adhesive crisscrossing the window. It was October, 1943. Under a pale blue sky, wintry sunshine showed up the scars and threadbare patches of wartime London. Across the street, drably dressed housewives queued outside a grocer's shop, waiting to have the coupons for their weekly allowance of butter, tea, bacon and sugar clipped from their ration books. Further away, men crowded around the counter of a tobacco kiosk displaying the legend *Regular Customers Only*.

There was a gap in the row of grimed four-storey buildings where three houses had been demolished by bombs. Between the temporary wooden buttresses shoring up the end walls of those on either side, a rectangular air-raid shelter with sandbagged entrances had been built on the rubble-strewn waste ground. Beyond its flat concrete roof, Lang could see a circular static-water tank for the use of firefighters, and then a green slope of park where men in blue RAF uniforms worked on a semi-collapsed barrage balloon tethered to a winch on a flatbed military truck.

Many of the houses on the block were pitted with the marks of bomb splinters. Most of the glass in the upper windows had gone, to be replaced by cardboard or blackout material, and those that remained – like the one through which Lang was looking – were subdivided by sticky tape to minimise fragmentation. The raw ends of the buildings on either side of the bombsite bore a patchwork of faded wallpapers punctuated by darker lozenges where pictures had once hung.

Lang sighed. This time it was total war all right. As he turned back into the room, the banshee wail of the air-raid sirens rose and fell over the roofs of the city.

The general was running his fingers through his sandy, thinning hair as he read. His shaggy eyebrows lifted in astonishment and then drew together in a scowl. Every now and then he exclaimed "Good God!" in a startled voice.

The file told him that Ian Lindsay Webster was the son of a Norfolk doctor and a suffragette from Edinburgh who had nursed in Flanders in 1917. It said that he had been born in 1903 and attended a minor public school in East Anglia – from which he had been expelled in 1921 for organising a series of roll-call deceptions enabling pupils to sneak out in relays to visit the local cinema. After that (according to the information in the dossier) he had sold Brooklands racing cars on commission, performed as a stunt wing-walker in an aerial circus, driven long-distance locomotives during the 1926 General Strike and started a radio station in Australia. He was suspected of running liquor from Cuba to the United States at the time of Prohibition, and it was known that he had worked as an adviser to the Emperor Haile Selassie during the Italian invasion of Abyssinia. He had joined his regiment with a short-service commission in the rearmament panic preceding Munich.

Character estimates from a succession of commanding officers stated that he drank too much, that he was a womaniser, that he was foolhardy and reckless, unwilling to accept discipline, disrespectful and the kind of officer whose attitude towards authority was lacking in seriousness if not downright flippant.

The general laid down the folder. "Good God," he said again. "Chap sounds as if he ought to be cashiered rather than put up for some special show!"

"That's just one side of the scales, sir," said Lang. "If you were to glance over the final sheet in the file, you would see that it was more than balanced by his *military* record."

"Meaning?"

"Webster gets results."

"H'mn. That doesn't necessarily mean . . ." The general relapsed into silence as he scanned the last page of the dossier.

He learned that Webster had won his MC cleaning up a German machine-gun nest that was harassing the Allied retreat from Belgium (the citation did not mention that he was at the time wearing a looted Nazi uniform belonging to a colonel in the Waffen SS). The first DSO award resulted from a one-man Normandy landing which the newspapers had got hold of and blown up before the Ministry of Information censorship division was properly established. In fact Webster's object had been to replenish his dwindling stock of Calvados. The bar to that decoration had come in 1942, when a unit led by Webster had destroyed a Nazi experimental base in North Africa and put back Hitler's development of the flying bomb by two years. In between these exploits, he had managed to put a Norwegian heavy-water plant out of action and steal a brand-new Stuka dive-bomber* which was delivered to the Ministry of Aircraft Production evaluation unit at Farnborough.

"Yes, Lang, that's all very well," the general said, closing the file. "But most of these are sort of one-off, solo jobs, aren't they? Kind of a Douglas Fairbanks wallah, what! But if the fellow can't obey orders . . ." He shook his head. "I mean, how the devil do we know what he'll do with the responsibility of two separate units to command, in the sort of show we have in mind?"

Lang cleared his throat. "I don't think, sir," he said carefully, "that you'll find any evidence that Webster actually disobeyed

* See *The Catapult Ultimatum*, also published by Severn House.

an order. He's got bags of initiative, that's all – and sometimes in the context of a changing situation . . . well, sir, you know how it is."

"No, Lang, I'm not sure that I do. How is it then?"

The commander swallowed. "Those of us at the planning stage," he said, "the backroom boys as it were – we don't always have a finger on the pulse, do we?"

"What pulse? What are you talking about?"

"We can't always size up what's going on in the field, sir, as well as the man on the spot."

"Are you trying to tell me that junior officers are in a better position to decide strategy than the General Staff?"

"Not strategy, sir. Tactics. In specific situations, in a limited way."

Beneath the bristling moustache, a row of yellow gravestone teeth appeared. The general was smiling. "You may be right," he admitted. "In a very limited way. But there's the question of command, y'know. However brave or resourceful a chap may be individually—"

"Webster may not be the most model soldier when it comes to carrying out orders to the letter," Lang interrupted. "But he's a great success giving them. He's respected, you see. The man's a terrific leader, I can assure you."

The general coughed. "Actually," he said, "I happen to have confirmation of that myself. As soon as I heard that this most irregular unit had been wished onto me, I sent a specialised squad up to Scotland to – um – stir things up a bit. Find out which way the wind blew an' all that. My chaps reported . . ." He reached for a sheet of paper on the desk and glanced at it. "Yes, they said the men were certainly tough, experienced and ruthless – but that the discipline was bang-on the moment this fellow Wendover—"

"Webster, sir."

"Just so. The moment Webster opened his mouth." The general laid down the paper. "Very rum, if you ask me. By all accounts the chap's a bit of a disgrace after all: CO only too glad to have him seconded to your death-or-glory lot. And the commandos up there are a pretty good collection of scallywags too, according to the bumf. Yet the moment Wellstead tells 'em to jump, they're through the bally hoop in a trice!"

22

Lang said: "They admire him, sir. As I said, they respect him. First quality required in a leader after all. Er – the name's Webster, Major Webster."

"Yes, yes. You don't have to tell me," the general said testily. "Major Webster. Seems a damned important job to give such a junior officer. Most irregular."

"It's an irregular unit, sir. You said so yourself."

"Quite, quite. And your people are absolutely convinced that they're the best chaps available – Webley and all – for this tomfool suicide stunt in the Baltic? Is that it?"

"We can't think of a more suitable team or leader, sir."

Before the general could speak again, the door opened and a bulky, silver-haired man in the uniform of a captain in the Royal Navy erupted into the room. His pink face was flushed with rage and his resolute mouth clamped angrily shut. "What the devil's all this rot I hear about you sending some blasted I-Corps spooks to mix it with my people in Scotland?" he demanded.

Captain Seamus M'Phee O'Kelly was Lang's immediate superior and the head of the Combined Operations (Security) Executive, that curious non-departmental organisation drawing its personnel from all three services and specialising in the less legal kind of undercover operation. O'Kelly was answerable only to the Combined Chiefs of Staff in person or to the Prime Minister, although when one or the other of those august bodies pushed a clandestine assignment his way he was sometimes obliged to consult and liaise with the commanding officers of other formations. He was a man who liked to make up his mind and act directly, and the committee-style repetitions which this involved frequently angered him. He was angry now. "I will not have it," he fumed. "Some of them may have dubious army records, some may have a history of insubordination, some may even be ex-convicts, but they are under my command! I can speak for them and I can speak for the man who leads them. If you want any information on the unit, Vane, you damned well come to me. I will not have your footling security bods unsettling them behind my back, is that clear?"

The general had fallen back in his chair under the outburst, his pale blue eyes startled. "Me dear fellow!" he protested. "No offence. Just checking up, you know. The top brass expect me to keep tabs on the kind of chaps I'm dealing with."

"Well, you're dealing with me now," O'Kelly snapped. "Remember that, please."

And then, as quickly as his rage had arisen, it subsided. "Just so that we understand one another," he said more calmly. "Very well, if your underlings have satisfied you that Webster and his men won't send postcards to Hitler outlining the details of Operation Andersen, and if you're prepared to accept Winston's recommendation that we should handle the first stage of the job, perhaps we could send a signal to the fellow concerned and bring him in for a briefing?"

Commander Lang repressed a smile. The old man was always a trifle choleric, and the more senior the character he was upbraiding, the more furious he became. Perhaps that was why he got on so well with Webster. Certainly Major-General Vane-Hyslop-Fortescue was still visibly shaken by the tantrum he had just witnessed. "As it happens," Lang said, "the major's in town on a forty-eight. Switchboard have his address. Perhaps, sir, you'd be good enough to lend us a dispatch rider, and then we could all meet this afternoon?"

The yellow teeth were gnawing at the general's moustache. "By all means," he said hurriedly. "Of course. With pleasure. Right away." He pressed a bell on his desk. An RAOC corporal came into the room and snapped to attention. "Sir?"

"I want a runner immediately," Vane-Hyslop-Fortescue said. "He's to take a message to a Major Webster and escort him to Captain O'Kelly's office in the Citadel as soon as possible."

Chapter Three

It was not the first time Webster had been bombed out while he was on leave. It was not even the first time he had been bombed out while he was in bed with a girl he hardly knew. He had missed the boat at Dunkirk because he had been in bed with a blonde whose house was shelled and he was determined to get his money's worth. It was this which had led him to steal the Stuka and fly himself home in it.

This time it was a blonde again – although there had been a fair proportion of brunettes and redheads darkening Webster's amorous horizon during the three years in between. He had recuperated this one from a nightclub in Leicester Square. He thought it might have been called the Four Hundred.

It was probably getting on for four in the morning when that night's raid began. "Bit of a late start tonight," Webster said thickly into the girl's hair. He was still a little drunk. "Thought we might have got off scot-free for once. They can't catch me, though: I'm the king of the bloody castle; they're the dirty rascals!"

The blonde said nothing. She was panting in the dark. As well as being an enthusiast, Webster was an accomplished lover.

"Bloody nerve," he said. "Trying to ruin the first night of my forty-eight!"

The wolf-wail of the sirens had scarcely died away in drawn-out moans when they heard the thwacking detonations of anti-aircraft guns in the Thames Estuary east of the city. Soon afterwards bombs began to fall – in Mayfair and the West End this time rather than in the dock area or around the railway marshalling yards.

"Must have known I was coming," Webster mumbled as a stick of high-explosives, advancing westwards towards them, burst with mathematical precision and increasing violence. Glass jingled on a dresser as the last in the series shook the block, which was in Kensington, just south of the park. In a sudden silence, they heard bricks and slates showering back to earth after a direct hit not far away. Air-raid wardens' whistles shrilled. A jangle of ambulance and fire-engine bells approached. Webster reached for the bottle and a pack of cigarettes on a bedside table.

They say you never hear the one that hits you. Either they are mistaken or the science of acoustics needs to be rethought. Webster heard the scream in time to drop the bottle, seize the girl and hurl her naked body to the floor on the far side of the bed.

The night dissolved in a thunder of unquenchable fury.

Through a tornado of flying glass and pulverised concrete, boards split, brick powdered and girders bent as easily as the stalks of daffodils in a high wind.

Astonishingly, although Webster had a cut above his left eye, they were otherwise undamaged. "Didn't have my name on it, you see," he told the girl when the flood of adrenaline pounding the blood behind the eyes and ears had ebbed. "Don't move though until I suss out the form. This could be a danger area!" He rose to his feet and felt along the wall.

A switch. To his amazement, the circuit was still connected. For an instant he screwed his eyes shut against the dazzle from a lamp on the bedside table. When he opened them, he saw that everything else in the room was in ruins. Glass from the martyred windows was everywhere, studding the flock-sprayed walls, transforming a sofa into a prison wall, littering the floor with razorlike shards. The carpet was strewn with picture frames, smashed ornaments and papers from a desk whose drawers had been sucked out by a freakish blast effect. From a pyramid of rubble and soot in front of the fireplace, one of Webster's non-regulation yellow gloves absurdly emerged like a drowning hand.

"No structural damage," he announced. "Direct hit two or three houses away, I'd say. Do you have a spare room, sweetie – what the French call a *chambre d'amis*, a room for friends?"

"At the back," the blonde said dazedly, "at the far end of

26

the corridor." They had been protected by the bulk of the high, brass-framed bed, and she was sitting with her arms wrapped around her bare knees on the only area of carpet not glittering with broken glass. "Don't move," Webster said. Treading with infinite caution, he left the room.

Obediently, the girl stayed where she was, waiting for the heaving of her breath to quieten. There was a lot of noise in the street now: angry voices, curt commands, feet hurrying in every direction. A woman, not far away, was crying. Light splashed the ceiling as a fire engine turned into the street, accelerating towards the pulse of flames further to the west.

In three minutes, Webster returned. His spare, muscular figure was still nude, but now his feet were splendidly encased in green velvet mules with ostrich-feather pom-poms.

"Meet the friend," he said. "The room's undamaged. Glass in every window." Stooping down, he picked the blonde up effortlessly, one arm around her shoulders, the other behind the knees. "Lower the left arm and pick up that bottle before we leave," he said.

"Darling, we can't leave like this!" she complained. "I mean I don't know if my clothes—"

"Not leave the house, idiot!" Webster said. "Leave this room. To go where there's glass in the windows, not on the ruddy floor. We have unfinished business, after all."

"Darling, we can't! It must be after six – and I have to get back to the War House. I'm on duty at eight." She had told him that she was in charge of some kind of intelligence evaluation unit attached to the Records Department ("Nepotism, really, my uncle's the department head").

"Not today you're not." Webster was carrying her plaster-dusted body towards the spare room. "Uncle will have to give you the day off. You just got bombed out, remember?"

"Webster, I can't. I'm in uniform: it's not as if I was a shopgirl, a factory worker, or a . . . a secretary or something. I'm on *duty*. Can't you understand—"

"You don't look as though you're in uniform," Webster said. "In fact you look gorgeous."

There was indeed a very special quality about the blonde's naked body. When she was wearing clothes, Webster found that she distilled that highly seductive quality of making a man tinglingly aware, with every movement, of the sensual ripeness of the body they concealed. Naked, she stimulated the excitement best encompassed by the phrase, "By God, I was right!" With her billowy hips, small waist and exceedingly generous breasts, she gave the impression at first of warmth and softness – almost slackness. But the cushioned hips were firm, the waist pliant and the big, full breasts taut and resilient below a bee-stung lower lip. Pillowed on the fleshy, shifting swell of her belly, Webster had thought her – in every sense of the word – the most *comfortable* lay he had ever enjoyed in his life.

Uncorseted, her friendly bust gave promise of pneumatic bliss! Who was it who wrote that, he mused as he laid her down on the spareroom bed?

It was later, much later – the beams of sunlight slanting steeply through the window, the organism craving coffee and the dispatch rider already waiting patiently in the hall – that Webster eyed the neatly tailored khaki of the ATS officer's uniform that the girl had rescued from the demolished front room. "Bit of a change from that shapeless WAAF corporal's gear, wouldn't you say?" he enquired as she buttoned the tunic.

She had begun to smooth down the narrow skirt. Now she stopped and straightened slowly, her violet eyes wide. "How did you know?" she asked.

Staring at the swell of breasts thrusting out the tightly belted material, he shook his head. "How could anyone forget a *poitrine* like that!" he said. "I'd seen you doing your number in the bar – just a glimpse through the open door; I had to resist the urge to join the queue myself, as a matter of fact. But I knew it must be a set-up the moment I saw the staff Humber that took you all away. The question is . . . why?"

She said nothing, the generous lower lip caught between her teeth, her eyes downcast.

"There is one other question," Webster pursued. "You followed me into that club where I picked you up last night, didn't you? You wanted to be approached, in fact. By me. In truth it was *you* who picked *me* up. Right?" He grinned. "I mean, no complaints. If it wasn't for the WAAF caper I'd have put it down to the manly charm, the old Errol Flynn smile. You know: Fearless Frazer strikes again, what!

28

But as it is . . . well, I'd just love to know why, that's all."

The girl looked up. "I suppose you do look a bit like Flynn," she said. "On a bad day."

She swallowed. "The set-up, as you call it, was because the powers-that-be wanted to check out how your rather – er – specialised unit ticked. How they reacted to provocation, to orders, that kind of thing. Not an assignment I'm especially proud of, but that was the job."

She met his eye. "So far as you personally are concerned . . . well, for a start, nothing to do with the job. I'd like you to believe that. But I knew you Special Service types have to report in every day, even when you're on leave, and I . . . happened . . . to see you leaving the War House – and I thought, well, it might be fun to see how *you* ticked!"

She smiled, reaching for the commandant's greatcoat with its insignia and stars. "It was fun," she said.

"Don't worry, there'll be a return engagement, that's for certain!" Webster assured her. "I still have twenty-four hours of my forty-eight to come, for a start." There was a glint of amusement in his rake-hell eyes. "So I insist that you give me your telephone—"

He stopped, leaving the sentence unfinished. "Good God! I just realised: I don't even know your *name*, old thing!"

"Actually, it's only Jill when I'm in the WAAF," she told him with a smile. "Among friends I answer to June. June Chandos."

Chapter Four

"You took your bloody time, Webster," Captain O'Kelly growled from behind his desk in the underground operations room below the Citadel – that strange concrete fortress built at the beginning of the war behind London's Admiralty Arch. "What the devil kept you?"

There was a telegraphist seated behind a battery of electronic equipment on the far side of the room. Webster studied the monitor screens above the man's head. "Very sorry, sir. Part of the new RIA conditioning plan for Special Service officers."

"RIA? What the hell's the RIA?"

"Ready for Instant Action, sir. Keep fit at all times – even when on leave. I was in the middle of a session with my masseur when the dispatch rider arrived."

O'Kelly stared at him. "I wouldn't be surprised," he said.

Webster allowed a discreet sigh of relief to escape and relaxed into a chair. The old bastard could be hell's own difficult but he did understand. The staff officers at Webster's own regimental headquarters in Rutland hadn't understood at all. To them he was a constant source of embarrassment: his special brand of reckless courage just didn't fit in with the *esprit* of that particular corps. "That bloody man Webster," they would say. "What in God's name is he up to this time?" And, as the general had discovered, they had been only too eager to release him for service with O'Kelly's CO(S)E – or Cosy Corner as the agents who worked for the old man irreverently termed the undercover organisation.

Once you stood in the Corner, life became much tougher. But Webster always sensed that O'Kelly was a kindred spirit. There were stories still circulating about his cadet days at Dartmouth. And for that reason alone Webster, detesting red tape and any kind of bullshit, would cheerfully have taken orders from him. But there was another reason. If you wanted to stay on the CO(S)E operational register, you did what you were told and no messing about. The fact was, nevertheless – and this was what attracted Webster – exactly *how* you did it didn't matter, just so long as it was done. An additional bonus was that most of the jobs were indeed, as the general had pointed out, one-off, non-routine ops that suited his talents and flair for improvisation very well.

O'Kelly was backgrounding one of them now, although this, non-routine though it might be, was to turn out to be anything but a solo exploit.

The old man had started with a rundown on the U-boat menace and the threat it posed not only to Allied shipping but to the continued independence of Britain itself. As he moved on to the alarming statistics of the problem, the door of the operations room opened and Commander Lang sauntered in with a slight, fair-haired young man on whose boyish upper lip an improbable moustache flourished.

O'Kelly rose to his feet. "Ah, Lang. Glad you managed to locate him . . . Believe you two have met before: Major Webster – Captain Fortune."

"Charles G," the young man offered, shaking hands. "The G stands for—"

"Goode," Webster cut in. "With an E. Like Goode Fortune. I remember . . . we met on that North African pilotless plane show in '42, right?"

"Too bally right," Fortune said. "You still owe me for that bottle of Arrack you sank before they shoved us on the boat to Alex!"

O'Kelly's fingers were drumming on the surface of his desk. "If you gentlemen could set your bibulous sights a bit lower," he said, "I'd suggest a quartet of pinkers before we eat. We're late for lunch already." He glanced reproachfully at Webster. "Archie, if you wouldn't mind . . . ?"

Lang opened a green metal filing cabinet and took out gin, Angostura Bitters and glasses. When they were all supplied, O'Kelly gulped down a mouthful and moved across to a six-foot wide map of Northern Europe hanging from a baton behind the desk. "Couple of minutes of background before we eat," he said, "and then you'll be in the picture when we form

31

up before the top brass this afternoon." He paused, looking first at Webster and then at Fortune. "You read the papers and you listen to the wireless," he resumed. "You know how serious the blockade's become since Hitler hotted up the U-boat war. We lost more tonnage last month than in the whole of last year. They're sending merchantmen to the bottom quicker than the Yanks can build Liberty Ships, and that's saying something! If we're ever going to open that second front the editorials keep bleating about, if we're ever going to stockpile enough munitions and supplies to mount an invasion of mainland Europe, this wastage has got to be stopped. And that means the U-boat threat must be mastered."

Webster exchanged glances with Fortune. Meeting the young man for the first time, he had been unfavourably impressed by his flippant demeanour and silly-ass conversation, but once they were in action together he had soon discovered that the boyish, almost asinine exterior masked a most unusual strength, determination and intelligence. Fortune was in fact among CO(S)E's top echelon of secret agents. He raised an eyebrow now and shrugged: he was as much at a loss as Webster to know what the Battle of the Atlantic, grave as the situation was, had to do with them.

O'Kelly was back at his desk. He sipped his pink gin and then returned to the map. "Intelligence reports suggest," he said, "that the Nazis are developing bigger, faster submarines – long-range craft that can refuel – and rearm – from mother ships in mid-ocean and stay out in the Atlantic indefinitely. Once they're in permanent service, our chances of winning the battle are halved. If luck was with the enemy, those subs alone could damned near bring the war effort to a standstill."

Webster nodded slowly. He drained his glass and Lang moved in to replenish it. "For the moment," O'Kelly went on, "the U-boat packs have to return to their bases for refuelling, recharging of batteries, loading of tinfish and supplies and that sort of thing. The most important pens are at Wilhelmshaven, Flensburg and Kiel. Here," – he tapped the map with the back of a forefinger – "here . . . and here. Now you'll see that Wilhelmshaven is both the easiest and the quickest for them to get to, being on Germany's North Sea coast, while the others are round the corner as it were, in the Baltic. To get to Flensburg or Kiel, either they have to pass through the Kiel Canal or else navigate the Skagerrak, between Norway and the tip of Denmark, and then go on down past the Kattegat and the Danish islands to get to their home ports. If you were on the German General Staff, which would you prefer?" The captain paused and glared accusingly at his audience.

"It's a question of balancing time against risk, isn't it?" Fortune said after a moment. "I mean to say, at Wilhelmshaven, they'd be in and out in a jiffy. And it would not take all that long to push on through the bally canal. On the other hand, Wilhelmshaven's vulnerable to our coastal patrols, and they're both easy targets for the RAF and the Flying Fortress boys. I'd feel pretty dicey if I had several million quid's worth of undersea-boat surfaced between two concrete towpaths and the boys in blue were overhead."

"Yes, absolutely not on the Henley programme," Webster agreed. "I'd say it was worth the extra time, taking the safer route. After all, Jerry's occupied Norway and Denmark, on either side of the Skagerrak, and bloody Sweden's neutral. They'd be in no danger at all, once they left the North Sea – but it's a hell of a long way round."

"You're both right," said O'Kelly. He sounded almost aggrieved. "Since they threw us out of Norway, the Boche have tended to favour the Baltic pens. And that's where they're testing out the new long-range U-boats."

Webster leaned forward in his chair. It sounded as though the history lesson was over and the briefing was about to begin.

"I don't need to tell you," O'Kelly said impressively, "how vital it is to us to learn everything we can about these new craft. And, for that matter, to check the movements of existing subs operating out of Flensburg and Kiel. Without this information, our chances lessen every day; with it we might just be able to turn the tide. Trouble, of course, is to get the right *kind* of information. We can plot sighting reports supplied by RAF Coastal Command, naval units and the the actual convoy escorts – any that survive. The Yanks provide plenty of high-level aerial recce shots of the ports. But none of these gives more than a picture of what's happening at one time on one particular day. What we want is a continuing picture over a period of time . . . and that's where you people come in."

Webster grinned at Fortune. The light of battle was in his eyes. It looked now very much as though a spot of action might be coming up.

"The Danish underground," O'Kelly continued, "tell us that there is a small, uninhabited islet in the Kattegat, about fifteen miles out from Kiel harbour. Jerry will have it on his naval charts, but it's too small to feature on the maps – not much more than a mudbank really; about an eighth of a square mile of reeds and stunted shrubs. They haven't bothered to defend it because, after all, it's surrounded by occupied, German or neutral waters. *Nevertheless, anyone sitting there with the right kind of equipment could spy on all the naval traffic in and out of Kiel, and maybe Flensburg too.* If they had a powerful enough transmitter, they could radio back detailed information on the programming and supply of U-boats that would be invaluable, absolutely invaluable."

"And you want us . . . ?" Webster's grey eyes were gleaming.

"The planners aim to plant a small, highly specialised observation unit on that islet. But, no – that part of the operation's not your pigeon. The unit will be made up of Norwegian volunteers, dedicated guerrillas who contrived to get out as the Germans came in. And it'll be kind of a suicide squad because it's bound to be detected and captured or destroyed within days. The radio transmissions alone will make that inevitable. But while it's there . . . well, you heard what I just said."

Fortune was looking puzzled. "So what is it that you want us to do?" he asked. "What kind of a show do we have to put up?"

O'Kelly went back to his desk and finished his drink. "The regular combined-ops johnnies are supplying, training and operating the observation unit," he replied. "General Vane-Hyslop-Fortescue's in charge of that. Our show – your assignment in fact – is to make it possible for them to get to the islet."

Webster and Fortune both looked puzzled now. Both of them were about to speak when O'Kelly held up a hand. "There's no point my going into details now," he said. "You'll get a proper briefing when we liaise with the general this afternoon. In the meantime the department will furnish you with luncheon at Scott's. The lobster soup there is uncommonly good."

"Wasn't there something about hearty meals and condemned men?" Fortune said lightly.

The sirens were wailing again as O'Kelly, Lang, Webster and Fortune arranged themselves around the general's desk in the second-storey room across the road from the bombsite. Above the slope of grass beyond the static-water tank, the barrage balloon was rising slowly towards the sky. A burly Intelligence Corps major stood by a wall map of Northern Europe similar to the one in O'Kelly's headquarters. Webster thought the man looked familiar, but failed to recognise him as the supposed sergeant who had provoked the brawl in the pub in Scotland.

"You chaps know the general picture," the major began. "The Danish cell that's been handling the other end of the operation's blown, but they did manage to get a message through before they were taken." He opened the lid of a small wire recorder that stood on a table beneath the map and fiddled with the controls. "This is what our monitoring station at Barnet picked up," he said. He pressed a switch.

Faint and scratchy, edged with an undertone of panic, the voice of a man who had been blown to pieces ten days earlier spoke from the machine.

Operation Andersen . . . Operation Andersen . . . Here is Hans transmitting with a Number One priority from Fairyland. Message begins. The tale can – repeat can – be told. The Snow Queen is alone in her Palace . . .

"That means that they checked, and the islet is still uninhabited," the intelligence officer explained. "The operation is cleared to go ahead as planned. The Queen is the observation unit."

. . . fourteen – one four – point seven two three miles from the Giant's Castle. The Queen can see the fairies coming and going . . .

"Exact distance of the islet from Kiel. The fairies are German naval traffic."

The Queen's treasure chest is buried within the Palace walls . . . Guess how many jewels . . .

"That," the major said, "is to tell us that the Danes have

35

already organised a dugout on the islet, ready for the unit and its equipment. The figures are for the navigator of the sub that lands them there. They give map coordinates for the four compass extremities of the place."

The wind is blowing. Message ends.

"It's not hard to decipher that one. They knew their time was running out. They certainly have their ration of guts, those people." The officer switched off the recorder. From outside the windows, a stammer of distant gunfire shivered the air. On the general's desk a teacup rattled in its saucer. An eyebrow scaled the lower ridges corrugating Webster's forehead, though whether this was due to the anti-aircraft fire or the recording he had just heard was not clear. None of the others moved.

Fortune was looking out through the window. Barrage balloons glittered like silver fish in the translucent sky. He cleared his throat. "Just now, old lad," he said to the major, "you did actually say the *sub* that lands them there?"

The intelligence officer smiled. "I did. We dare not drop them by air, because of the risk that the drop would be monitored. Obviously. The equipment could be damaged or lost altogether too: some of it's heavy stuff and the islet's a pretty small target to hit from operational height over enemy territory."

"Yes, but . . . ?"

"I know, I know. Running them all that way by submarine, through such heavily defended waters, would be impossible. Just the same, that's what we have to do."

Webster's predatory face split into a grin of pure delight. "Tell us about it," he said.

Chapter Five

"There are mine-fields," the intelligence officer told Webster and Fortune, "at the entrance to the Skagerrak. We reckon we have those charted all right. In any case that's a risk that does have to be taken. But once you've turned south, in the middle of the Kattegat, thirty miles from occupied Denmark and ten from the coastal waters of neutral Sweden, there's a fair-sized island called Anholt. And here, defending the outer approaches to Kiel, Jerry has installed a battery of 360-degree turret guns, and the latest sophisticated radar and sounding gear. The island's like a moored bloody battleship, covering the passage on either side: the turrets are identical to those on the *Tirpitz*. With these and the depth charge equipment they have, they can annihilate anything suspicious picked up by their scanners, above or below water."

The major picked up a pointer and indicated an area high up on the wall map. "Here, closer to the Kattegat entrance, there's this bigger island. It's called Laeso. There are similar batteries there too, though the radar base isn't completed yet. These defences explain why we can't run our observers in by submarine." He paused to allow his words to sink in, then added: "But if the radar and guns on these two islands could be put out of action . . ."

The general had thrust out his feet and was scrutinising the polished toes of his shoes. Lang and O'Kelly were looking out of the window (the gunfire had started again). They'd heard it all before. But Webster and Fortune sat on the edges of their chairs, faces alive with interest.

"It wouldn't need to be total destruction," the briefing officer went on. "Even the short time it would take Jerry to repair or replace the damaged stuff would be sufficient for a sub to make a one-time run, land the unit under cover of darkness, then race back for the open sea."

"Suppose the sub's rumbled on the return journey?" Fortune asked. "Will it run for a Swedish port and expect to be interned as a belligerent illegally found in neutral waters?"

"No. It'll have orders to make an apparent *kamikaze* raid on warships leaving Flensburg or Kiel. There's got to be a believable reason for it to be there, without the Boche having to look any further. Such an operation would explain the raids on the islands too."

"What about getting the observation unit back?" Webster queried.

The I-Corps man turned away. "I'm afraid there's no question of that," he said gruffly. "Now, gentlemen, your briefing—" He broke off and glanced involuntarily at the ceiling. Somewhere above, the wavering drone of synchronised aero-engines manifested itself. A series of thudding explosions shook the building.

"Must be a couple of months since he tried a daylight raid," the general observed. He too stared out of the window, blinking at the vapour trails smudging the sky above the balloons.

"As I was about to say," the major resumed, "your briefing is simple. Take a small commando unit to each of these islands, silence the radar and batteries to coincide with the passage of the sub carrying our observation unit, then get the hell out. But, believe me, it's not going to be simple to carry out!"

"You mean . . . how do we get there, for instance?" Webster said.

"Right. For you – as for the sub on its own – a sea assault would be out of the question."

"A drop, then?" This was Fortune.

O'Kelly spoke for the first time since the briefing had begun. "Wouldn't work," he said. "On Laeso, you might have a chance. The island's shaped like a tennis racquet or frying pan. But Anholt's a long, thin triangle, only two miles wide at the base. And the German installation's at the tip. You could lose fifty per cent of your men and equipment in the sea, even if the radar didn't track you coming down. They'd be on extra alert anyway: what would enemy aircraft be doing, overflying that non-strategic area?"

"Maybe," Webster said slowly, "we could land on the *North Sea* coast of Denmark at night – and then make our way across the Jutland peninsula in small groups, rendezvous on Denmark's Baltic coast and take it from there?"

This time it was the general who replied. "Wouldn't have a hope," he grunted. "Place is thick with Huns. Patrols all over the shop. Roadblocks everywhere and checkpoints in each village. And apart from your arms and your explosives, you'll need to have perishing *boats* with you! No, that's out of the question."

"Dammit, sir, we're supposed to be guerrilla effectives, aren't we?" Fortune said. "Surely we could knock off a couple of—"

"Don't be an ass, Fortune," Lang cut in. "In the unlikely event that you could arrive on the Baltic coast with enough men left to mount an attack; in the even less likely event that you could get away with a couple of boats—"

"One large boat, then?"

Lang smiled. "The islands have to be attacked simultaneously. Two boats. But you'd be blown out of the water before you were a quarter of the way across, man. There's thirty miles of open sea between Anholt and the nearest point on the mainland – and to reach that point you'd have to cross the country at its widest, which is exactly a hundred miles!" He gestured at the wall map.

The intelligence major had been waiting patiently during these exchanges, leaning with both hands clasped around the tip of his pointer, which was in fact an old billiard cue. Now he straightened up and approached the map once more. "Frankly," he said, "our chaps have already tested all those ideas – and chucked 'em out. But the backroom boys have been working on a project for a couple of weeks. Research in depth is the fashionable term. In any case they've come up with a scheme that looks to me—" Once again he stopped in mid-sentence and looked upwards.

The crump!—crump!—crump!—crump!—*crump!* of an appoaching stick of high-explosive bombs filled the room with an appalling clangour. There was a sudden express-train screech –

and the officer, together with O'Kelly, Lang, Fortune and the general, was flat on his face on the floor, covering his head with his arms.

The explosion seemed to go on for a long time, shuddering the foundations of the building and thundering in their ears. Bricks, tiles and other debris were still clattering back onto the neighbourhood roofs as the five men picked themselves up. Webster was sitting in his chair. He appeared not to have moved.

"That was bloody silly," the general told him, brushing off the knees of his khaki trousers. "You could have been cut to bally ribbons by flying glass, propped up there like a stuffed dummy! That one was pretty close, you know."

Webster shrugged. "If it has my name on it . . ." he said.

One of the window-panes, cracked by the detonation, dropped from its frame and fell to the floor through the white dust swirling in the sunbeams. "You see what I mean, sir," Webster said.

The general stared at the wicked shards of glass glinting in the pale light, shook his head and went out of the room to satisfy himself that there had been no casualties among his staff.

The Intelligence major picked up his pointer. "As I was saying, they have come up with a plan. For the reasons we have discussed, it was finally decided that your approach would after all have to be by air." He raised a hand as Fortune and Webster both began to speak at once. "But it won't, hopefully, be in a way that could arouse enemy suspicions. It will not, in other words, be by means of a parachute drop. On the night you go in, there will be a thousand-bomber raid on the U-boat pens at Wilhelmshaven, Flensburg and Kiel. The RAF are doing them all the time. Only this particular time there will be two supernumerary planes in the second wave. Inside those planes will be your two assault groups."

The pointer swept across the map. "They'll come in over Holland, turn north and then east to bomb the three ports, and then swing west to return home over the sea, right? Now, as you know, all hell breaks loose during these big night raids. The sky's chock-a-block with Pathfinders, bombers, German night-fighters, flak, searchlights, flares . . . and aircraft that have been hit and are going to crash. Among the casualties in this raid – or at any rate the *apparent* casualties – will be the two planes carrying your men."

Fortune whistled softly between his teeth. "Not *bad!*" he said admiringly.

Webster still hadn't got it. "When the main force swings west after the raid," the briefing officer explained, "your two planes will continue towards the north, gradually losing height. The backroom boys will have kitted them out with special equipment to trail what looks like smoke and flames, just as if they were really crippled. You should be safe from attack that way: the gunners and night-fighter grid controllers are not going to waste ammunition on a crate that's done for anyway. The first will ditch in the Kattegat near – but not too near – Anholt; the other will limp on, staggering lower and lower, until it's off Laeso. You chaps can make the rest of the distance in each case in rubber dinghies . . . and after that, it'll be up to you." The officer grounded the billiard cue. "That's the main outline of the scheme. Now – any questions?"

"Yes," Webster said at once. "Two."

"Fire ahead."

"First of all, what do we do with the pilots of the two planes? Do we have to take them with us?"

"Fortune can drive one of them," said O'Kelly. "He's a bit of an expert: used to ferry bombers across the Atlantic for the ATA, an' all that. We'll second you Joe Constantine for the other, I think you've worked with him before anyway?"

"The Canadian? Yes, he was with us in North Africa," Webster said. "OK, pilot problem scrubbed. Second question: what happens when Jerry finds traces of two plane wrecks floating in the sea – but no bodies to go with them? Won't the absence of dead aircrew – or of survivors, for that matter – tip him off that there's something fishy about the crashes?"

"You'll be supplied with the right number of corpses," Lang said, "properly identified as aircrew, with the right kind of injuries, to be left in the water when you take to the boats."

"Good grief, your backroom boys think of everything, don't they!" Fortune exclaimed. "But tell me one thing, O wise man of the sea. Suppose our esteemed enemies are cretinous enough not to catch on that we're not really part of the bomber force?

41

Suppose the Krauts are rude enough to hit us and we are genuinely shot down in flames? What then, sir?"

For the first time that day, O'Kelly smiled. "We thought of that too," he said. "There'll be a back-up team in training before you leave."

General Vane-Hyslop-Fortescue came back into the room. "Everything all right, sir?" Lang enquired.

The red-tabbed staff officer shrugged. "Direct hit on a small hotel in the street behind," he said. "'Fraid there may be a lot of casualties. Nothing serious here. We lost all the windows at the back and one of me sergeants has rather a nasty cut on his head. That's all." As he dropped back into his chair, the clanging of fire-engines and the shrill ring of ambulance bells cut through the sounds of running feet from below. There were several more bomb bursts, but they were further away to the east.

"Right," the general said. "Everyone in the picture now? Good. You, Webster – you'll have been wondering why you've been sitting on your backside in the wilds of Wick for the last few weeks, with a crowd of roughs to command and nothing to do, hey?"

"Yes, sir."

"Well, you know now. Fortune can fly you back there tomorrow in an Auster, and you can start trainin' right away. My Norwegians will be ready to go two weeks from today. We'll give you three days on the islands to do the job. That means you'll have exactly ten days to make your plans, lick your rascals into shape and rehearse the attack."

Lang was on his feet by the broken window. In a gap between two houses, he could glimpse early autumn leaves on the trees bordering the Thames Embankment. It was just after high tide and the river raced silently under the bridges towards the sea.

"We'll supply you," he said without turning round, "with large-scale maps, aerial reconnaissance photos and sand-table models of the two islands. Plus whatever gen we have on Jerry's local defences. Which may not be much. In a couple of days, I'll move the lot of you out to the Orkneys: that's the closest match we can find to the terrain on Anholt and Laeso, and it's about the same latitude."

He swung around to face Webster.

"But you'd better put your chaps through their paces on survival routines and on camouflage. The actual show will last three days, remember, there's precious little cover on the islands, and bugger-all to eat except shellfish!"

"Oh, well," Fortune said over the strident wail of the all-clear sirens, "at least the diet should agree with the lobster soup."

Chapter Six

A cold autumnal wind blew across the aerodrome in East Anglia. Beyond the line of blue lights marking the perimeter track, a wedge of pale green in the west still separated the flat, dark country-side from the night sky. An RAF 3-tonner drew up at the door of the hut where the aircrews collected their parachutes. "A Flight here!" the WAAF driver called. There was an ironic cheer from the crowd of airmen gathered in the blackness. Twenty-eight young men detached themselves from the group and climbed aboard, laughing and joking a little too loudly. It was the third time the squadron had been sent on nights raids over Germany that week, and according to the Met type there would be bright moonlight and little cloud cover over the target. The tension in the air was an almost palpable thing.

The B Flight transport collected its human cargo, and after it a third lorry braked to a halt. This time the girl driver leaned out of the cab and said: "Members of the Special Flight, please." From behind the twenty or thirty RAF aircrew left outside the hut, eighteen shadowy figures marched compactly to the vehicle. One got in beside the driver; the rest scrambled over the tail-board.

"Who the hell were those blokes?" someone asked as the truck accelerated away. "The Führer's secret weapon?"

"Yanks," another voice called through the laughter. "I heard them talking before the briefing: there were a couple sitting at the back of the hut."

"No," said a third man. "Those were Canadians: I saw their shoulder flashes."

"Well, there was at least one Scot with them. An Irishman too, I think."

"Anyway, the Yanks don't go on night raids: they bomb

44

from seven million feet in daytime, preferably before they reach Jerry's defence grid."

"Why the hell are they flying with us?"

"Well, they must be flying Yank *planes*: they'll be using those two American kites the ATA girls ferried in today. Mitchells, I think they were."

"Do me a bloody favour, Alan: there were *eighteen* of the blighters! You're not going to tell me there are nine aircrew on a fucking Mitchell. Even the Yanks don't go that far."

"Yes, but talking about those ATA girls—"

"Christ! Did you see the dark one? What a smashing piece of crumble!"

"I wouldn't mind wading through that barefoot, Jimmy boy!"

"If we have any feet left when we get back from bloody Kiel, mate, I'll be happy to wade through anything on offer. Next to the Rühr, that's the hottest flak concentration Jerry has. And the night-fighter grids are—"

"Ah, pack it in, Nobby, for God's sake! You'll have the bleeding violins playing next!"

A fourth transport drew up. "Taxi for the gentlemen of C Flight!"

Archie Lang sat next to the driver of the Special Flight lorry and stared at the gaunt silhouettes of the four-engined Lancasters dispersed in tarmac pans around the aerodrome perimeter. Most of the flyers had been decanted from their transports now and were chatting with the ground crews gathered around the bombers. "I'm afraid I'm not a hundred per cent on about the position of your aircraft, sir," the girl said as they bumped across the main runway. "American medium bombers, aren't they?"

Lang nodded. "B-25s," he said. "Twin-engined crates with a high, cranked wing and a double tailplane. According to my information, they're parked in an oversize pan on the inside of the perimeter, just after your Lancasters O for Orange and L for Love."

"Right you are, sir," the driver said. And then, as she pulled up beside the two Mitchells a little later. "I don't know where you're going, but good luck, anyway."

Lang smiled. "Thanks," he said. "As it happens, personally

I'm simply going back to your officers' mess for a drink: I'm just the chairborne briefing type. Save your good luck for the boys in the back, my dear: they're going to need it!"

Captain O'Kelly jumped down from the rear of the truck and assembled his assault groups some distance from the two planes, which looked almost toy-sized beside the huge Lancasters. "All right, chaps," he said briskly. "This is it. You've done all the rehearsing you can; now you know where you're going and what you have to do. You've been given lists of safe-houses and details of the Danes' underground escape network in case you get hit and have to bail out. If you make it, you head for Sweden once the job's wrapped up. All I have to say to you now is – go on out there and hit the bowling for six! We're counting on you. And I personally am counting on at least one bottle of schnapps for my Christmas stocking. Are you with me, Webster?"

"All the way, Captain," Webster acknowledged with a crooked smile. "Steinhaegger or Dornkaat?"

"Both," O'Kelly said decidedly. "One from each island." He turned back to the commandos and said: "All right men, prepare for embarkation: Number One squad in the first plane, Number Two in the other. By the left, quick *march!*"

As the grim-faced assault teams in their Mae Wests, battle-dress and parachute harnesses wheeled away and began piling through the hatches of the two Mitchells, he drew Webster and Fortune aside to where Commander Lang was waiting by the transport. "This is Monday night," he said. "You should have made landfall on the islands before dawn tomorrow. Zero hour for the passage of the sub is 0100 hours on Friday morning. That gives you all day tomorrow, Wednesday and Thursday to reconnoitre, make your dispositions and sabotage the defences on both islands. You should aim to have the whole bang-shoot out of action by midnight on Thursday at the latest – but not more than a couple of hours earlier than that, or Jerry could call up naval units which would make it as difficult for our sub as the stuff your lot are going to neutralise. Timing is everything on this show, and ideally I'd like to receive a signal – a radio message from you – confirming that it's safe for the sub to go ahead, around 2300 hours on Thursday night, right?"

Webster and Fortune nodded. Most of their teams were

aboard the two B-25s now. "Very well," said O'Kelly. "Now, if you get away with it, make for Falkenberg, Varberg or Göttskar, on the Swedish coast. I'll be at the Hotel Metropole in Göteborg from noon, Thursday, waiting for that signal. As you know, you'll be interned as belligerents if the Swedes catch you in uniform or with arms, so you'd better junk everything before you're sighted. They won't bother you with too many questions if you're clean. Assuming you get away with that, we shall repatriate you via the Embassy in Stockholm. Clear?"

"Yes, sir."

"There's just one thing I want to say to you . . ."

"Sir?"

"Good luck," O'Kelly said gruffly. "We'll be keeping our fingers crossed."

The four men shook hands and then Webster and Fortune saluted, turned about and strode off to the planes. Webster was leading the party charged with sabotaging the guns and radar on Anholt. His aircraft had been assigned the code letter U for Uncle. Fortune, heading for the Laeso batteries, was flying Z for Zebra.

They stopped beneath Zebra's tailplane. Fortune grinned. He looked more boyish than ever, despite the huge moustache. "Well," he said, "another balloon to go up, eh? Bracing sea air and a health farm diet to go with it, all included in the price of admission. They're even paying us to take the jolly old cure!"

Webster still felt twinges of guilt every time he remembered how he had once mentally dismissed this brave young man as a brainless fool. "There's one thing, Fortune," he began awkwardly.

"Yes, old chap?"

"I'd like . . . well, I'd like you to know that . . . I mean, there's no one I'd rather . . . Dash it all, I'm happy to have you as my Number Two. Confidence one hundred per, and all that."

"Oh, I say . . . Good show! . . . I mean, gosh . . ." Fortune was embarrassed. "Very decent of you. That is to say . . . likewise. Er, tell you what: we'll sink one together in Göteborg on Friday night, eh?"

"It's a date," said Webster.

47

"What-ho!"

Webster hesitated, staring at the young man for a moment in the dim radiance reflected from the blue perimeter lamps, and then hurried away to his own aircraft.

In the freshening breeze, his pilot and navigator were talking to the RAF ground crew by the Mitchell's entrance hatch. The plane had been painted in Bomber Command camouflage with red and blue roundels. At first they had hoped they might be allowed to use twin-engined English aircraft – Whitleys or Wellingtons or even Ansons – to further the deception when Nazi salvage units found the floating wreckage. But in view of the tremendous losses sustained by Bomber Command on its nightly raids over Euope, and the perilous supply situation, Lord Beaverbrook, the press baron who was Minister of Aircraft Production, had flatly refused to sanction the sacrifice of two precious machines. Even when the request had been pushed through the highest echelons of Eisenhower's Supreme Headquarters. The RAF was already using American Bostons for aerial reconnaissance, O'Kelly was told: the Nazi intelligence system was unlikely to unmask the whole operation just because they found the wreckage of two Mitchells in the Kattegat after an RAF raid on Kiel. And so finally they had to content themselves with these two clapped-out B-25s grudgingly supplied by the USAAF.

Webster approached the small group beneath the wing. "Everything wrapped up?" he asked.

The flight-sergeant fitter saluted. "Just reportin' to your skipper, sir," he said. "We been all over the crate from stem to stern and as far's we can see, she's all tickety-boo, allowin' for her age! Course, we ain't too familiar with these aircraft and all. But the only problem as I can see might affect your port carb. She just might ice up if you run into high cloud. There's a tendency for your needle valve to stick there. If she does, bung 'er onto fully-rich and that should do the trick."

"Thank you, Flight."

"One other thing," a grizzled rigger added. "You want to watch your oil temperature when you're near your ceiling. If she gets too cold, it could stiffen up your pitch control, see."

Lieutenant Joe Constantine, the Canadian-born pilot, nodded. "OK," he said. "I'll keep my eyes skinned for that."

Webster looked at him covertly. He was a tall, rangy man with a high-bridged nose and a lantern jaw. They had worked together on a secret mission in North Africa, and the Englishman had come to respect Constantine's strength of character, his inventiveness and above all his endurance. Reilly, the navigator, was more of an unknown quantity. He had volunteered for the RAF in 1938 and transferred to CO(S)E only six months previously, since when his record of AWOL junketings, minor insubordination and drunken behaviour ran to three pages of typescript – excessive even for that untraditional organisation. He had been chosen for Operation Andersen simply because, as an ex-pathfinder expert, his navigational expertise was beyond reproach. Renard, the other Canadian, who was navigating for Fortune, had been with the outfit for more than a year.

"Right you are, then: up you go . . . and good luck, lads!" the flight-sergeant said perfunctorily. With the RAF aircrew, whose planes they knew and loved and serviced, the ground crews were on affectionate and jokey terms, but the commandos were strangers; their mission was secret; they would never meet again. There was really nothing else to say.

Webster motioned the others ahead, then ducked under the belly of the plane and climbed up through the open hatch just forward of the bomb bay. He found himself standing in a narrow cabin lit only by the dim red and blue bulbs glowing on the instrument panels ahead of the pilot's and navigator's seats, which surmounted a steep step in front of him. Above the heads of Reilly and Constantine as they settled themselves before the controls he could see stars through the Perspex panels of the greenhouse. Beside the step, a narrow tunnel led forward to the bomb-aimer's position in the nose blister.

He turned around. The soundproofing material jacketing the stressed metal of the fuselage was veined with a complex of cables and control conduits, scarred with patches where flak had penetrated the skin. Beneath the empty gun turret, the five remaining members of the team sat strapped into temporary iron and canvas seats only installed that afternoon, and behind them the box-like bomb bay blocked off most of the machine's after end. In the bay, wrapped in quick-release tarpaulin . . . Webster put the thought of the gruesome contents from his mind and swung back to face the front.

Constantine had slid back the blister's side panel and was peering down at the RAF men fifteen feet below him. As the counterbalanced hatch swung shut below Webster's legs, they heard the shattering roar of one of the engines on the nearest Lancaster bursting to life. It was followed by another and another until the close, oil-and-petrol-smelling interior of the Mitchell was vibrating with the thunder of their unsilenced exhausts. Constantine pointed at his port starter motor and turned a gloved thumb up. On the tarmac below, the flight-sergeant jerked his head at the engine cowling and revolved his index finger. The pilot pressed the Energize switch.

The control lamps dimmed. Webster heard the stuttering of the booster pump over the noise of the Lancasters. Gradually, a faint whine began in the B-25's port starter motor as the flywheel built up energy. Constantine flicked the switch to Mesh; the airscrew wheezed, coughed and then spun. As he stabbed the Prime button and thrust the throttle forward, the Wright Cyclone caught with a racketing bang that shook the whole of the aircraft and drowned out all other sounds. By the time the starboard motor fired, Webster's whole world was conditioned to the insane reverberations of the bombers as the entire raiding force warmed up. And then, as suddenly as they had started, they all stopped. There was nothing to do now but wait until the control tower gave them the signal to take off.

Over the silence ringing in their ears, they could hear the subdued conversation of men in the nearest Lancaster. An owl hooted somewhere in the trees beyond the perimeter. The keyed-up commandos in U for Uncle, tense with anticipation, remained mute.

Webster lowered himself into the one empty seat and stared at his team in the half light. Next to him was the monolithic form of Sergeant Hawkins, a large, unflappable cockney regular whose courage and initiative Webster had been grateful for on more than one occasion. Behind them were Hunter, who had once been a ship's engineer, and the Pole, Zygmund, a German-speaking refugee seconded from the Pioneer Corps. The two rear seats were occupied by a dark, wiry little Scottish sergeant named McTavish, and Hewitt, the giant West Country man who had smashed the chair during the pub brawl. Webster had complete confidence in all of them – except perhaps the Scot, who had only joined the unit at the last moment, sent up to the Orkneys by O'Kelly because of his talent for survival in impossible conditions. McTavish, who had spent most of his life fishing in the wild waters off the west coast, had a host of skills that no army could teach him, yet there was something about his attitude – a reserve? a near-insolence? a seaman's contempt for the landlubber, perhaps?—that inspired in Webster a vague disquiet. A suspicion that sometime, somewhere, the man could prove to be a source of trouble.

In any case, Webster thought, buckling his safety belt, there was no point worrying about it now, when they were about to take off on the first stage of the operation.

In fact it was almost nine o'clock before the first Lancaster moved out of its pan onto the perimeter track. One by one, engines roaring, the big planes trundled around the outside of the airfield to line up at the south-west end of the main runway awaiting the green light from the control tower. Constantine edged U for Uncle in at the tail end of the queue, followed by Fortune in the second B-25. As soon as one bomber was accelerating down the runway towards the tower – and the target – the next was in place flashing its identification code letter. In a surprisingly short time, the tail-light of Lancaster O for Orange was receding into the dark and Reilly was signalling his 'U'.

They gave him a green immediately. Constantine shoved the throttles up to 30 inches of boost against the brakes and took a last look at the instruments: throttle and pitch locks off . . . booster pumps to Emergency . . . supercharger to low gear . . . mixture control okay . . . engine and oil temperatures with the needles flickering on the red lines. He checked the flaps, the security of the hatches . . . and finally flipped off the brakes.

The Mitchell surged forward down the runway, gradually gathering speed as the dry clatter of the Wright Cyclones rose to a roar. Fifty, sixty, seventy m.p.h. came up on the dial, the pedals hardening and the wheel growing stiff in the Canadian's hands. At eighty, he made the tiniest dab at the brakes and feathered in a touch of right rudder to counteract the leftward

51

pull of the motors. At eighty-five the nose wheel came unstuck
. . . and then, smoothly, with the indicator on 110, they were
airborne, the white runway marker lights streaming beneath
the wings like tracer, the control tower and then a line of trees
flicking away into the dark as he heaved the column back into
his stomach, banked and settled the plane into a long climb to
operational height.

"Gear up," Constantine called into his microphone. Reilly
jerked a lever. There was a sudden hollow roar while the
undercart doors opened and the oleos folded inward to tuck
the big wheels into the aircraft's belly – then they were alone
in the night with only the blue-white flames from the Mitchell's
exhaust stubs on either side for company.

A modern traveller accustomed to high-speed, high-altitude,
pressurised transport would hardly recognise a 1943 warplane
as an aircraft at all. Oxygen masks were obligatory at anything
over 8,000 to 9,000 feet. Conversation without headphones
was impossible since the entire machine shook and rattled
and shuddered with the appalling racket of the piston engines.
Owing to their low power – weight ratio, the planes pitched
and yawed, or dropped and rose like an elevator at the mercy
of the slightest turbulence in the air, and it took all of a pilot's
strength to keep the non-power-assisted control surfaces in the
airstream.

As Webster and his men thundered toward the bomber
stream assembly point over the east coast, the leader unstrapped
himself and crawled forward into the transparent blister in the
Mitchell's nose. Lying flat on his face, he plugged in the
bomb-aimer's headset and called up the pilot sitting somewhere
above and behind his position. "What-ho! Everything spot on
in the engine-room?"

He listened to the Canadian's acknowledgement and then
peered through the curved Perspex panels. Four hundred
yards away to the south, quadruple flame patterns from the
second B-25 twinkled in the blackness. A mile ahead, the
dim silhouette of a Lancaster showed up against a cloudbank
silvered by a moon which had yet to rise above the horizon.
Otherwise, despite the fact that the bomber stream that night
was two hundred miles long and anything up to fourteen miles
wide, the immensity of the dark sky appeared empty.

Below them now the undulating, milky curve of the English coast slid rearwards to vanish beneath the wings and engine pods. It was penetratingly cold in the exposed, unheated nose of the plane. "Constantine – what's our height?" Webster demanded. His pulse was racing and the low temperature was causing him to breathe in fast, shallow gulps.

"Eight thousand seven hundred."

"Have Reilly order the chaps to clip on their oxygen masks, will you?" Webster reached for his own mask. "And tell that bonnie Scotsman to shin up into the turret, plug in the mike and watch out for night-fighters. From now on, we're a sitting duck for Jerry sharpshooters."

"Wilco. Get out the earmuffs, boss: we're still climbing."

Webster himself anxiously scanned the sombre wastes of the sky as the B-25 clawed its way up towards the stratosphere. There were no guns in either of the turrets. They carried no radio operator, so they were unable – by tuning in to the German controllers' frequencies – to find out if they had been spotted on the coastal defence radar screens. In addition to that, if a night-fighter could be directed to within two miles of them, at approximately the same height, the Mitchell would show up as a blip on the Nazi crew's own screen. The enemy's radar-controlled searchlights could probe almost seven miles into a clear sky and the deadly 8.8 cm flak could reach as high as 18,000 feet.

Webster swallowed. He had never felt quite so defenceless in the whole of his career. Despite the intense cold, there was sweat on his forehead. As his eyes ceaselessly swept the dark, his mind, unwilling to dwell on the negative aspect of whatever hazards lay ahead, roved over the recent past. He had done everything he possibly could to prepare the teams for the near-impossible task they had been set (and Webster had no illusions about the odds stacked against them). He had made them practice silent assault landings night after night on the low-lying Orkneys. Hewitt and Crisp, who was flying in Fortune's plane, had learned to construct seaweed and driftwood bivouac shelters that were indistinguishable among the rocks at a distance of more than twenty feet. McTavish had demonstrated the art of making a smokeless fire from wet sticks and then cooking the molluscs and fish that they speared. All of them, Fortune and Webster himself included, had spent many hours submerged in the icy water around one of the tiny fishing ports, planting dummy limpet mines on the slime-covered jetty walls. They had studied the maps and sand-table models of Anholt and Laeso until they felt they knew every contour of the terrain they were to attack better than the streets around their own homes.

And, as a final test, they had been ordered to make a secret night landing on a heavily guarded islet housing a British naval radar station, Webster's unit on its north coast, Fortune's on the south. Their briefing was to conceal their rubber dinghies, rendezvous in the middle of the island, then complete the two-way crossing to re-embark in one another's boats – knowing that the Royal Marines patrolling the defences, who had not been warned of the exercise, would shoot to kill if they were discovered. In fact not a shot was fired and O'Kelly had pronounced himself satisfied – the highest accolade he could bestow – with the operation.

Looking down through the transparent nose of the machine carrying him at more than 200 m.p.h., towards the genuine target, Webster hoped that the real thing would prove equally 'satisfying' to the old man.

They were at 17,000 feet and still climbing when they crossed the Dutch coast and saw the yellow TPMs – the turning-point marker flares – which the Pathfinders had positioned over the seaside resort of Zandvoort. The garish brilliance illuminated the pillboxes of the Nazis' Atlantic Wall and the dolls-house façades of the town among the dunes. Inland, searchlights stabbed the sky over Leiden and there were pinpoints of fire twinkling through the blackness to the north. The Mitchell banked over the flares and turned towards them.

The main bomber stream was routed south of Amsterdam, with a second batch of TPMs scheduled to be dropped near Hanover in the hope that this would mislead the enemy defences and persuade the controllers that the raid was destined to pulverise Hamburg. Without radio, the two Mitchells had been left to pursue a maverick course, with no specific ETA over the assembly point and no precise position in the stream: they were simply to tag along and keep out of everyone's

54

way until it was time to start the pretence that they had been shot down.

"Steer zero-eight-zero," Reilly's brogue ordered suddenly over the intercom. "Sure, we don't want to run into all that shit around bloody Amsterdam . . . Bejasus, would you look at all them searchlights!"

Webster was already staring at the bright fingers probing the sky ahead of them. In each searchlight battery there was one beam that remained vertical and stationary. This he knew was the unit's radar-controlled master beam. It only shifted when they had a fix on some poor sod. Then all the others automatically homed on it, and God help the plane they caught! He peered left and right, scanning the night for the fleeting, tell-tale shadow of an enemy aircraft. They had long since lost sight of the Lancaster ahead of them, but the other B-25 was still visible, half a mile to starboard and a thousand feet lower down.

As Constantine followed the navigator's directions, the searchlights veered away to the left. Seconds later, flak hosed up at them. Pale streaks of tracer rose lazily from the flickers of gunfire pricking the dark below . . . suddenly to accelerate with incredible speed and flash past the blister or curve away harmlessly beneath it. Now the blackness ahead was punctuated by sparkles of orange as anti-aircraft shells burst among the invisible raiders. The Mitchell tilted, shook. Black smoke whipped past the Perspex. They had flown through their first near-miss.

Webster could hear the Canadian cursing as he wrestled with the controls, hauling the plane back on course. Then the central beam in the nearest group of searchlights moved abruptly towards them. Inexorably, the shaft of light traced a path through the dark as the others converged on the thin cone of brilliance. The pilot muttered something inaudible and Reilly's suddenly indrawn breath hissed sibilantly in Webster's earphone. But the beam stopped moving a quarter of a mile to the north and they could see the shape of a bomber trapped in it. The aircraft was a four-engined Halifax flying on a course crossing their own about fifteen hundred feet below. The skipper tried the time-honoured manoeuvre of sideslipping down the main beam, but the others moved relentlessly in, pinning the machine against the night as definitively as an insect on a board. The Halifax twisted, turned, banked and dived, desperately trying to escape the blinding lights, but flak was already peppering the air around it with puffs of smoke and flashes of red. They could see the silver streaks of bombs falling away as the plane jettisoned its load – and then the crucified silhouette seemed all at once to stagger in midair. A ball of fire flamed from the centre section, blooming quickly into a whirling maelstrom of crimson that paled to whiteness, and then livid green, before it vanished to leave only a stain of smoke in the converging beams.

"Holy Christ!" Constantine said in a shocked voice. "You'd think they'd have— My God! There goes another!"

Further away to the east, a burning torch erupted in the sky, blazing furiously downward until it spread in a slow explosion that lit up the rectangular strips of polder fringing the canals below in a momentary orange glare.

"Bandits!" McTavish's voice shouted urgently in the intercom. *"Night-fighter above and astern, closing fast from port! For the Laird's sake—"*

His words choked off as Constantine flung the Mitchell into a vertical left bank and put down the nose. Webster heard the roar of the fighter's engine over the Cyclone's protesting scream – then the squat shadow of a Junkers JU-88 swept past above the blister, spraying tracer and cannon shells innocuously into the night.

"Wacko!" Webster yelled. "Show the blighter, Joe! . . . But don't lose too much height shaking him off if you can avoid it."

The Canadian was too busy to reply. Slamming the throttle levers to full boost, he dragged the wheel savagely back and brought the B-25 lurching up into the first part of a loop, and then flipped the machine over in a half-roll to complete a perfect World War One Immelmann turn, facing back the way they had come.

Webster saw the tilted clumps of light that flickered below swing crazily away. They wheeled into sight again above his head, then dropped from view as the pilot banked steeply to turn back onto his former course.

Before the shouts and jeers of the men so unexpectedly thrown about in the cabin had died away, the Mitchell had flown into the comparative safety of the cloudbank they had been approaching ever since they crossed the coast.

Chapter Seven

Lost in the marrow-chilling darkness of ten-tenths night cloud, Constantine missed the TPMs over Hanover and, flying on Reilly's estimated reckoning, turned north fifteen miles too soon. They were at 21,000 feet when the Mitchell sailed out of the cumulo-stratus front into a magic world silvered by a three-quarter moon riding in a clear sky behind them. Astonishingly, the other B-25 was still in view, about a mile away to port now, still below and behind.

Beyond Z for Zebra, McTavish from his empty turret could see ten or twelve four-engined bombers flying towards an irregular pattern of red, white and yellow lights twinkling around a sheet of water glinting in the moonlight. They were approaching the first of the thousand plane raid targets. "That must be bluidy Kiel there," Reilly shouted. "Would you believe it, that stinkin' ould wind has carried us to the west! Laird save us, we're between Oldenburg and bloody Hamburg. Stand by, everyone, for all the shit Jerry can put up."

But there were no shells exploding among the bombers on their left now: they had crossed into a night-fighter grid and faint streaks of yellow and white etched into the sky marked the position of enemy planes as they fired or were fired upon. Abruptly McTavish yelled: "Och, away! There's a bleedin' Kraut on Fortune's tail! Can ye no' see it, man? Is there nobody can see the bugger? Oh, Jasus! Oh, God – why dis'nae the prick *do* somethin'?"

Webster jerked his head to the left, eyes straining to see through the Perspex bowl. The drama was clearly visible in the diffuse light. A single-engined FW-190 was approaching the other Mitchell in a shallow climb, closing for the kill in the blind spot beneath the B-25's belly. He watched in horrified disbelief as the night-fighter, its complex radar antennae

58

gleaming in the milky light above the matt-black body and wings, drew relentlessly nearer the unsuspecting American machine.

Powerless to help or even warn his comrades, he cursed impotently and pounded the surface of the blister with a clenched fist while the distance between hunter and quarry narrowed.

Flame streaked from the leading edges of the FW-190's wings as the pilot eased back his stick and thumbed the firing button to rake the unprotected Mitchell with armour-piercing, high-explosive and incendiary shells from its 20 mm cannon. The helpless watchers in U for Uncle saw the converging missiles strike home all along the underside of the doomed aircraft. Portions of fuselage broke off and whipped away in the slipstream. The starboard cowling detached itself from the engine pod, flapping over the wing like an angry bird before it vanished into the void. The engine glowed red, brightening to orange as tongues of fire licked at the pod, spread inboard and then, teased out by the 200 m.p.h. airflow, enveloped the whole of the B-25's flank.

The flaming plane seemed to halt in midair. Its starboard wing dipped. Then the nose dropped sickeningly and the fuel tank exploded with a dull roar, blowing off the wingtip to send the Mitchell hurtling earthwards in a blazing spiral. The sinister alto whine of its death dive was clearly audible over the racket of the engines in the surviving B-25. Hawklike, the Focke-Wulf circled down after it.

Webster followed the fiery corkscrew path of the stricken machine with his eyes, but the flash of the explosion when it hit the ground 20,000 feet below was lost in the inferno beneath him. He gritted his teeth, trying not to think of the fighting companions he had trained and lost – sardonic Renard, the other Canadian in the group; Crisp, the camouflage expert; Marron and Goldberg and the Free Frenchman, Duplessis. Worst of all, Charles G. Fortune, with his fool's mask disguising a will of iron, Fortune who looked so unbelievably innocent that if he didn't join in a fight you knew it was because he was afraid of killing someone! Well, this time the G in his name stood for gone. They were all gone now, all dead, blown to pieces, incinerated or flung from the wrecked plane to split open like slaughtered beasts on the earth far below . . .

For over a minute after the disaster the Mitchell's headsets were silent. The snarling Cyclones dragged the plane on, shuddering, towards the fiery hell pulsating along the waterfront four miles beneath them. Then Constantine's voice said softly: "Poor bastards."

"McTavish?" Webster demanded. "Did you see any parachutes?"

"No, I didna," the man in the upper turret replied huskily. "I looked guid but I saw naethin'."

After another pause, Constantine asked: "Orders, Major?"

"Orders? What the hell do you mean, orders?" Webster rasped, still not entirely in control of himself. "You got your blasted orders back in the briefing hut. Carry them out."

"Orders were that, if one plane was hit, the other was to turn back and—"

"I don't give a fuck what the orders were!" Wester shouted with a splendid disregard for consistency. "I'm in charge here, Lieutenant, and I say we have a mission to complete and we are damned well going through with it!"

"OK, OK, OK," the Canadian soothed. "But there are two islands and they are fifty miles apart."

"I know that as well as you do. We'll just have to look after both of them ourselves now, that's all. You'll have to work twice as hard for your pay."

"Yeah, but which—?"

"Carry out your orders. Go ahead and ditch near Anholt . . . and leave the responsibility for the other island to me."

Constantine's theatrical sigh was audible in every earphone on the plane. "Yes, sir," he said.

Searching the moonlit sky for night-fighters, Webster shook his head, grinned a little shamefacedly and transferred his gaze to the incandescent earth below. They were much nearer to Kiel now. He could make out the flash of bursting bombs around the shipyards and U-boat pens. Beyond the quivering glow of incendiary fires and the canopy of flak arching over them, red and green flares floated above Flensburg, forty miles further along the coast. Every now and then the street plan of the city under attack leaped alive for an instant as a seven-million-candlepower photoflash exploded to enable the raiding planes to record the accuracy of their aim. It was beginning to get a trifle noisy down there, Webster decided. It was time for him to put the final phase of his own operation into action.

"Reilly, release the first battery of FF-10s."

"Right away, sir."

"Constantine, the moment she blows, take us out in a wide curve over the sea and start to lose height. Do your crippled kite number like billy-oh and have Reilly vector you in on the island from the south-east, right?"

"Wilco."

"McTavish, for Christ's sake keep your eyes skinned for Huns."

"Aye, I'd be a fool if I didnae," the lookout man said sourly.

As the pilot banked away from the fires below, the navigator pulled a lever beneath the instrument panel. At once dense clouds of red and orange smoke poured out from special canisters fixed by the CO(S)E armourers below the centre section of the B-25's wings. Illuminated by powerful red spotlights projecting rearwards from each side of the plane's cabin, the billowing vapour, whirled back by the slipstream from the airscrews, looked from a distance exactly like flames. At the same time Constantine began a spirited impersonation of a flyer trying desperately but unavailingly to keep a crippled machine in the air. Alternately feeding his engines over-rich and too-weak fuel mixtures, jockeying with the throttles and occasionally feathering the propellers, he forced the Wright Cyclones to splutter and cough while he worked at the wheel to bring the aircraft lower in a series of yawing lunges.

The wrinkled silver sheet of the sea slid past beneath them as they jolted down from 20,000 feet to 17,000 and then to 10,000.

Twenty miles out from the inferno of Kiel, when the invisible bomber stream of which they had been a part had swung away to the west, the Canadian completed his half circle and turned north over the Baltic to bring them back on their original course. Flensburg was a distant flicker of lights to port and the Danish island of Loland was immediately below. Over

61

the ten-mile-wide strait separating Odense from the island on which Copenhagen was built, Webster called up his navigator again. "Tally-ho, Barry! Give 'em the works now. Release the second FF-10 battery and make it a real cremation – give the buggers value for money, what!"

Reilly yanked at a second lever and a fresh set of canisters added their smoke to the long plume of artificial 'flames' streaming behind the apparently disabled Mitchell.

They were down to 4,000 feet when the last strip of land vanished beneath their wings and the plane flew out over the open waters of the Kattegat. "Zero-eight-seven," Reilly's voice intoned on the intercom.

"Are you sure?" Constantine's acknowledgement was tinged with doubt.

"Am I sure? Sure I'm sure. Holy Mother of God, Constantine, who's navigatin' this ship? You or me?"

"I figure we're too far to the east. An over-correction maybe. Don't forget, we already made one fuck-up. While we were in that cloud, the wind blew us—"

"Ah, forget the bloody wind, man, will you? Steer zero-eight-seven. You'll have us all end up in Norway, else!"

"It's a very small island," the pilot said stubbornly. "Shit, if we were to miss—"

"*Constantine!*" Webster's voice cracked across the conversation like a whip. "What the devil d'you think you're doing? Reilly's the navigator. Do what he tells you."

"Just as you say."

Fifteen minutes later, when the B-25 was at less than 1,000 feet, the Irishman exclaimed triumphantly: "What did I tell you! There's your bloody island, for God's sake – and *it's* still to the east of *us*! Look, man look! But would a person be after apologisin' for doubtin' me word? Would he hell!"

Webster stared through the blister. The low-lying stretch of land was smudged across the silver-grey sea off to his right. Even with the moonlight it was impossible to make out any details of the topography. "Put her down about seven miles offshore," he ordered. "That way, we should be out of sight over the horizon if any of their sea-level patrols see us ditching."

He unplugged his intercom and crawled back through the

tunnel into the main cabin. McTavish was still propped up in the empty turret, his sparrow head twisting this way and that as he scanned the bright sky for enemy aircraft. The rest of the team sat strapped into their seats, grey-faced with anxiety and fatigue. Unable to see out and follow the course of the flight, powerless to converse or hear the exchanges between Webster, the turret and the men in the greenhouse, they had found the ordeal more severe than they expected.

Webster plucked at the lookout man's trouser-leg to attract his attention and signalled him back to his seat. Together, they strapped themselves in and waited for the perilous crash landing. The Mitchell planed down towards the sea, the roar of its engines faded to a subdued clatter. "Flaps down," Constantine said tensely. "Pitch." Stroking the control column back as tenderly as a lover, he flattened the aircraft out ten feet above the grey waters that were now rushing up to meet them. The air-speed indicator needle sank back past the 150 mark to 100 . . . 90 . . . 85 . . . 80 . . .

At the last moment, as the B-25 slowed to its stalling speed, he cut the motors and lifted the nose. The plane flopped down onto the waves like a shot duck.

The impact was harder and louder than any of them expected – a tearing, splintering crash overlaid by a screech of tortured metal that jarred every bone in their bodies. In the silence that followed, the slap and gurgle of encroaching water sounded almost deafening.

"All right, chaps, let's go!" Webster shouted. They flipped open the safety belts and leaped into action. They had between one and a half and two minutes before the sea chased out the air lending the wreck its buoyancy and the machine sank. Each man had specific tasks allotted to him. They had rehearsed it all a dozen times. Zygmund and Sergeant Hawkins opened the special escape hatches which had been cut above the bomb bay in the Mitchell's tail. McTavish and the towering Hewitt unclasped the quick-release clips securing the tell-tale seats and threw them out into the sea. Hunter freed two rubber dinghies, already packed with their arms, supplies and equipment, that would automatically inflate in contact with the water. Webster drew the tarpaulin off the grisly contents of the bomb bay.

There were four dead men packed inside, kitted out as

aircrew complete with identification tags, ID papers and letters. Three of them had died from impact injuries and one was burned. Webster didn't know, and he didn't want to know, who they had really been, how and when they had died, and how O'Kelly's backroom boys had got hold of them. With the help of Reilly and the pilot, sweating as the Mitchell sank lower in the water, he manhandled two of them into the greenhouse and propped them up in front of the controls. The third they left lying beneath the empty mid-upper turret, sightless eyes staring fishlike at the moonlight filtering through the Perspex. The burned one, who also had bullet holes in his chest, they dragged up through the escape hatch and consigned to the waves. It was better that he should be washed up somewhere ashore rather than found in the wreckage of a plane without a scorch mark on it.

And, now that he came to think of it, without gun mountings in either of the turrets. But that was a mystery he could leave to the German or Danish salvage crews if and when the crashed plane was recovered.

The rest of the party were now in the inflated boats – Hawkins, Hunter, McTavish and Hewitt in one; Zygmund waiting for Webster and the two aircrew in the other. Three of the B-25's formers had snapped when they hit, leaving her sprawled on the surface of the sea like a bird with a broken back. She was already awash, one wing submerged and the other canting skywards. The tailplane had broken off under the impact and floated away, and the transparent canopy over the cockpit was about to vanish beneath the surface of the sea.

Consantine was the last to leave. Before he stepped into the bobbing dinghy, he patted the shattered fuselage and murmured: "She was a good ship: an old lady, but game to the last!"

"Game as a dead pigeon already!" said Zygmund, who had learned his English on New York's East Side. "But does she have a sister – I mean like a girl she should fly us home?"

Webster grinned, pushing the dinghy away from the sinking plane. If they were making jokes – even acid ones – that was good: it meant that morale was high.

The night was achingly cold, with an icy breeze ruffling the surface of a slight swell. The hissing of water against hot metal suddenly ceased as the port engine sank from sight. The wingtip tore free and eddied away. Then the sea poured with a rush and a roar through the open hatch; the B-25 slid slowly beneath the wavelets and vanished in a widening circle of bubbles. A few pieces of debris floated back to the surface – a log-book, a seat cushion, part of a safety harness and some unidentifiable fragments of wood – and then they were alone under the high, cold sky, the last link with their base cut and only the impossibility of their mission ahead.

Webster looked up and gave an exclamation of satisfaction. The cloudbank through which they had flown earlier had followed them up from the south-west and was about to blanket the moon. While its dark shadow was still racing across the sea to overtake them, they spun the dinghies around and started paddling steadily towards the invisible island.

Part Two

The Tinder Box

"No, this is it, surely – why, here's a cross too!" cried all of them together on discovering that there were crosses on all the doors. It was evident that their search would be in vain and they were obliged to give up.

Chapter Eight

Webster lay flat on his belly between two clumps of coarse grass and surveyed the flat land through his field glasses. He was on the lip of a low bluff at the south-western corner of the island. Behind and below him, the seven members of his team were concealed among the rocks at the foot of an overhang in the twenty-foot cliff. The dinghies had been deflated and stowed out of sight. Webster had issued machine-pistols, American Buntlines, bowie knives and grenades. The primacord, detonators and C3 explosive were packed in eight separate waterproof bundles. After emergency rations had been eaten, a convincing rampart of boulders had been constructed to hide the lower part of their makeshift bivouac.

Although they had encountered no obstacles or obstructions on the foreshore, when the two rubber boats were paddled into the lee of the bluff just before dawn, it had taken them all day, working silently with two lookouts posted above, to arrange things to Webster's satisfaction. He preferred to establish a solid base first, take his time reconnoitring the terrain, and only then carry through the operation in a single decisive action.

Just as well, too, he thought as he refocused the glasses. Although they had seen no sign of a patrol or an enemy soldier all day, the reconnaissance was proving to be unusually difficult. To start with, the batteries at the other end of the island bore little relation to the high-level aerial photos of those they had been briefed to destroy. There were large-bore naval guns in the emplacements all right – he could see the wicked grey muzzles thrusting through slits in the concrete with his naked eye – but they were on fixed traverses pointing west, not mounted in 360-degree turrets the way he'd been told. In addition there were Oerlikons, pom-poms and two 8.8 cm flak batteries. As for the radar, he could make out conventional scanners swinging easily in the late afternoon sun, the complications of a Freya antenna, but there were no Würtzburg bowls and no sign whatever of the sophisticated new sonar installation that everyone had been so worried about. It almost looked as though the island's defences were geared to repel air attacks rather than seek out and destroy intruders from the sea.

Was he expected to put the flak out of action too? If so, they were going to have to ration the supply of C3 like sweets among a crowd of wartime schoolboys, especially as they already had to reserve some now for the guns on Laeso. He shook his head and repeated to himself the eternal complaint of those on active service: Those stupid pratts at HQ! As usual, the chairborne wonders at Staff had got it all wrong! The bloody planners knew fuck-all about the actual job – it never failed!

This time, though, they seemed to have put up an exceptionally colossal black, for not only was the briefing on the armaments out by a mile: the rest of the gen they'd been fed was equally off. The island conformed near enough to the general plan they'd studied so hard, yet the topography bore little relation to the sand-table models. There should, for example, have been a tiny fishing port less than a mile from the spit where they'd made landfall, but he had neither seen nor heard any activity in that direction. Nor was there a roof, a chimney or a church tower visible above the shallow undulations of the coast. The batteries, also, were at least half a mile from the locations charted on the maps. Could Jerry have altered the entire defence plan of the place? Since the Intelligence bods had received their information? If he had, why on earth would he have substituted inferior, out-of-date stuff for the top-secret material they were supposed to be installing?

In any case (Webster thought) where were the traces of the original emplacements? You didn't just obliterate every sign of modern, reinforced and pre-stressed concrete coastal batteries in a matter of days. A more likely explanation was that the Danish underground types furnishing the gen were double agents. In which case he and his men could be walking into a trap. But no – why the hell would Jerry go to all that trouble just to lay hands on a few commandos?

Whichever way he looked at it, the thing smelled off, decidedly off. He didn't like it at all. And he was damned if he was going to make a single move towards those bally guns before he had found out a whole lot more about the base and the way it worked.

Yet again he stared through the field glasses. In the magnified circles of vision he could see between the bluff and the emplacements a swell of land divided into fields planted with cabbages and potatoes and some root crop. *Cabbages*, for God's sake! On a top-secret Nazi base! About a mile away on the far side of the slope there was a group of white-walled, slate-roofed cottages with men and women working around the barns behind them. The military quarters must be behind the knoll housing the batteries: he could just see the hooped corrugated-iron roofs of army huts above the terraced concrete. But of the troops manning them, there was at the moment no sign. He swept the glasses from coast to coast along the narrow island. No patrols marched the hilly clifftop path, and the white dirt road cleaving the fields was deserted. He shook his head again. Knowing the exploits of the Danish underground, he would have expected barbed wire and watchtowers.

Webster pushed himself back on his elbows and knees and slithered down the bluff to the shore. Over the swash and suck of waves, he could hear the pulse of a motor-boat beyond the headland at the southern tip of the island, but otherwise everything was quiet. He picked his way back to the cave along the rocks.

"Something decidedly rum about this place," he told the team. "I want to take a shufti at the other end: we must have a whole heap more info before we even think of a plan. I don't know, but it looks to me as if someone, somewhere, has put up the most almighty ricket." He looked at his watch. "It'll be dark in less than an hour. I'm going to take a patrol of five men and circle the whole blasted island, paying special attention to the casemates and pillboxes I've seen. Then maybe we'll know where the fuck we're at!"

He went across to one of the waterproof supply packs and took out two small transceivers. "I wasn't going to break radio silence until we had the whole thing wrapped up," he said, "but I suppose you have to break even your own rules in an emergency. Reilly – go back up to the top of that bluff and keep watch while we're away. Joe – you must be flaked out after the strain of driving that plane. I'm leaving you here as longstop, to guard the clobber and look after the boats." He handed Constantine one of the transceivers. "If anything breaks, call me up on the walkie-talkie. The island's not much more than a mile, maybe a mile and half, across, so the range should be OK. The long, thin tip at the top of the triangle must be flatter than we thought: it's out of sight beyond the installation, and you can't see it from the bluff."

A few minutes later he led Sergeant Hawkins, McTavish, Zygmund, Hewitt and Hunter out into the dusk, while Reilly climbed to the clifftop observation post.

In their proofed, olive-drab battledress zigzagged with camouflage markings, the steel-helmeted figures were soon lost to sight among the rocks. Constantine watched them melt into the gloom, marvelling that six men could move so silently: he couldn't hear a single footfall over the breaking of the small waves running obliquely in to the shore from the west.

For a while he stared out over the grey water, listening to the distant beat of the motor-boat engine that had been puttering away behind the promontory. Perhaps the missing port was hidden on the far side? But no – the sound increased in volume and a small fishing craft with three men aboard slid into view. Constantine froze, shrinking back against a lichen-covered slab of rock, not daring to duck down in case the sudden movement attracted their attention. But the boat sailed on, about a quarter of a mile offshore, and disappeared around a curve of the coast to his left.

He expelled his breath in a long sigh of relief, stamping his feet and slapping gloved hands against his shoulders to restore the circulation in his limbs. It was bitterly cold. The pale glow which had flushed the sky above the western horizon had died, leaving a single star glittering over the sea. He turned around and went back to the bivouac that formed their base.

It was dark now and just as cold beneath the overhang: he could scarcely make out the dim bulk of their equipment piled against the cliff. A loose stone rattled somewhere to his right. As he swung around with an exclamation of surprise, something moved in the blackness close to his face.

Automatically, the Canadian flung up an arm to protect himself, but a great weight descended on his head. For a split second he was aware of breath playing hotly on his chilled face, and then he pitched forward into a roaring void.

Webster led his men around the tip of the low promontory and halted to survey the terrain. The shoreline looped out in a shallow curve to the higher ground on which the gun emplacements were built. Within this bay, a crescent of hard sand separated the rocks and shingle from the sea. Beyond it was a stone jetty sheltering half a dozen small fishing boats, and then the near-vertical walls of the stronghold plunging sheer into the water. The beach was deserted, the skyline on top of the cliff innocent of patrolling figures, the tiny harbour protected by the jetty unmanned.

Webster's experienced eyes took it all in, estimating distances, measuring angles, working out the odds. The gun muzzles pointed out to sea above high stone walls. A couple of well-placed charges on the waterline could bring the whole shebang tumbling down into the Kattegat and blow the place to hell.

But below this semi-automatic calculation, this professional's expertise, the devils of doubt were gnawing industriously at his self-confidence.

It was all wrong; everything about it was wrong. Apart from the geographic anomalies, it looked too easy. A piece of cake. And what the hell was the port doing on the wrong side of the island? Something most definitely smelled stronger than ever . . .

He stared at the desolate shore. The tide was low, but on the way in. A thin line of wrack, near the outer curve of the sandy crescent, indicated the last high-water mark. The men were carrying their long-barrelled Buntlines in shoulder harnesses, with the grenades slung around their waists. This left their hands free as they moved among the slippery rocks . . . but it would be much quicker if they could cut across the sand. The incoming tide would erase any Man Friday footmarks, and the bluff would still hide them from any late workers in the fields above. Webster lifted the glasses, which were hooked next to the transceiver on his webbing shoulder

73

strap. There was no sign of sentries on this side of the gun emplacements.

The beach was littered with rock outcrops surrounded by pools of sea water. The sound of the fishing boat's engine had died away on the far side of the island. With the long northern twilight, if they made a series of dashes from pool to pool, they could be a mile away beneath the wall of the fortress before it was really dark. He decided to take the chance: they might never get such a good opportunity again.

"Right," he said crisply. "Now we're going to take the straight line across the sand, hoping the tide will cover us before anyone notices. Spread out and make for the shelter of the jetty, using those rocks with the pools as much as you can. And if any silly bugger puts as much as one foot above that high-tide line, I'll . . . I'll jolly well send him home without any tea!"

"A fine thing," Zygmund said bitterly. "He brings us to the beach – and not an ice-cream man in sight!"

"Christ, you must be a bloody masochist, Ziggie!" said Hunter. "Ice bloody cream? A fish and chip stall would be more like it. Or, better still, one of those Yankee hot-dog stands. Jesus, but it's cold here!"

Webster grinned malevolently. "You want a warm-up? Right – I want every man down behind that jetty wall in eight minutes flat. Come on, now . . . move!"

Dodging, sprinting, ducking and weaving, they raced from rock to rock across the foreshore, to reassemble, panting, in the shelter of the weathered, barnacle-encrusted stone wall. Webster and Sergeant Hawkins were the first to arrive. The huge NCO, who could only be dwarfed by unnaturally large men like Hewitt, took a battered Ingersoll from the breast pocket of his battledress tunic. "You're cuttin' it bleedin' fine, those two men," he said to the last pair. "Next time, I want to see you fuckers in the first three, right?"

There was a narrow path zigzagging up from the jetty to a stone balustrade linking the cliff with the gun emplacements. "We'll swan up here to take a closer look," Webster said in a low voice. "Hewitt, Hunter – you stay here and cover our retreat. We should be back within an hour. But if we can't find out what we need to know, we'll have to swim around that blasted wall beyond the jetty and suss the place out from the other side." He shivered. "Let's hope it'll all be laid on, or we may need your hot-dog man after all, Hunter!"

Silently, in single file, the four men crept up the stony path in the fading light. There really were a hell of a lot of questions that wanted answering, and Webster wished fervently that a closer view of the installations might provide some of the clues he needed. Why were the damned guns pointing west, for instance? That was the most urgent question of all. Were there others which had been hidden from him in his lookout position on top of the bluff? Where was the top-secret radar and sonar equipment they had been told about? You couldn't hide that kind of stuff in the boot of a staff Mercedes: you needed masts and aerials and reflectors. And if it really was here somewhere, why was the coastline so lightly guarded? The questions repeated themselves ceaselessly in his mind.

Motioning the others to lie low, he raised himself on tiptoe at the top of the path and peered through a gap in the balustrade. He was looking at a tiny village square. In the middle of a space between two clusters of fishermen's cottages, there was a rusty pump. Beside it stood a handcart piled with driftwood. And beyond the rectangular outlines of the military base bulked against the oncoming night.

The square was deserted and there was the scent of wood smoke in the chilled air. Cautiously, Webster raised himself higher and looked over the top of the balustrade. He could hear voices in the cottages now, and somewhere a radio was playing dance music. A bit non-Aryan, he thought! Craning his head to one side, he saw a sentry standing by a striped barrier pole at the entrance to the military camp. From beyond the concrete walls came the tramp of marching boots and a guttural command. But the army huts he had spotted through his field glasses were outside the compound: he could see them in a gap between two of the cottages, on a slant of land dipping down beyond the square. They appeared to be unguarded. Why? And why – again the problem clamoured for a solution – why *should* those bloody guns face west, towards occupied Denmark, rather than towards the wider expanse of sea through which any raiders might be expected to pass? He could distinguish no sign of other emplacements, apart from the anti-aircraft batteries in the centre of the complex. If there were any, he supposed, they must be on the low-lying tip of the island he had not yet seen. There was nothing for it but to continue their clandestine circuit of the coast. But first he wanted to have a closer look at exactly what was here and make an estimate of the German garrison's strength.

Sliding back to rejoin the others, he murmured: "There's something about this place that simply does not make sense. I want to go in on my own and take a closer look. Sergeant Hawkins – you should know more than any of us about liberating gear: you've been serving longer than anyone! There's a collection of army huts beyond the square up above. I want you to sneak up there and swipe me some kind of Kraut uniform – overalls, anything. If you nip around behind the cottages you should be able to get in easily enough: they don't seem to have posted any sentries there. But watch for the man on the gate leading into the compound; he's on the left of the square."

"Very good, sir."

"In any case" – Webster chuckled – "no offence, Sergeant, but if anyone can convince the local peasantry and the honest burghers of Anholt that he's a Jerry, it's you!"

It was true that the big sergeant, with his pale eyes, bull neck and thatch of sandy hair had a certain Teutonic look about him. But he was a man of few words . . . and those he did use were as a rule unmistakably Anglo-Saxon. All he said now, however, was a simple, "Yes sir."

"We'll wait for you down by the jetty," Webster said.

"Sir."

Moving with a catlike agility for a man of his size, Hawkins climbed to the balustrade, glanced warily from side to side, then vaulted over the stone rail and disappeared. It was almost an hour before he returned, and Webster was growing anxious. Hewitt complained continuously about the cold; Hunter was angry because he couldn't smoke; even Zygmund's flow of whispered cynicism eventually dried up. The only man who hadn't spoken at all was Sergeant McTavish; not for the first time, Webster surprised an oddly hostile look on the tough little Scot's face. But by the time Hawkins materialised from the dark, Webster himself was growing irritable.

"What the hell kept you?" he demanded. "Something good showing at the local cinema? Did you run into any kind of trouble?"

"Sorry, sir." The sergeant was unperturbed. "Not exactly trouble, leastways not as far as the Krauts were concerned. It was them fuckin' lights." Strength of feeling translated the Hawkins vocabulary from the military to the domestic. "And it ain't too easy for some bleeder to move around undetected when the whole soddin' place is lit up like some holiday bloody fairground."

"Lights?" Webster exclaimed incredulously. "*Lights?*"

"Yes, sir. Oil lamps, electric bulbs, floods. All over the perishin' shop, soon as the dusk thickened. But I got your duds, sir. Officer's clobber an' all—"

Webster brushed aside the dark bundle the sergeant was offering him. "But you must be joking," he interrupted. "Surely, Hawkins, there cannot be lights in a wartime—"

"No joke, sir, I can tell you. You can see for yourself."

"Too bloody right I will!" Webster said. "Don't make a sound, any of you."

He hurried back up the path to his vantage point. The sergeant hadn't exaggerated: oil lamps burned now in most of the cottage windows. Through the nearest he could see a family, seated around a table, evidently eating their evening meal. The sentry stood beneath a powerful electric bulb; the compound behind him was floodlit; naked lamps shone over the door of every army hut. They must have been switched on a moment after he'd dropped out of sight before. He could hear a generator thumping in the distance.

But lights? All over a top-secret base? In wartime? Somebody must be joking indeed – and it wasn't Sergeant Hawkins.

Speechless with astonishment, he scrambled back to rejoin his men. Hawkins was proudly displaying his acquisitions. "There's these officer's togs – I nicked 'em from a hanger just inside the door of one of the huts . . . a large-scale map of the area, a fuckin' sight better than the bugger they issued to us . . . a bottle of booze I snatched because some cunt had left his window open—"

"Ar, now that we cud use!" Hewitt's West Country drawl sounded curiously alien in this northern latitude. "Nobody but a gert fule would leave a window open in this weather . . . less he was so tough Oi wouldn't want to meet 'un. But me, Oi ben in the maarket for a drop o' the haard stuff ever since the minute we landed!"

"I told you not to talk," Webster snapped, squatting beside them on the cold, damp stones. "Show me that uniform, Sergeant." He produced a small pencil flashlight and, shielding it with one hand, directed the beam onto the insignia decorating the collar of the field-grey material.

Field-grey? The uniform was a dusty blue.

A dreadful suspicion began to form in his mind. "Let me see the bottle," he said huskily.

"That's a nice piece of cloth," Zygmund said, reaching for the stolen tunic. "Feel the—"

"*Holy Christ!*" Webster breathed. He was staring at the red lettering on the label of the bottle. *Akvavit – Sölertalje SA, Malmö.* "That's a *Swedish* officer's uniform, for God's sake! This is Swedish booze. You know what's happened? That stupid prick Reilly has only landed us on the wrong fucking island!"

As the others gaped in amazement, he grabbed the map from Hawkins' hand and spread it out on the ground. It was a chart of the Kattegat. And – the sergeant had been right – it was far more detailed than their own. There was the squat shape of Laeso with its panhandle projecting to the east; to the south was the extended triangle of Anholt; and – yes! just inside the thick blue line indicating the limit of Swedish territorial waters – there was another island. It was called Karlsö. And according to the legend it was a Swedish coastal defence base.

Its shape corresponded with the wider, south-western half of Anholt. But it was hardly surprising that Webster had been unable to make out the long, thin north-eastern tip: it simply was not there. No wonder the topography bore little relation to the sand-table models on which they had been briefed; no wonder there was no blackout, no landing obstacles, no hostile patrols! No wonder the guns were angled towards the west: the installation was designed to repel a possible air-sea invasion by the Germans!

Christl

Landing, in uniform, with offensive weapons, on neutral territory . . .

They could have blown a non-belligerent's defences sky-high in a commando raid that would have made headlines all over the world. They could have killed Swedish soldiers. They might even have been caught. Webster's blood ran cold at the thought of the possible repercussions. "Come on – we've got to get out of here!" he whispered. "About three times as fast as greased bloody lightning."

On the way back to the base they had so carefully concealed his mind seethed with the implications of his discovery. Karlsö and Anholt were on the same latitude but fourteen miles apart. How could an experienced navigator like Reilly, an ex-Pathfinder, have made such a mistake? Webster remembered the dispute between the Irishman and Constantine which he had interrupted on the plane. Why had Reilly been so certain he was right? Why hadn't he noticed from his maps that the two islands were so close – and that there was a similarity of shape in their southern extremities, the aspect he would see first from the approaching B-25? Why hadn't he double-checked, especially after the pilot had expressed doubts about the course they were on? Was the man such an egotist that he would risk blowing an important mission and jeopardising the lives of eight men just to avoid admitting he'd made a mistake?

Those questions – more numerous and more urgent than those the discovery had answered – were themselves damned well going to be answered, Webster promised himself grimly. But for the moment the number one priority was to get the hell out before anyone saw them. They were already a whole day late on their schedule because of that cretin of a navigator – and they had two operations to handle instead of one. Reilly's cock-up could imperil the whole show.

Leading his men around the end of the promontory to approach the overhang in the low cliff, Webster flashed the prearranged signal – two short and three long, repeated – to warn Constantine of their approach.

There was no answering flash from the darkness ahead.

Cursing, Webster felt his way warily between the boulders, pausing every few yards to listen. He heard nothing but

79

the rhythmic splash of waves on the shore. Dear God, he thought bitterly, was there nothing and nobody he could rely on? He reached the rock rampart they had built and called Constantine's name softly into the blackness.

Silence.

In the salt, sandy chill of the night air, Webster felt the hairs at the nape of his neck prickle. Holding it well away from his side, he shone the flashlight over the barrier. Constantine was lying face down on the shingled floor. There was blood on his face, a swelling behind one ear.

"Jesus!" Webster exclaimed. "He's been coshed by the look of it. What the *hell* goes on here? Hewitt – go and fetch that bastard Reilly down from the top of the cliff. This is another piece of criminal carelessness he'll have to answer for."

But there was no sign of the Irishman in the lookout position – or anywhere else. He seemed to have vanished from the island altogether.

So had one of the rubber dinghies, the second transceiver and their entire stock of provisions.

Chapter Nine

Captain Seamus M'Phee O'Kelly took the decoded flimsy from the cipher clerk's hand and settled gold-rimmed spectacles on his nose. The signal had been radioed top priority from an FBI contact of his in Washington and then telexed, still in code, from the MoI monitoring station at Barnet to the old CO(S)E centre in Regent's Park. It was Winston Churchill himself who had persuaded O'Kelly, when the Luftwaffe stepped up their raids on London, to move his operations room to the sub-basement below the Citadel. But the old man had always regretted the move, and he still retained the original premises as an armoury, a registry for the less urgent files and a clearing-house for cables arriving from his agents all over the world. "Good thing I happened to be passing," he said genially to the clerk. "Save you fellers the sweat of typing the thing out again and sendin' it on to me below stairs, eh?"

"Yes, sir," said the clerk, who would in any case have to recode the message and send a confirmatory copy to the Citadel for the top-secret files there.

O'Kelly smoothed out the flimsy on his desk and read the neatly typed lines of capitals in a single comprehensive glance. "Holy Mother of God!" he exclaimed. The spectacles fell from his nose. He jammed them back in place and read the signal again, more slowly this time. Then he looked up at the clerk and said: "Fisher – have my car brought around at once. And tell Mary to call General Fortescue at the War Office right away. Tell him I'll be with him in fifteen minutes . . . and tell him I want to be shown straight in. Something's come up on Operation Andersen."

"Right away, Captain," the clerk said.

O'Kelly ran down the stairs and climbed into the back of the civilian Lagonda V12 that he used for security purposes.

The car carried diplomatic plates and the commando sergeant who was ostensibly its chauffeur had a pass that would get him at once through most roadblocks, cordons and police checks.

Even so, it took them twice as long as O'Kelly had estimated to reach the general's official home in a tree-lined square between Whitehall and the river. There had been a heavy raid the previous night and traffic was still chaotic. Three times, they had to make time-wasting detours because the road ahead was cratered or strewn with rubble from bombed buildings. A land-mine had gouged out a hole seventy feet wide and thirty feet deep in the middle of a crossroads near Trafalgar Square. Beyond the raw earth slopes spined with fractured gas and water mains, salvage teams and rescue workers clambered over a gigantic slant of masonry in search of trapped survivors. Near a direct hit in Northumberland Avenue, the mangled scarlet wreckage of a double-decker bus perched incongruously on a second-floor balcony.

Fuming with impatience, O'Kelly left the Lagonda in another traffic jam on the Embankment and completed his journey on foot. The swirling, leaden surface of the Thames was pitted with raindrops, and yellowing leaves had started to fall from the sycamore trees bordering the quiet square.

At the guarded entrance to the discreet red-brick house commandeered by the general's department, he showed his pass and was escorted to the inner sanctum at once.

Vane-Hyslop-Fortescue was sitting at his desk reading a thick sheaf of reports which had come in during the night. He looked up as O'Kelly strode through the doorway and nodded. "Mornin'. What can I do for you, Captain?"

"You can read this," O'Kelly replied. "It'll put you in the picture more quickly than I can."

He unbuttoned his tunic pocket, took out the folded flimsy, opened it out and laid the paper on the desk.

General Fortescue in his turn adjusted his spectacles. Leaning forward with his arms on the desk, he read the message it contained.

URGENTEST PROKELLY 6973–131043 REGRET PREVIOUS
SECURITY CLEARANCE 3927604 REILLY BARRY MICHAEL
NEGATIVED REPEAT NEGATIVED LATER INFO STOP FILES

UNEARTHED RAIDWISE FORMER GERMAN-AMERICAN
BUND HQ REVEAL REILLY RECRUITED NAZI INTEL
NETWORK PREMUNICH STOP BELIEVED ACTIVE
SENDING MILINFORMATION VIA HITLEMBASSY DUBLIN
STOP REILLY THEREFORE UNSUITABLE ATTENTION
UNSUITABLE YOUR OPANDERSEN BALTICWARDS STOP
PLEASE DETAIN AND ADVISE STOP REGARDS ===
ROBERTS FBI.

"Good God!" the general exclaimed. He looked up at O'Kelly over his glasses, shaggy eyebrows raised. "So we sent those poor buggers off complete with a built-in spy?"

O'Kelly sighed. "That's the way it looks, sir. In Webster's unit. Reilly was to be his navigator." He thumped the desk with his fist in a sudden gust of rage. "Damn it all! The kind of opportunity every spy dreams of. The swine, the traitorous bloody bastard! God knows what damage he'll do – blow the entire blasted operation, most likely."

"Reilly, eh!"

"That's right, sir. B. M. Reilly. Acting Flight Lieutenant, seconded from Bomber Command. Man was actually a bloody Pathfinder. Dropped his flares to guide the crews away from their targets, I suppose. And into the most active night-fighter grids." O'Kelly's voice was bitter.

The general grunted. "Irish," he said. "What can you expect?"

"Oh, now look," O'Kelly began angrily, "just because a man's name—"

"My dear fellow," the general said hastily. "No offence, I assure you. But you know how it is."

"No, I don't know how it is. If you don't mind me saying so, you're in the wrong war, sir. Nineteen sixteen was a long time ago. What I do know is that there are twenty thousand Irish volunteers – Free Staters, I suppose you would call them – in the British Army alone." O'Kelly's pink face had flushed a deep red.

Fortescue cleared his throat and shuffled the papers on his desk. He drew a handkerchief from the sleeve of his jacket and blew his nose. "There's – er – no chance of contacting Webster and warning him about this . . . about the situation?"

"None. They've been instructed to maintain radio silence until the show's over. We are monitoring a certain frequency twenty-four hours a day in case they have to call us in an emergency – but there's no way we can get to them: they won't be listening."

"This feller whatsisname – Tyler? Miley? – the bally traitor: think he could have briefed the Hun, contacted his control before your crowd pushed off?"

"You mean could he have genned up Jerry on the whole operation before it started?"

Fortescue nodded. It was probably safer not to talk.

"I wouldn't think so." O'Kelly wrinkled his brow in concentration. "They were in the top security bracket from the moment they left for the Orkneys. At that time, apart from Fortune and Webster himself, they knew nothing. Up there in the north, they never left the base except for exercises; never saw a soul except for Archie Lang and the briefing officer. And although they boned up on maps and models, they weren't told the names of the targets until the final briefing just before take-off. No – Reilly couldn't possibly have passed on anything of value before he left. Except possibly the code-name of the operation. And even then, what chance would he have had to contact a control? In any case, only Webster and Fortune knew *why* the islands were to be attacked." O'Kelly stared out of the window. The rain was falling more heavily. "If Reilly could have had knowledge of all the details," he said, "surely he'd have chickened out of actually going with them? I mean AWOL once he passed the stuff on."

"Ha! So it looks like the second part of the operation, my sub runnin' in with the observation unit, isn't directly at risk; but the assault on the islands may be?"

"I should think so. The bastard will be playing it by ear – but all he has to do, at any time, is tip off the Boche that they are *there*. Once Jerry knows that, Webster might as well pack his bags and come home to mother."

"It's a damned bad show all around," the general said. "There's nothing at all we can do about it?"

"Not a bloody thing," O'Kelly said. "All we can do is sit on our backsides and wait . . . and put another team into training in case the balloon goes up."

Fortescue plucked at his lower lip. The horse teeth gnawed his moustache. "You think the sub should continue to cruise off Norway, waitin' for a possible green light? It's due to put to sea this afternoon."

"Certainly I do. Webster's no fool, and Reilly's in his lot. There's just a chance that the swine will make a mistake and give himself away. He may find it harder to pull the wool over the eyes of our gallant major than he thinks. If Webster did cotton on, we could still pull it off." O'Kelly was pacing up and down. "I think we should give 'em the chance. I'll go to Göteborg as planned and wait until Thursday midnight. If I haven't heard from them by then" – he shrugged – "well, we shall just have to call off the submarine and start again from scratch."

"Right you are," the general agreed. "Don't see what else we *can* do in any case." From outside the sobbing wail of the air-raid alert rose and fell. He pushed back his chair and walked to the window, staring at the low clouds scudding above the river. "Not to worry," he remarked. "Just the usual recce plane the Hun sends over every morning after a big raid. Jerry likes a record for the files. Fat lot of good it'll do his blasted photo-analysts on a day like this!"

"D'you think I could use your good offices to send a reply to this message?" O'Kelly asked. "I have a lunch date, and it'll save me going back first to that underground prison where I work."

"My dear chap! I'll have my PA come in right away and take it personally to the coding room. Here – take a pew and make yourself at home." The general ushered O'Kelly into his chair and pressed a bell button set in a platen on the desk. "'Fraid you'll have to excuse me, though. Pow-wow with the Old Man at the War House. That feller Rommel's gettin' uppity again in North Africa. Have to do somethin' about him soon. Talk about a second front! Ask me, there are a sight too many blasted fronts already."

There was a tap on the door and a voluptuously built blonde in the uniform of an ATS Commandant came into the room. Fortescue murmured instructions to her while O'Kelly drew a sheet of paper towards him and began to write.

"This is June Chandos," the general said when he had

85

finished. "Invaluable girl. Most reliable. Well, you'll be in good hands now. Everything under control, so I'll push off."

When he had gone, O'Kelly read through what he had written and then handed the paper to the ATS officer. The message he had composed read:

URGENT PROROBERTS 2239–141043 YOUR SIGNAL 6973
TOO LATE REPEAT LATE REPEAT LATE STOP BALLOON
ALREADY UPGONE STOP CANCEL ERASE ALL FILE
REFERENCES OPANDERSEN SUBSTITUTE CODEWORD
FOLLOWS SOONEST STOP FYI SWEDENWARDING
PLANWISE TOMORROW IN HOPES SUCCESS DESPITE
REILLY UPCOCK STOP NEXT TIME TRY CARRIER PIGEON
STOP REGARDS === OKELLY COSE.

The blonde had been patiently standing by the desk. As she took the paper, O'Kelly looked up. She wasn't actually moving, but somehow she gave the impression that there was an inner life pulsating, investing the hips and belly and breasts beneath the well-tailored khaki uniform with a vibrant existence of their own. The breasts, he realised, looking more closely, were quite splendid. "By Jove," he said. "You must be . . . aren't you the gel Vane sent to Scotland to stir up trouble with my chaps?"

June Chandos smiled. Her lips moved as sensuously as a cat stretching. The flesh around her worldly, violet eyes crinkled. "It made a change," she said huskily. "I find office work gets so boring, don't you?"

"If ever you feel like a change . . ." O'Kelly cleared his throat. "There's always room for a girl with . . . enterprise . . . in my outfit," he said.

She looked at him speculatively. The tip of a pink tongue moistened her lower lip. "That," she said slowly, "might be an idea."

"Would he wear it? Old Vane, I mean."

"I'm only on loan," she said. "And I have a friend in Records. If you made the request strong enough . . . if you have any pull . . ."

"Leave that to me," O'Kelly said. "Perhaps we could discuss the details over dinner tonight? The food at the Carlton's still

86

quite edible. If you don't mind being seen out with an old codger like me, that is."

The slow smile tantalised him again. "I always did prefer the older man," June Chandos told him. "There's no substitute for experience, is there?"

"I say!" O'Kelly was suddenly boyish. "If you can wangle a forty-eight, how would you fancy a weekend in Sweden?"

"I think that would be *smashing!*" the girl said. "Perhaps you'd better let me take this signal to the cipher room now, otherwise everybody will have migrated to the canteen for lunch."

As she was gliding from the room, a bespectacled corporal clerk appeared in the doorway. "Beg pardon, ma'am," he said hesitantly, "but there's a telephone call switched through for Captain O'Kelly. The caller won't give his name, but he says – excuse me, ma'am! – he says as how he's ringing from . . ." the corporal gulped . . . "from Denmark, ma'am!"

Chapter Ten

Like Webster in the other Mitchell, Charles G. Fortune was lying face down in the bomb aimer's blister when Z for Zebra was attacked by the German night-fighter. He had handed over the controls to Bryan Marron, an ex-RAF pilot who was one of the tougher members of his team, so that he could more accurately correct their position once they flew out of the cloudbank into the bright light of the moon. Fortune was staring down through the Perspex dome, marvelling that a mere 20,000 feet could transform a holocaust of flame and high-explosive and sundered masonry into a Fifth of November firework display, when he saw the tracer.

It raced past the B-25's nose and then arched gracefully down to lose itself in the kaleidoscope of multicoloured fire mapping the hell below them. Fortune had time to register surprise that they had already passed through the fighter grid and back into the flak zone before the truth hit him.

Flak zone be damned! The stuff chucked up by the ground batteries appeared to lift off slowly and then accelerate past the plane at about a million miles per hour. This was doing precisely the reverse: it shot rapidly past them and then floated lazily *down*. It wasn't being flung at them by zealous Jerry gunners defending Kiel; this was air-to-air tracer, fired at them from behind!

There must be a Nazi fighter sitting under their tail . . . and that was the one place where Marron and the chap in the mid-upper turret wouldn't see the blighter.

Fortune screamed a warning into the intercom. Before the first syllable left his lips, the Focke-Wulf 190's second burst was ripping into the Mitchell's belly.

The 20 mm cannons slotted into the leading edge of the fighter's wings each fired sixty-round drums at a rate of 520 shells a minute. The rounds were loaded with a repeating series of three – one high-explosive, one armour-piecing and one incendiary that burned at more than 2,000 degrees centigrade for one-seventieth of a second. The burst, which the German pilot restricted to just over three seconds, launched more than a hundred rounds at the Mitchell's fuselage and starboard wing. Twenty-seven of them struck the aircraft.

The first HE shell to pierce the stressed skin of the tailplane exploded against one of the formers and severed the rudder controls. A tenth of a second afterwards, another demolished the bulkhead behind the navigator and wrecked the intercom. The third hit the mid-upper turret mounting ring, blowing off the legs of the man standing beneath the blister. In the meantime, armour-piercing shells had smashed holes through the floor, jammed the escape hatchway and decapitated the man sitting strapped into the rearmost seat. An incendiary had set fire to the gruesome contents of the modified bomb bay.

The Mitchell yawed as the rudder controls were lost, and the last dozen rounds sprayed the starboard wing and engine. The cowling was dislodged, the fuel tank punctured and a feed line fractured. At the same time, an incendiary shell lodged in the aileron hinge bracket and another exploded in the heart of the Wright Cyclone.

Marron never heard Fortune's warning. The aircraft was dead before he felt the limpness of the control column signalling that he had lost directional control. The figures on the instruments blurred into non-existence as a terrible vibration shook the main spars and the cabin. Flames from the blazing starboard engine streaked back and set fire to the high-octane aviation spirit fanning out from the punctured fuel tank. The navigator had been flung forward across his instrument panel by the shellburst which had destroyed the intercom. Marron thought he must be dead.

In the nose blister, Fortune hunched himself around and tried to crawl back through the hatchway into the cabin. A heavy thumping from the loose cowling of the burning engine drowned the racket of the remaining motor. There was noise too from the interior of the stricken machine. Metal clattered and squealed. Men shouted. Someone was screeching in an unnatural, high-pitched voice: *"Mother! . . .*

Oh, Jesus! Oh, God! Oh, Mother! . . . Christ Jesus, my chest, my chest . . ."

It was always Mum, Fortune thought. Dad never got a look in; they never called for him. He stared through the hatchway as Z for Zebra dropped her nose and plunged sickeningly earthwards. The cabin was garish with the pulsating light of the flames, choked by smoke from the smouldering clothes on the corpses under the tarpaulin in the bomb bay. Suddenly the fierceness of the heat was excruciating, unbearable.

Two men were frantically trying to free the jammed escape hatch beside the puddle of blood and viscera under the damaged turret. Another slumped in his seat with a leg from the dismembered lookout across his knees. A yard and a half in front of him, Fortune saw the rugged face of a Welsh commando on the floor. The mouth was open and so was one of the eyes. Where the other had been, there was only a pulped red hole.

He reached forward to drag himself through the tunnel into the cabin, thinking that he could hear Marron shouting instructions somewhere above. At that moment two things happened. The starboard smoke canisters, ignited by the fire, filled the plane with dense red fumes; the loose cowling finally tore itself free, smashed another hole in the fuel tank and disappeared into the blackness.

The Mitchell dropped its right wing and howled into its death dive.

Fortune couldn't move. Centrifugal force was plastering him to the shuddering floor; the extra G rendered his body so heavy that he was not strong enough to move it. Giddily, he watched a pattern of red and yellow stars twinkle up the side of the blister, slide across the roof and then sink slowly down the other side. The bitch was going into a spin! He had to get out, fast, and he was powerless to shift his own blasted body. Dash it all, he couldn't budge an inch! It was ludicrous, but he simply could not move . . .

The fuel remaining in the starboard tank exploded, blowing off wingtip and engine pod. As the doomed aircraft rolled over, the entire nose blister tore free, smashing into the windshields and carrying away part of the tailplane as it was whirled back in the 200 m.p.h. slipstream. Fortune saw the ruddy

90

inferno beyond the tunnel incomprehensibly receding from him in a slow spiral. Then suddenly he was alone and it was bitterly cold.

For some time he didn't realise what had happened. The centrifugal force which had drained his blood to his feet had at the same time starved his brain and induced a mild anoxia – a condition producing an exaggerated sense of well-being and optimism. He was pissed, by Christ! Alone in the sky without a responsibility in the world, he was pissed as a bloody newt! And he hadn't had a single slug from the emergency flask in his hip pocket . . .

He watched a plane streaming a long tail of fire behind it drift slowly away on his left. O'Kelly's backroom types had certainly put up a wizard show with those canisters. It was the most convincing thing he had ever seen! He was sorry he couldn't stay with the chaps for the rest of the op – but, dash it all, he had a right to stay where *he* wanted to be, didn't he? Anyway he wouldn't be much use to them if he was juiced, twinkled, plastered, tiddly, stinking, tight – what a lot of words there were to describe you when you were smashed out of your mind.

It was nice up here, Fortune thought dreamily, almost four miles above the earth, with those flickering coloured lights wheeling around his head. It was queer, just the same, how slowly the plane moved away. Marron must have throttled her back like crazy: why the hell didn't the silly sod get on with it and leave him in peace up here with his parachute?

It seemed a long time later that the truth hit him. And then it was the cold rather than the lack of oxygen that tipped him off. He was up here with his parachute all right . . . *but he hadn't pulled the fucking ripcord*. The Mitchell appeared to be moving away slowly because they were falling at almost the same speed . . .

Christ! Spread-eagled like a diver, plunging head first Fortune yanked frenziedly at the ring clamped to his chest by the rush of air.

The coruscating pattern of bomb busts and fires and flaming gun barrels revolved lazily towards him. And then suddenly it was all coming fast, too bloody fast, swinging up and away over his head.

Quite steadily his body reversed his position, so that now he fell feet first. The lights settled beneath his legs. But now they were rushing up with terrifying speed, growing larger every instant. He could make out burning city blocks, individual batteries, the flash of isolated bombs. For the first time he was conscious of his location in the void: 165 pounds and 9 ounces of bone and flesh and blood and cartilage hurtling earthwards at what must by now be his terminal velocity – more than 230 m.p.h.! Sweat started on his forehead and between the hairs of his moustache as he remembered the time-honoured joke of the stores clerk issuing the air-crew parachutes: "If she don't work, mate, bring 'er back and we'll fix you up with another."

If she didn't work . . . Fortune gasped as the opening 'chute wrenched at his shoulders and thighs. The air sucked into his lungs cleared his head. He remembered it all now – remembered the horror and remembered too that he must have been holding his breath ever since he was sucked out of the disintegrating nose of the B-25.

He had been plummeting through the sky for half a minute! Because of the inebriating effect of the anoxia, he had inadvertently pulled off a delayed drop of some 8 or 9,000 feet. The time lag had probably saved his life: had he drifted down slowly from somewhere near 15 or 18,000, he could have been asphyxiated through lack of oxygen; he could have been carried out to sea or dropped into the flaming hell of Kiel. As it was, he seemed now to be floating towards what looked like a patch of open country. The blazing Mitchell had vanished. The explosions and the continuous drone of the invading bomber stream were somewhere behind him; the lights had swung out of sight in the way things do, seen from the air.

The moon – he hadn't even noticed its absence – swam out from behind a cloud. The nebulous blur of land below abruptly gained depth and dimensions. In the pale light he could see woods and fields, a ribbon of road, a church spire rising from a huddle of roofs. Some way to the north, water gleamed. That must be the Kiel Canal. Fortune hoped the wind would carry him to the far bank. He didn't know why – because it was further from the centre of Germany? – but he wanted to land on the far side of that damned canal.

He tugged at the shrouds rayed out on either side of his

shoulders, trying to coax the parachute more to the right. But the easterly breeze was taking him obliquely away from the raid, at an angle to the waterway. He could see that he wasn't going to make it.

The low moan of wind through the shrouds was now drowned by a harsher, more sinister noise. A single-engined aircraft was approaching from the north. Fortune judged from the sound that it was lower than he was . . . and climbing. It must be a night-fighter that had just taken off to stalk the bombers far above. He bit his lip. He had heard enough stories of pilots from the Nazi *staffeln* amusing themselves by shooting up survivors dangling helplessly from parachutes . . . and he knew too that British and American pilots were not always averse to the same kind of murderous target practice. If the wretched moon stayed out, he'd be a sitting duck for any killer within half a mile. He tilted back his head and squinted upwards. Beside the bellied canopy the moon rode in a clear sky. Fortune cursed: it would really be the giddy limit if he was to make a miracle escape from a doomed plane . . . only to fall to the guns of some Prussian playboy with an itchy trigger finger!

The snarl of the fighter's engine was very loud. Suddenly he saw it: a winged shadow racing against the undulating, moonlit country below. It seemed to be flying straight towards him. The pilot couldn't fail to see him below that great white canopy in this brilliant bloody light! Was this, then, the way it was to end – after so many adventures in so short a time? A riddled corpse on a nylon gibbet, the blood teased out by the wind before it even reached the ground?

He tensed his muscles, anticipating the flicker of flame from the wings, the blinding impact of tracer smashing into his body. The snarl rose to a scream. Fortune recognised the rounded snub nose and squared-off wingtips of an FW-190.

The fighter zoomed past, climbing steeply a little to his right and no more than thirty feet above him. For the second time that night, Fortune realised he had been holding his breath. He expelled it in a long sigh of relief. Either the German pilot was a gent – or he was flying on radar instruction, husbanding his ammunition for the bomber on which his controller had a fix. In any case, some other poor sods up there would feel the draught of his cannon.

Fortune looked down again. He had lost a lot of height while he was getting hot under the collar about an attack that never materialised. Trees and hedges were speeding up to meet him.

He was going to land in a large, sloping field about 300 yards short of the canal.

He sailed over the outbuildings of a farm, planed down across a shadowed, twisting lane and just avoided a line of telephone cables slung between posts along the edge of the field. A moment before he hit the ground, he drew up his knees and shielded his face with his arms.

The impact knocked the breath from his body and he was dragged twenty yards before he could twist around, seize the shrouds and spill the air from the canopy. Panting, he hauled in the nylon cords, rolled up the 'chute and unclipped his harness.

He looked cautiously around him. No torchlight beam. No tramp of jackboots. No guttural shouts from a Nazi patrol. Just wet grass, the smell of cold, damp earth, a creak of branches as the breeze stirred the trees at the foot of the slope. By God, he had made it! Fearless Frazer strikes again! he thought wryly, recalling a favourite line of Webster's. Good Fortune smiles on Charles, miracle man of the moonlight!

But, thinking of good old Webster, what had happened to the other plane? Had they been luckier and passed over Kiel unscathed? Had they noticed that Z for Zebra had bought it? They had been flying fairly close, so they might have done. If they had, would they have obeyed orders and turned for home? Not on your bloody life, Fortune thought to himself; not knowing the jolly old madcap major! He'd carry on regardless and try to pull off the whole show himself.

In the meantime, Fortune was on his own too. Stumbling to his feet, he hurried across the field and stowed the parachute in a hedgerow. All right, he had made it: he was alive and well and living in enemy territory . . . unarmed, with no papers and no money. So what was he going to do now? Just how do you propose to deal with this situation, Fortune?

What does A do, in fact? Write your answers, clearly and legibly, in the space provided. Candidates will hand in their papers promptly at the end of the test.

Suddenly the young man felt an overwhelming sense of solitude. His career as an agent – and a brilliant one – had taken him behind enemy lines often enough before, but never with so little preparation, never at such a loss for the most elementary means of existence. Until this moment, he hadn't given a thought to what he must do after he landed: all his energy had been directed towards staying alive until he felt the solid earth beneath his feet. Well, it was solid enough under him now: the time had come to make decisions. But decisions between what and what? Most choices in the field involved balancing one set of facts, of parameters, of possibilities against another. Here he had no data: he was at point zero. But whatever he did, he was going to have to do it on his tod; there wouldn't be a soul to lift so much as a finger to help him in Hitler's Germany. The words of an old twenties song came into his mind:

Everybody knows that he's just Good-time Charlie,
The lonesomest guy in town . . .

Lonesome or not, Fortune thought, it was time this Charlie pulled his finger out and got a move on. He remembered O'Kelly's parting words: "You know what you have to do . . . you've been given lists of safe houses and details of the underground escape network in case you get hit and have to bail out . . ."

So they'd been hit and he'd bailed out. The only one to make it, too. The other poor bastards had simply got hit. Period. He had the safe-house list and network details committed to memory. Fine. But these were just names and addresses and passwords: before he could use them, he had to know where the hell he was. Otherwise, how could he tell which of the addresses was the nearest?

So far, all he knew was that he was a few hundred yards south of the Kiel Canal, in the centre of what used to be Schleswig Holstein – and that the Kiel Canal must be one of the most heavily guarded areas in northern Europe. Before he made occupied Denmark, where the safe-houses were, he had somehow to spirit himself to the far side of that perilous stretch of water and then cross the frontier between the two countries. Just that.

Fortune sighed. The wind couldn't have blown him to some place where there were mountains or forests of fir, where the border would be an imaginary line impossible to survey: it had to be in lush, rolling pastureland, where every blinking inch could be barricaded and covered by strongpoints and pillboxes – probably under observation from watchtowers too.

Just to prove the immutability of Murphy's Law – what can go wrong will go wrong – without a doubt!

Well, he might as well make a start: he'd have to wait until the moon was obscured by clouds before he attempted the canal, but there was no point hanging around here. It would be a long time before the sun rose; at least he could take a shufti at the guards on the canal bank, so he'd be ready to go as soon as it was dark again. Besides, his feet were getting wet, staying in one place on the waterlogged earth of this field.

He stared across the hedgerow at the farm. Dense shadows on the side away from the moon made the buildings as sharp as cardboard cutouts in the wan light. Better not go that way: there could be dogs who would bark and give the alarm. Keeping to the shady side of the hedgerows, he stole silently towards the belt of trees beyond which he had seen the canal. He traversed a field of sleeping cows, stumbled through another waist-high with some leafy crop, his feet sinking deep into the moist furrows of ploughed earth, and finally found himself in a meadow. On the far side of this stretch of coarse grass and bramble clumps were the trees.

He stopped to survey the terrain. The meadow was huge. It would be three-quarters of a mile if he followed the hedge all the way round its perimeter. If he walked straight across, on the other hand, there might be guards below the trees who could see him in the milky light. He held his head on one side and listened. Far off to his right, the noise of the bombardment muttered and thumped. Nearby, he could hear leaves rustling in the wind, the stealthy drip of moisture falling onto a stone, a sudden scurry as some nocturnal creature he had startled made its escape through the undergrowth. A long way behind him, a dog barked fretfully. But still there was no tramp of military feet, no tell-tale clink of equipment from the far side of the field. What the hell, he thought: time was precious while the night shadows could hide his movements; he would take the risk – and the straight line – and walk across.

He was still a hundred yards short of the trees when his foot caught in a briar. He tripped and fell headlong in the wet grass. There was a loud coughing noise a few feet in front of his head. Involuntarily, Fortune gave a stifled cry of alarm. Something large and dark rose from the far side of the bramble clump, momentarily blotting out the moon. With a shrill whinny, a horse cantered away across the meadow.

In Fortune's ears, the thump of his own heart was as loud as the drumming of the animal's hooves. He lay for a moment breathing in the scent of earth and stalks and leaves, suppressing the temptation to laugh aloud. Charles G. Fortune scared witless by a sleeping horse! That was a new role for Fearless Fucking Frazer: now it was Frightened Frazer, fooled by a filly! That would be one for the chaps in the Mess all right!

He rose to his feet. If he didn't get a move on, he wasn't going to be in any place where the chaps could be told . . . except maybe in some Jerry PoW camp. If, of course, he hadn't been shot first as a spy. Hurrying now, he plunged in among the trees.

The wood wasn't extensive, perhaps 150 yards wide and half as deep. But there were fallen leaves, crisped by the cold night air, lying in the gaps between the underbrush. It was dark, too, beneath the interlaced branches. Moving a step at a time, testing the ground before he dared place his weight on a foot, he crept forward. Even so, the noise of his progress seemed to Fortune terrifyingly loud. The dead leaves rustled. A twig snapped. Saplings thrashed his face and hands. But at last he could see the glint of water between the close-packed trunks ahead. He crawled the last few yards, infinitely slowly, on his hands and knees.

He was at the top of a grassy slope shelving gently down to the canal. He didn't quite know what he had expected – barbed wire, lookout posts, guards patrolling a concrete towpath ruled straight as a die across the countryside? Perhaps a surfaced U-boat moving slowly towards the open sea? What he saw was a placid, deserted reach, curving away through the wood to where the arches of a low bridge blocked the view about a quarter of a mile to his left. So far as he could see in the moonlight, the current appeared to be quite strong, shivering the reflections of trees on the far side of the water. He could hear the ripple of the stream over the creaking of branches behind him.

Fortune frowned. The canal was wide – though not as wide as he had expected – but it didn't look the kind of waterway that could take deep-draught cargo vessels and the largest submarines to a major port. How the devil could they pass beneath that bridge, for a start? He shrugged. Perhaps there were locks bypassing this particular section. His not to reason why, in any case: he should thank his lucky stars that he'd happened across a stretch that was unguarded . . . and then get the hell over to the far side. It would take him that much nearer Denmark.

He looked longingly at the bridge. The further end was hidden by the curve of the canal – but even if it was as deserted as the end he could see, he dare not risk crossing it. Somewhere near, there was bound to be a roadblock. No, he would have to swim for it: there was no alternative.

The water was colder than he could possibly have imagined, an icy, freezing chill that numbed his bones and produced an ache in his head that reached from his throat to behind his eyes. He remembered that ache: he'd had it often as a child on the beach at Bournemouth when he had taken too greedy a mouthful of old man Ancarani's vanilla ice cream cornet!

All right, he told himself: so it was colder than Goose Bay in Labrador, where he'd once spent an uncomfortable winter tracking down a German agent infiltrated into an RCAF radar installation. But it would still be madness to strike out in an attempt to keep the blood circulating, and maybe attract the attention of some Nazi sentry with the splashes he'd be bound to make. He decided to float with the current and let it carry him to the darkness beneath the bridge; then perhaps he could wade silently ashore and sneak up the opposite bank. Or at least see what the form was on that side before he tried.

He saw his mistake as soon as he had drifted to the curve in the canal. Beyond it, the trees gave way to a stretch of open ground with houses on either side of the road which had crossed the bridge. There was a blockhouse too. And, in the centre of the open space, their rakish, uptilted barrels gleaming in the moonlight, a mobile battery of 3.7 cm flak guns were jacked up on their fat, rubber-tyred wheels. Fortune could see the crews moving around them, but they weren't shooting at the moment: this must still be a PAZ – a pre-alert zone.

He would have done better to take a chance and swim straight across where he had first come upon the canal: it was the story of the meadow all over again, only this time he had made the wrong choice. Well, he couldn't go back; there was nothing he could do about it now. He submerged all of himself except his mouth and nose and willed the rapid current to carry him beneath the bridge.

As soon as its dark shadow passed across his eyes, he began to paddle gently with his hands, manoeuvring himself in towards the bank. He grounded on shingle under the furthest arch, turned over onto his hands and knees and dragged himself out of the water. Wading cautiously ankle-deep, he edged around the corner of the stonework into the pale radiance diffused by the moon.

Light blinded him, searing across his eyeballs so that he screwed up the lids momentarily to ease the pain. Voices shouted, boots scraped on stones, rough hands seized him and he was hauled, still cascading water, up the bank.

He was standing in a ring of German soldiers wearing coal-scuttle helmets. They carried Bergmann-Schmeisser machine-pistols. Beside them, a flatbed truck parked by the bridge carried a powerful spotlight which was directed down at the water. An officer – an *oberleutnant*, Fortune thought – shouted questions at him.

His teeth were chattering so much that he wouldn't have been able to answer even if he wanted to. The officer shouted again and struck him in the face. Fortune was so numbed with cold that he didn't feel the blow.

There was a squeal of brakes and a dark blue station wagon with an amber light on its roof drew up alongside the truck. One door on each side of the vehicle was white, with the word 'Polizet' painted across it in black letters. The door opened and men in uniform piled out and ran to the group surrounding the Englishman. They were holding revolvers in their hands.

"It's all right, sir," one of the policemen said to the officer.

"This one's one of ours. We've been chasing the swine all night. We had him cornered at Drem, but he jumped into the river and got away."

"Got away?" the *oberleutnant* echoed. "You mean this man is—?"

"A black-marketeer. One of the worst. The commissioner has been after him for weeks. He'll go up for at least five years, you'll see."

"I suppose that is in order. I thought he might be an escaped—"

"Don't bother yourself, Herr Oberleutnant," the policeman said. "You leave him to us. I'm sure you have more important things to do than deal with scum of this kind." He pushed his way through the Wehrmacht men and snapped handcuffs on Fortune's wrists. "Come on, you tricky bastard," he rasped. "We have a nice clean cell waiting for dirty traitors like you."

Fortune spoke good German. He stood, utterly bewildered, feeling the steel of the bracelets cold against his cold flesh. Feet clattered on the roadway. A runner sprinted up to the officer and saluted. "Permission to speak, Herr Oberleutnant?" he said breathlessly. "Sir, a message from the Flugwachkommando: PAZ to AZR. It's AD-10 for the whole area sector."

Fortune knew what that meant. The pre-alert had become a full alert. AD-10 meant danger in ten minutes. The next wave of raiders must be on their way. He thought he could hear the distant drone of bombers already.

The officer had been looking dubious. Now he made up his mind. "Very well," he said to the policeman, "we'll leave it to you. In any case I must get back to the battery now."

The policeman saluted again. "Come on, you," he snapped at Fortune. "Start moving if you don't want a few broken bones." Pushed roughly and cuffed, Fortune was bundled into the back of the police car. The door slammed. Through the steel mesh covering the rear window, he watched the officer lead his men back to the guns. His mind was reeling. He'd been to enough courses on uniform recognition, and he knew these cops weren't Germans; they were Danish. What the hell were they doing, twenty-five miles inside the Reich? And why hadn't the Nazi officer been surprised to see them? Evidently there was mistaken identity involved, but why had the German allowed him to be taken away so easily? Even if he had been a black-marketeer, it seemed all arse over tip! Because surely it would be German rather than Danish business to lock him up and punish him in that case? It was bad enough being in the hands of any cops on enemy territory, Fortune thought, but he supposed he should be thankful they were Danes rather than Germans. Shivering in his sodden clothes, he wondered what was going to happen next.

He didn't have to wait long before he found out. Two of the Danes had climbed into the back with him. The other two settled in front. The engine started. The station wagon accelerated away down a narrow tarmac road.

"I think perhaps you may be freezing coldly, eh?" the cop who had been doing all the talking said in English. "So maybe you better can drink a liddle of this?" Leaning forward, he unlocked the handcuffs and then proffered Fortune a flask of colourless liquid.

Fortune stared uncomprehendingly as the road twisted through a wood, crossed a bridge, and then began climbing a swell of pastureland on the far side of the valley. Behind them, orange light flashed balefully behind the trees as the flak battery fired a salvo. The wired windows of the police car shuddered in their frames.

The policeman chuckled. "Is true we have follow you for some time," he said as the echoes of the gunfire rolled across the countryside. "We have see your parachute come down, and go there as fast we can."

Fortune went on staring. So they knew who he was – or at any rate what he was. So why the black-marketeer charade? He didn't get it. The flak battery fired again. And again.

"We are sorry, being rough," the cop explained. "But when we see you are already with the Nazis, we think it best pretending you are criminal. This way, we get you free, eh? Come. Drink now." He shook the flask invitingly.

If Fortune hadn't been half dead with cold, the penny would have dropped sooner. "Do you mean to say," he began slowly, "that you fellows are . . . that it was all a jolly . . . Oh, no! You *can't* be in the Danish underground! That would really be too rich!"

The policeman was nodding delightedly. "Of course," he said. "Of course."

"Not true," Fortune kept repeating. "Not true, not true!" He frowned. "But, God, that must be a hell of a risk you're taking, impersonating policemen and all that kind of thing."

The second cop laid a hand on his arm. He shook his head. "Not impersonating," he said.

"You mean you're genuine members of the constabulary? You're actual, dyed-in-the-wool, long arms of the Danish law?" Fortune was astonished. He grabbed the flask and drank. The fiery, aniseed-tasting schnapps scalded his throat and exploded a soft, comforting warmth in his belly. He began to feel better. "I say," he exclaimed, "this is a turn-up for the bally book all right. Real coppers! I thought you meant you were partisans or—"

"In Denmark," the first policeman interrupted, "everybody is a partisan. We are *all* in the underground. Except maybe a few ones in the black market, and even these do not like the occupiers. So naturally, when we see a flyer in a parachute, we try to get there first, to save him from the Germans. There is no law," he added proudly, "to say that a policeman he cannot also be a patriot."

Fortune shook his head in admiration. "Frightfully decent of you," he said. "I really am awfully obliged. I mean, *Skol!* to you chaps, then." He raised the flask, drank again, and then handed it back. "All the same," he said reflectively as the policemen drank in their turn, "you must be taking one hell of a risk, putting the arm on me right down here. How did you get away with it? And what happens when we make the border?"

"Border?"

"The frontier. Even if your country is occupied, I imagine there must still be some kind of demarcation line between Denmark and Germany. Will the guards be as easy to fool as that young Kraut officer? And how is it that you are permitted to operate right down here – even if you are genuine policemen?"

It was the Danes' turn to look puzzled. "We are driving north," one of them said. "Not south."

"That's what I mean. That's why I'm asking you about the frontier and—"

102

The other cop burst out laughing. "I think you don't look too good where you are going in your parachute," he said. "The frontier, you passed it already. You are not in Nazi Germany, man. This is Denmark. Occupied but still Denmark."

Fortune's jaw dropped. "In Denmark? How can that be? We haven't passed any . . . I mean, OK, you arrived in the nick after those Jerries had pulled me out of the Kiel Canal, and—"

The policeman laughed again. "Not the Kiel Canal."

"Not . . . ? But it must have been: I saw the city burning as I came down, way over to the east!"

The Dane shook his head. "Not Kiel. Flensburg."

"Good God!"

"You are landing between Rends and Tinglev," the first cop said. "About four miles inside Denmark. Where you have swim is the Sonderaa – a river that rises by Graasten, and then flows by the lakes at Neukirchen and so into the Nordsee by the island of Sylt."

"It cross the country in a slant," his companion explained, "just like the canal, but not so large. If you have swim in the Kiel Canal, believe me, you *would* have trouble, my friend!"

Fortune was silent. He rather prided himself on his geography and it was a shock to him – although an agreeable one – to find that he was forty miles out in his reckoning. So the flaming city he had drifted across was Flensburg and not Kiel. It just showed how easy it was to cock things up from a height. The Mitchell must have made a lot more ground than he thought, before she went into her death dive. Or maybe the error was due to the fact that he'd believed he was pissed! He grinned suddenly. "Tell you what," he said. "Let's celebrate with another drink! One for the road, as we say."

They drove through a village, a long street of pale houses shuttered beneath the tall, steep northern roofs. The road crossed a stretch of moorland where the moon-bleached grasses bent beneath the wind. Presently they came to the outskirts of a small town. "Lönderslund," the policeman who seemed to be in charge announced. "Here we put the handcuffs back on you because there is a Nazi control."

They stopped by a concrete pillbox and the driver exchanged pleasantries with the two Wehrmacht men on duty. Evidently they knew one another well. One of the soldiers shone a flashlight into the rear. Fortune scowled, doing his best to look like an arrested black-marketeer. With his waterlogged clothes, his moustache bedraggled and his face disfigured and scratched by briars, the impersonation didn't call for a great deal of histrionic talent.

"What do we do now?" he asked when the striped barrier pole had risen and they were driving on into the town.

"We hand you over to the men running the escape line," one of the policemen replied. "But that is for tomorrow. Tonight you must have rest. And perhaps some hot food, yes? We take you to a safe place where you can sleep."

"You fellows certainly lay on a spiffing service," Fortune said. "I really can't thank—"

"It is the liddlest thing," the second cop told him. He jerked his head towards the south, where the sky was still livid with the flashes of anti-aircraft batteries firing at the raiders overhead. "You people don't do so bad for us, eh?"

The driver swung the wheel over and they jolted through an archway lit by a shaded green lamp. The station-wagon lurched to a halt in a cobbled yard surrounded by high stone walls. Through an open doorway, Fortune could see a man in uniform sitting behind a high desk. "This is my hotel for the night?" he asked, trying not to sound apprehensive. "Where exactly am I, if you don't mind the question?"

Both the policemen laughed this time. "The police station," one of them said. "What safer place to hide a man than where the Germans believe him to be!"

"We fix you up good in a prison cell," said the other. And ten minutes later, refreshed by a hot shower and kitted out with corduroy slacks and a fisherman's sweater, Fortune was taken by his rescuers down a flight of stone steps and pushed along a basement corridor lined with steel-barred cell doors.

"This is where you belong, you swine," one of the cops who had been in the front of the car called loudly for the benefit of the other inmates. "In there with a couple of your gangster cronies!"

Keys grated in an iron lock. The Englishman was shoved into a cell comfortably enough furnished with a table, a washbasin and three bunks. There was a bottle of schnapps and three glasses on the table. The cell door clanged shut behind him.

Fortune took a step forward . . . and froze.

"Good Lord!" he said.

Peering at him over the rough blankets covering the two occupied bunks were the faces of his Canadian navigator, Renard, and one of the crewmen, named Crisp.

Chapter Eleven

"It was the escape hatch," Renard explained. "She was jammed up good by that first squirt. I was kind of knocked for a loop by the shell that took out the intercom and the bulkhead. But as soon as Marron saw that I hadn't kicked the bucket, he told me to go back and help Crisp here free the bastard. We were halfway there when the goddam fuel tank blew. The ship rolled over and the hatch freed itself and fell plumb into the cabin – I guess the blast must've shifted it the way it blew your blister. So as soon as she turned on her belly, we just dropped out."

"Just you two?" Fortune queried. "None of the others?"

Crisp shook his head. He'd been a corporal in the Tank Corps and he was very conscious of rank. "No, sir. Evans was killed. The bloke in the turret was blown in half. Meredith bought it with the first burst: cannon shell took his head clean off. Goldberg should've been okay, but he was shocked, like. Still strapped in his seat with half the turret man's guts in his lap. Squadron-leader Marron was still at the wheel, sir. He must have gone down with the plane, trying to right her."

"You don't think either of them could have got away, Marron or Goldberg?"

"Not on your life." Renard's headshake was decisive. "We watched her all the way down, saw the flash when she hit the deck. If there'd been any other 'chutes, we'd sure as hell've seen them in that fuckin' moon."

Fortune nodded and sighed. "Bad show," he said.

They drank for a little while in silence, and then Crisp said: "What do we do now, sir?"

Fortune frowned, caressing his resuscitated moustache with a forefinger. "Your guess is as good as mine, old lad. The orders were: if one kite goes for a burton, the other's to turn back and abandon the mission. If those orders were followed, the others should be back home by now. Provided they saw our plane hit, of course. We don't know if they did. But even if he had proof that every one of us was beneath the sod, I can't see Fearless Frazer . . . that is to say Major – er – Webster . . . letting a little matter of orders change his plans. He never abandoned anything in his life."

"You mean he'll go on in and waste those guns?" Renard said. "But what about the batteries on the other island, the one we were supposed to do? There's no sense just silencing half the defence: that sub could as easily be sunk by the guns we don't knock out as it could've been by those he does."

Fortune grinned. "If you knew Major Webster," he said, "you'd lay every penny you had on him trying for the double himself."

"Maybe we could try to help some way," the Canadian said.

"Just tell me how. First, we don't know for sure if he *is* going to try for both. Secondly, if he is, how the hell could we help him? Thirdly, if he isn't, three blokes are going to look pretty silly, storming a heavily defended Jerry base on their own without arms, ammunition or explosives."

"Maybe these Danish underground people could help?" said Crisp.

"Maybe. It's more likely they'll have plans of their own," Fortune said. "Anyway, they've got jobs: they can't just take time off to ferry three foreigners to the top of bloody Jutland."

"Shucks, it's not far," Renard protested. "I looked at a map."

"My dear old lad! You and your wide open transatlantic spaces! It may not *look* far, but did you think to check the scale of the map? I mean like how many miles to the inch? It's a hundred and forty miles to the stretch of coast opposite Anholt – and that's Webster's target; ours is another sixty or seventy, and that's without counting the sea trip afterwards. You're nuts if you think we could pull off that kind of a stunt on our own."

"Guys have done more. I heard tell of a flyer shot down over the Rühr who walked clean through Luxemburg and half of France to get to—"

"Quite. To get out. Once he'd made the distance, he could relax. We'd only be starting when we'd made the distance. If we made it." Fortune shook his head. "'Which I doubt, he said'."

"Come again?"

"It's a quote. From *Winnie The Pooh*."

"Oh," Renard said blankly. "Yeah?"

"Perhaps it would be better, sir, if we let these Danish blokes repatriate us, the way they suggest?" Crisp said sleepily.

"Perhaps. In any case, it's no earthly use making plans until we chew the fat with them. I think it's about time for a spot of shut-eye." Fortune lowered himself gingerly to the vacant bunk and pulled the blanket over himself.

Different policemen brought them rolls and steaming cups of coffee late the following morning. Hidden beneath a tarpaulin in the back of another squad car, they were driven for more than an hour along smooth country roads and through several towns. Neither the driver and his mate nor the two men in the back spoke during the journey. Perhaps they didn't know any English. More likely, Fortune thought, they were scared of the consequences if the Germans caught them helping shot-down airmen to escape.

The car finally bumped along a rough track and stopped with a squeal of brakes. The tarpaulin was lifted, and one of the cops signalled them to follow him.

Clambering out, they stretched gratefully and saw that they were in the yard of a farm. Two sides of the rectangle were blanked off by huge barns with steep tiled roofs; the third by the farmhouse itself. A wall ran along the fourth side of the yard. Through the open gateway at one end of this, they could see the track twisting away across a flat, featureless landscape patchworked with fields of stubble. In the distance, there was a leaden gleam of water beneath the grey sky.

A tall man of about thirty emerged from one of the barns. His hair was straw-coloured and he was wearing dungarees. He greeted the policemen in Danish and then smiled at Fortune and his companions, displaying large, uneven teeth. "Welcome," he said. "Please to go within the house." Fortune turned to thank the policemen, but they were already climbing back into their car. As the driver accelerated away, Fortune looked curiously around him. The farm buildings were in good repair, but the place had an air of neglect about it. It was only October, yet the hay loft was almost empty. Beyond the gate, the nearer fields were choked with weeds, and grass had pushed up between the cobbles of the yard. Near the front door, a solitary black hen pecked around a rusting truck which had had its engine removed.

In a back room with closed shutters, a short, bearded man sat at a table greasing the parts of a Sten gun in the light of an oil lamp. "Nils Bergg," the farmer announced as he ushered the fugitives in. "I am called Olafsson, and we are happy for you gentlemen to be with us."

Bergg looked up and smiled. "Also," he said.

Fortune nodded and shook hands with both men. "That goes for all of us too," he said. "Almost as happy as those coppers were to get shot of us!"

"It is difficult for them," Olafsson explained. "Our people will not permit that they do not help the partisans. But so it is with the Germans: the police are supposed to aid them too. It will be very severe for them if they are discovered bringing you here."

"Of course. My God, I didn't mean to criticise," Fortune said hastily. "I mean to say, it's fantastic what you chaps have done for us already."

Olafsson shrugged. "Some perhaps are more enthusiastic with their help than others," he said. "Things are very difficult here. It is not possible to find labour for the farm: the Nazis draft all the young men away to work in their munitions factories. What we do produce, they take to feed their armies. Life is not so easy."

Renard said: "Gee, it sure burns us up, having to trouble you guys. It's tough enough, I know, without the responsibility of smuggling people outta the country under the noses of the Krauts."

"No, no. It is not that. We are pleased to help. Only just now we have received radio message ordering us a sabotage operation – and this must be done tonight. So we are not sure how we do with you. There is no time to pass you away before the operation . . . and if we do not return, you will be blocked here with no contacts to take you onwards."

Fortune exchanged glances with Renard and Crisp. "We're in your hands," he said. "All the way. You must do whatever suits you best. How would you normally get shot of us?"

"To Sweden, of course. There are three ways. We take you to the island of Fyn, past Odense, and then across to Sjaelland, where Copenhagen is built. From there you must cross the sound to Malmö, in Sweden, which is very close. Only the route is all main roads and there is much, much Germans. Also the two sea passages are greatly patrolled."

Bergg completed his task and began to reassemble the Sten. "Not enough of these," he said, patting the open frame stock of the gun.

"Another way," Olafsson continued, "is to find some deserted part of the coast, in the north, and take you there in a fishing boat. But here is much wider sea – eight hours to cross, at least – and much Nazi naval patrols, with radar, who will search any boat they see."

"Very dangerous," Bergg said with a rumble of laughter.

"Best of all," the farmer concluded, "is to go straight to the tip of Jutland and make you stowaways on a scheduled steamer service that goes from Frederikshavn to Göteborg. But for this we have to wait for a ship where we have friends in the crew – also a night when the right men is on duty in the port."

"Göteborg?" Renard echoed. "Shit, that's where we're headed anyway, ain't it? How far is it from here to Frederikshavn, then? And where is here, if it comes to that?"

"Here you are near Vamdrup, west of Kolding," Bergg said. "One hundred sixty-two miles to Frederikshavn. Also very dangerous." He laughed again.

"Maybe we could make it on our jack, without troublin' you guys further?"

The bearded man shook his head. "Never. Besides, how would you get aboard the boat?"

Fortune plucked at his lower lip. "Look – is there any way we could help with your sabotage operation? Which of your three routes is it nearest to? If you can tell us, that is."

"Sure we tell you," Olafsson said. "No secrets between allies, eh? We have to blow up a Nazi telephone exchange. He is beyond Aarhus, on the way north."

"On the way to Frederikshavn?"

The farmer nodded. "Ya. Sixty mile from here. Must be important all right, because we get a special message from London. Priority. Has to be done tonight because it tie up with some other operation. That's what they tell me."

For the second time, Fortune exchanged glances with Renard and Crisp. He sat down at the table. "You have been very frank with us," he said. "I'm not supposed to breathe a word, not a syllable to a soul – straight into the Tower and off with his head if anyone finds out! – but I'm going to be frank with you in return. For my money, your 'other operation' is in fact one of ours."

"Yours?"

"We are not even supposed to tell Resistance types," Fortune explained, "but we are not, to tell you the truth, shot-down airmen. We came by air all right, we were certainly shot down, but we too are on a mission connected with sabotage."

"But this is magnificent!" Bergg burst out. "Please to explain." He grinned. "If you can tell us, that is."

"Whether or not I *can*," Fortune said, "I certainly will." As simply as he could, he filled them in on Operation Andersen, on his own part in it and on his doubts about what he and his companions should do now. "If you ask me," he said, "you have been requested to destroy this Nazi exchange as part of the same plan. To muck up the Jerry communications, so it'll be easier for Webster and us to do the job. Only London doesn't know that the plane my lot were in didn't make it."

"You may be right," Olafsson said. "Certainly we have hear about the Andersen code and what happens to Bergstrom and Hanson and Telder and the others. Very bad."

"Exactly. So I have a suggestion to make," said Fortune. "As your operation has been dreamed up to help us, why don't we go along with you chaps to help with yours? Then, when it's all over, you can put us on the boat to Göteborg – all aboard for the jolly old *Skylark*, what! Dammit, we'll be halfway to Frederikshavn already, won't we?"

Olafsson and Bergg were delighted with the idea. They could always use extra hands, they said; and it would save them having to come all the way back to the farm to collect the fugitives afterwards. If there was an afterwards. The only difficulty was to find arms for them. They had so few. But

111

they would contact friends in another cell and try to borrow some. The farmer strode to the door, his horse teeth bared in a happy smile. "Anya!" he called. "Coffee for our friends – and bring down the bottle of akvavit."

Renard was frowning. "What do you figure we should do when they get us to this port?" he said to Fortune. "Do we just get the hell out – or do we still try to find some way to sabotage the goddam guns? You think maybe these guys would come along for the ride? I mean like would they help out? After all, we're gonna lend a hand with their war. And the two islands are still part of Denmark."

Fortune shook his head. "I don't know, old son. We'll just have to play it by ear again. In any case, if we're decanted onto a steamer running a scheduled service, we couldn't get to Laeso."

Crisp spoke for the first time since they arrived at the farmhouse. "Excuse me, sir. Why don't we contact Captain O'Kelly or Commander Lang and ask for orders? Then we'd know we was doing right."

Fortune stared at him. "Contact . . . ?"

"It's all right, sir. I haven't gone stone bonkers."

"But, Crispie . . ." Renard began gently.

"It's a telephone exchange they're attacking, isn't it?" Crisp said doggedly. "They'll have lines to Sweden, won't they?" He turned to the two Danes. "Can you see any reason why we couldn't put through a call to London before we blow the place up? I don't mean directly, of course. But we could route it through your contacts in Sweden, couldn't we? If we could get through to a Swedish exchange, I can't see why they shouldn't make a connection with London and then hook us up."

Bergg's laugh rumbled once more around the shuttered room. "Sure you could do it," he said cheerfully. "Call Roosevelt if you want. Just so long as we make time enough to finish off the switchboard after."

Fortune was looking at Crisp appreciatively. "Jolly good show," he said. "That's positive thinking."

Light footsteps clacked in the passageway outside. A girl of about twenty came into the room. She was carrying a tray loaded with glasses, a bottle and mugs of hot coffee. "My daughter Anya," Olafsson said. "She is art student. She will make papers we carry when we go. Anya can make photos also."

"Wizard," Fortune said, smiling at the girl. "That's service! Tell me, though: as it's sixty miles, how exactly *do* we go?"

Anya smiled too. She had big teeth like her father. She was robustly built, with wide hips, a small waist and a neat cap of dark hair. "As everyone else in Denmark today," she said, "we go on bicycles."

Including the three fugitives, there were nine of them in the party. Ten miles from the farm, Bergg and the two Olafssons collected a trio of young men who could have been brothers. Each of them was between twenty-five and thirty years old; each was blond and slightly built; each had a ruddy complexion roughened by exposure to the northern winds. Their names, the farmer said, were Svenderup, Bramming and Peters. All of them worked on the land.

They rode in a group, wearing the blue-and-yellow windcheaters and close-fitting, long-peaked caps of a local cycling club. This way, Bergg explained, they would in one sense attract less attention. The sport was recognised by the occupiers as part of the Danish way of life, and it would be believable enough that the members of a club might go on a long-distance training ride – whereas several small groups apparently unconnected but all following the same route might arouse suspicion if one Nazi control point happened to check with another. Olafsson, with papers identifying him as Secretary of the Vamdrup Wheelers, carried ID documents for all of them, including expert fakes forged by Anya for Fortune, Crisp and Renard. Weapons were to be collected from contacts nearer the target, but Bergg's Sten had been dismantled and the components skilfully incorporated in the frame of his heavy machine.

It was after dusk when they made the rendezvous. The land had been flat most of the way, the roads mainly straight, but they had made many detours to avoid known roadblocks and the larger towns, such as Vejle, Horsens and Aarhus itself. In fact they were stopped only twice, once for a routine check at a contol point, and once by a motorised patrol whose officious young commander insisted on searching every member of the

113

group, including the girl. Although he knew they were clean, Fortune found himself sweating more from the suspense than from the unaccustomed exertion of the ride when at last they were waved on. He spoke fair Danish himself, and the Germans were foreigners there anyway, probably not too hot on the local accent, but supposing Renard or Crisp had been asked a direct question . . . ?

The arms takeover was outside a small village. The gate-keeper at a level-crossing came out of his cabin to give Olafsson a message pinpointing the exact location while they were waiting for a long goods train to pass. "There goes everything we produce to feed the fat swine in Prussia, Bavaria and the Rühr," Bergg said bitterly as the milk tankers, cold storage vans and slatted boxcars full of lowing cattle trundled past.

Two miles further on, Olafsson halted them by a huge grain barn standing on the corner of a narrow lane. Outside the barn, unattended, a horse harnessed to a wagonload of hay nibbled the grass verge. The weapons were hidden beneath the hay, just ahead of the tailboard.

They found another Sten, five revolvers, a small quantity of plastic explosive wrapped in oiled silk, a canvas satchel of ammunition and four grenades. "It is very difficult," Olafsson confided to Fortune. "The RAF parachute us supplies some times, but the Nazis find much of them. So we must – how do you say? – pool what little we have between cells, you know."

Concealing the arms in their saddlebags, they rode up the lane and then pushed the bicycles through a gate on the edge of a small wood. North of the town of Aarhus, from which ferries sail several times a day to Sjaelland and Copenhagen, the coast is indented by a deep, irregular inlet on the far side of which the Fornaes peninsula projects into the Kattegat. It was at the inner end of this lagoon, not far from Ronde, that the telephone exchange was located.

The wood in which Olafsson and his band were hidden lay a mile and a half further south. Beech trees and pines, firs and oaks grew closely together here on a slight rise overlooking the eight-mile stretch of water. From the gloom beneath their branches, the saboteurs looked out over the darkening landscape.

Immediately in front of them, a grass-grown track led through flat, rectangular fields towards a line of dunes marking the sea and the shore. Aarhus was a smudge of smoke blurring the horizon to their right. Away to the left, beyond the square concrete buildings of the exchange, the long, low line of the headland framed the grey waters of the inlet. Forty miles further out was the island of Anholt. Fortune wondered if Webster and his men were there.

He shivered. A cold wind blowing in from the north-east was stirring the surface of the shallowing sea into whitecaps. "When were you thinking of going over the top?" he asked Olafsson.

"Over the . . . ? Oh, just before dawn," the Dane answered. "The night shift will be tired. Their tour end at six. Also there is less guards during the night."

Anya Olafsson produced a meal from her rucksack – slices of black bread with sausage; cheese; pickled herring. There was even beer in a huge stone bottle which Peters had strapped to the rear of his machine. After they had eaten, they drew baggy overalls on top of their cycling gear and gathered around while Bergg and the farmer explained the plan of action. The place was lightly guarded, they said. Facing an inland sea, the coast was not fortified, and the exchange was simply isolated by a double line of barbed wire with a sandbagged machine-gun post by the sentries at the entrance. They would, however, be obliged to approach the site through the dunes, because the road from Ronde, along which the relief shifts would be driven at six o'clock, was straight and flat, with no cover whatsoever.

"We knock out the guards with grenades," Bergg said, "and after is the piece of cake, yes? We take their guns and go inside. There is not much personnel and only two more guards. *Boum!*" He mimed an explosion with his hands. "Finished."

Svenderup switched on a masked flashlight while Olafsson scratched a plan of the installation in the sandy earth and Bramming, who spoke good English, assigned each member of the team his or her task. "This is a special military exchange," he said. "Automatic, with land lines to each army headquarters in the sector. The Nazis can call each other without having to go through the post-office system at all."

"What-ho!" Fortune breathed. "So if we manage to throw a

jumbo-sized spanner in the works that should put the kybosh on Jerry's entire communication network, eh?"

"Certainly. They can still use the public system, of course. But we understand there may be – er – certain delays. Especially tomorrow. Line repairs and suchlike. Defective relays. Our apologies, Mein Herr. Normal service will be restored as soon as possible. You know."

"You chaps certainly have it all buttoned up," Fortune chuckled. "Tell me one thing, though: do we really have to take the young lady in with us? Couldn't we handle it on our own? Now that we've brought you three extra pairs of hands, I mean. *Noblesse* jolly well *oblige* and all that. I mean to say, I hate to see a girl—"

"Of course I have to come." Anya interrupted the inane pleasantries decidedly. "I have work as a switchboard girl in Odense, so I know best how to damage the equipment quickly and with best effect. Also I am very good shooting with the pistol."

"The female of the species!" Fortune said resignedly. "You must do as you think best, of course."

They slept fitfully, taking it in turn to keep watch until three o'clock. Then they left the wood, stole down the track and started the long slog through the dunes. It was extraordinarily cold. Wind moaned through the tall grasses, stinging their faces with salt spray and grains of sand. The stars and the moon had been blacked out by low clouds, and they were constantly thrown off balance, pitching down unexpected slopes or brought up short by steep rises impossible to distinguish in the blur of paler darkness below their feet. The going, in fact, was tough – but there was the advantage that any noise they might make would be drowned by the sound of waves crashing on the shore.

They reached the barbed wire soon after four thirty and began the laborious crawl around the perimeter to the entrance. Split into two parties, with the wind now howling across the flat land above them, they moved painfully over the uneven ground on elbows and knees. Bergg, armed with his Sten, led Fortune, Crisp and Bramming around one side; Olafsson, who had the other Sten, took Svenderup, Peters and Renard the other way. Anya, carrying the explosive, followed her father.

Bramming had taken charge of the grenades; the other men had a pistol each.

Thirty yards short of the entrance, Bergg halted his team and lay flat on the sandy earth. Squinting through the dark, Fortune could make out the black outline of a hut and an irregular shape beside it that must be the machine-gun nest. Further away, a flat-roofed building bulked against the sky. From time to time he heard guttural murmurs of German snatched away by the wind.

He stared at the luminous dial of his watch, feeling his heart thump away the seconds. As the minute hand eased on to the sliver of phosphorescent paint marking the hour, the creaking call of a nightjar sounded from the far side of the entrance. Bramming stood up and drew back his arm.

For an instant the wind had dropped. Fortune heard the rustle of the Dane's garments as he threw. A livid flash split the night. In the fiftieth of a second before the detonation cracked his ears, he saw imprinted on the dark the shapes of steel helmets, sandbags, the grooved cooling jacket around a Spandau. Then Bramming was cursing under his breath: the grenade had fallen short, striking the earth and bursting against the sandbags protecting the nest. Feverishly, he pulled the pin of another and threw again.

But the Nazi guards were well trained. Taken completely unawares as they must have been, they had nevertheless seen enough in the first grenade flash – and been sufficiently alert – to aim their weapons. Flame stabbed from the Spandau; the calico-tearing stammer of Schmeisser machine-pistols ripped out from the doorway of the hut. Bramming dropped like a stone as his second bomb exploded over the sandbagged emplacement.

All hell broke loose then. Bergg fired a short burst from the Sten and then rolled frantically sideways before the sentries could aim at the flashes jetting from the muzzle. The roar of Fortune's .45 and an 8 mm Luger that had been given to Crisp were drowned by another volley from the Schmeissers. Slugs scuffed the earth around them and whined over their heads. Bergg fired the Sten again. Someone cried out by the gates. They heard the clatter of metal as a body slumped noisily to the ground.

For a moment there was silence and total darkness. A fresh gust of wind flattened the grasses. Then two sentries, believing the attack came from Bergg's side only, stepped out from the shelter of the hut and blazed away for the third time.

This was what Olafsson had been waiting for. It was all part of the plan. Three revolvers and the second Sten spat fire from the darkness behind the Schmeissers. The sentries were cut down in a hail of lead. As the ringing in his ears died away, Fortune felt for Bramming's body. His hand came away wet with warm blood. There was no point feeling for heartbeats: the man's chest had been smashed in by the steel-jacketed slugs from the machine-pistols. Fortune's fingers touched splinters of bone pricking through the rough denim of the Dane's overall. Pocketing the two remaining grenades, he stumbled to his feet into the stink of cordite.

Olafsson was calling from the far side of the gates. One gleam from the masked flashlight told them all they wanted to know.

Bramming's second throw had been a good one. The Spandau was a tangle of twisted metal still smoking amid the welter of blood and entrails strewn over the interior of the sandbagged nest. One guard lay inside the hut with nothing but blood showing between his greatcoat collar and the brim of his helmet. The others sprawled where they had fallen outside the gates. "Come!" Olafsson yelled. "Take their guns and follow me!"

Fortune, Peters and Renard grabbed the Schmeissers and pelted after the others up the fifty-yard macadam driveway separating the gates from the entrance doors. They could hear shouts and the clatter of feet from inside the building. Olafsson hurled himself into the shelter of a portico as rifle and revolver fire cracked from the blacked-out windows of the upper storey. Svenderup, Peters and Renard dropped down behind an Opel delivery van parked at the end of the drive, returning the fire sparingly.

Fortune found himself standing with Bergg, Crisp and the girl in the lee of an old Mercedes tourer a little further away. "We must get in quick," Bergg panted. "Already they will have called the base to report the attack. It will take only fifteen minutes for reliefs to come from Ronde. We must be gone before then."

Olafsson was firing the Sten at the locked doors. After a short volley the harsh clamour of the gun ceased. "Bastard!" they heard him shout. "Always they are jamming!"

"Look," Anya said urgently. "Inside there are two guards with Schmeissers, three night operators, German ones, and a maintenance engineer. Maybe they do not all have guns. They cannot cover all the building at once."

"Right. We go," Bergg said. He called something in Danish to Olafsson, took one of the grenades from Fortune and sprinted for the corner of the building, followed by Crisp and Anya. Clearly, they were going to try for a rear entry. Fortune ran to the front wall, about twenty feet from the portico. As he crouched down, floodlights beneath the parapet bordering the flat roof blazed into life, illuminating the ground in front of the exchange with glaring brilliance. A shutter above the Englishman banged open. A machine-pistol chattered. Enfiladed in his position behind the Opel, Svenderup clawed at his chest and fell with scarlet spurting between his fingers.

Almost in reflex action, Fortune swung his own gun up and squeezed the trigger. The marksman vanished from the window embrasure, his weapon dropping to the ground at Fortune's feet.

Olafsson's Sten was still jammed. Fortune signalled to him and lobbed the remaining grenade, with the pin still in place, in his direction. The Dane scooped it up, withdrew the pin and rolled the bomb across the step against the doors. "Well fielded, sir!" Fortune murmured. Olafsson sprinted towards him, dropped face downwards to the ground and crossed his arms over his head.

A blinding flash; a shattering concussion.

Peters and Renard were dashing for the portico with guns blazing. Fortune ran after them. Olafsson scrambled to his feet, picked up the Schmeisser which had fallen from the window and followed.

The doors, blackened and splintered to matchwood, sagged on their hinges. Beyond, a hallway lit by a green-shaded overhead lamp swirled with brown smoke. As they kicked down the remains of the doors and burst in, a man in Wehrmacht uniform

119

ran down a flight of stairs leading to the upper floor with a machine-pistol cradled in his arms. Renard fired before the man could aim his gun, sending the soldier crashing over the guard-rail. At the same time they heard a volley of small-arms fire from the back of the building, followed by the coughing of Bergg's Sten gun.

It didn't take long after that. Both the guards were dead. Bergg had killed one of the defenders at the back; Crisp and the girl between them had accounted for another. The last two men holed up in a store-room at one end of an upstairs corridor, firing blindly through the door until Olafsson dragged himself along the floor and emptied the magazine of a Schmeisser upwards through the perforated panels. Then it was just a question of gathering up all the arms while Anya placed the charges that would blow the installation.

Fortune went with her into the operations room. The place was warm and heavy with the odour of stale tobacco. Red and green pilot lights flashed and glowed on the main control board. Tumblers with gothic numerals fell. Over the quiet hum of electrical equipment, the spiral selectors moving along the banks of automatic dialling machinery clicked busily as they rose into place. He watched, fascinated, as the big-hipped Danish girl lodged tiny parcels of the plastic explosive in strategic positions among the maze of transformers and looms. "What about this call you wanted to make?" she asked with a smile when the last charge was in place.

Fortune wiped his overalled sleeve across his brow. "Frankly," he said, "I don't know. It would be a great help – but I don't know how to get hold of my chief at five o'clock in the morning. I don't know his home number, you see . . . or the number of the bint he's after, the old rascal!"

"The . . . bint?"

"Never mind, old girl. No, but I'd like to check with him really. If only it was possible."

"It is possible," Anya said. "Do not worry. These charges can destroy only the automatic dialling equipment, not the cables themselves. I make a connection to a friend's home, and it will stay in place until the Nazis have repaired the damage. Maybe until tomorrow afternoon. You can call from her house later in the morning then." There was a manual dial in front of

120

the control board. She spun off five digits, spoke quietly into the headset for a moment, and then replaced the mouthpiece on its hook – with the lead still plugged in to its socket.

With Fortune's help, she levered up a cast-iron manhole cover in the cement floor. She lowered herself into the spider-web of blue and red and white cables beneath, with connectors, wire-cutters and a pair of American Kleins in her hand. "I loop in the circuit I have just make where the bangs cannot hurt it," she explained. "So my friend remains linked with the exchange's outside line until you have your call. So you speak to your boss from a Nazi army headquarters unit!"

"By Jove, that'd be super," Fortune enthused. "But won't they . . . I mean, will they be able to trace her in any way? I couldn't accept—"

"No, no. A line is plugged in here, but there is no way for them to know what is on the other end. So long as my friend's receiver is replaced."

In fact the explosive charges were relatively small. Huddled in the dunes as the sirens screamed along the road from Ronde, they could only just hear the detonations over the sound of the sea; it was more by counting the flashes as each charge printed the shapes of the windows on the night that they knew the raid had been a success. That and the quantity of weapons which would swell the partisans' secret armoury hoard.

And so Fortune, some six hours later, was able in a fisher-man's cottage twenty miles to the north to dial Stockholm direct and put through his call to O'Kelly.

But long before that, tragedy had struck. Olafsson was calling urgently: "Anya! Hurry! We have the guns. We must be outside the perimeter in three or four minutes."

"Coming," the girl shouted. With a last look around at the cheap watches fixed to the detonators as timing mechanisms, she led Fortune back to the entrance hall.

Olafsson, Bergg and the others were waiting by the smashed doors. "Where do we go now?" Fortune asked.

The Dane chuckled. The horse teeth gleamed. "The last place they look," he said. "You have see the island she lie between here and Ronde?"

Fortune nodded. He had seen it in the distance before darkness fell: half a dozen acres of stooked corn, a couple of grazing fields and a neat farmhouse in a grove of poplars. It was joined to the mainland by a short causeway.

"We go there. It is the last place they look," Olafsson said again. "First because it is a cul-de-sac. No escape, they think. Second because there are already Nazi guards: the colonel in charge of this exchange is billeted there. But there is a boathouse – and hidden there is a dinghy, slung beneath the roof. We use her later, after they put up roadblocks around here and catch nobody."

"We shall pass by Ronde and head for the peninsula," Anya said. "It is only ten, fifteen minutes in the boat while it is still dark. We better can – *Look out! Behind!*" she screamed.

The saboteurs whirled around as one man. Leaning against the shattered doorpost was the sentry they had left for dead on the floor of the hut. Blood had soaked through the field-grey cloth of his greatcoat and splashed onto his boots. It stained his sleeve and streaked the white-knuckled fingers of the hand clenched on the splintered wood. From the gory mask of his face, a single eye glared balefully into the savaged building.

But the Walther pistol in his other hand was steady. And it was trained on the thin, gangling figure of Crisp.

Bergg dropped the wounded man with a single shot from the .45 he had found in one of the dead guards' holsters.

The two guns roared simultaneously, shockingly loud in the smoky hall.

Crisp took an abrupt step forward. A thick gout of crimson pumped obscenely from the bib of his overall. "Christ!" he said plaintively. "Awfully sorry, sir, but I seem . . ."

For an instant he swayed on rubber legs, and then he pitched heavily to the floor with outflung arms.

Part Three

The Marsh King's Daughter

A storm arose; the Viking's wife heard the rolling of the waves east and west of her from the North Sea and the Kattegat. The Gialler horn sounded – and away over the rainbow rode the gods, clad in steel to fight their last battle.

Chapter Twelve

Webster's reactions on discovering Constantine unconscious, then the absence of Reilly and the stolen boat, ranged from astonishment through outrage and furious anger to determination, in that order. So he had been played for a bloody sucker, had he? Very well, just to show them, he would go ahead and complete the mission . . . and the hell with any dangers, difficulties and obstacles in the way.

At least he was no longer puzzled. You didn't have to be Albert Einstein to work out the score: if a guard had been knocked unconscious and a boat stolen, and if the second guard was missing, then you didn't have to go through the Army List to find the culprit. It followed therefore that since Reilly was responsible for them being on the wrong island, his navigational error must have been deliberate and not a mistake. Why should he have done that? To Webster, suspicious by nature and by training, there could only be one answer. Reilly was a traitor – if an Irishman could properly be called a traitor to England – or at least he was on the other side.

There was no point wasting time on recriminations, on the moral values of team loyalty or pondering the hows and whys. You played with the cards you had been dealt.

So there had been a Fifth Columnist aboard . . . and the bastard had shoved them in the shit. OK, for the moment the only thing that counted was how fast they could get out.

Landing them on Karlsö couldn't have been planned in advance, because Reilly hadn't known what the real target was until just before take-off. It must therefore have been a clever piece of improvisation; he *had* noticed the closeness – and the topographic resemblance – of the two islands on the map. And he had taken advantage of it. Why? For two reasons, Webster thought, each equally important. One, to gain time, so that he could get to his German masters and warn them of the impending attack before it went in; two, to trick the team, hopefully, into an armed assault on a neutral base, with the natural embarrassment to the Allies that would follow.

Well, thank God the second trap had been avoided. As for the first, well that was why Reilly had taken the dinghy: at this moment he would be paddling like blazes for Anholt, not realising that the lights of Karlsö would have tipped Webster off so soon and cut short the planned tour of the island's coast. Looked at in this light there was just one imperative for Webster and his men. Reilly must be caught and silenced before he could alert the Germans on Anholt. After that – Webster assumed with his usual daredevil optimism – the operation could be completed as planned, and then they would be free to tackle Fortune's show on Laeso.

There were of course inconveniences. The Canadian, still groggy and sick, said that as far as he could tell, he had been knocked out within a few minutes of the patrol's departure. This meant that Reilly had at least two hours start on them: he had been in such a hurry to get away that he hadn't even taken the time to sabotage the second dinghy.

"Unless, of course . . . ?" Webster began. He shook his head. "The man's not an idiot. He may simply have allowed for the fact that we might not fall for an attack on the base here. In which case it would be better if we did get the hell out and make the genuine attack . . . too late. A failed commando raid beaten off by the Jerries is better propaganda than a handful of chaps marooned on neutral territory – who would in any case have chucked their weapons into the sea before they were nabbed."

"You mean if we *had* sussed out that he'd done the dirty on us, but *hadn't* flown the coop?" Hunter said.

"Exactly. Playing both ends against the middle and covering every angle." Webster's voice was bitter. "Cocky bastard must have all the confidence in the world; thought we'd never be able to catch up with him, even if we did have the bloody dinghy! Well, it's up to us to prove the bugger wrong."

Reilly had almost fifteen miles of open water to cross, Constantine pointed out, with no lights to guide him. But he was a navigator: they couldn't rely on him losing time

126

by steering a wrong course. He could be damned near halfway there already.

On the other hand – this was Sergeant Hawkins – these rubber dinghies had no rowlocks; nor were they designed to be paddled by a single person. The Irishman's progress would therefore be slow – half a dozen strokes on this side, shift across the thwart, half a dozen on the other, and so on. Webster's boat would be grossly overloaded, but there were six paddles. Theoretically, he would have six times the power available on less of a zigzag course.

There were nevertheless other factors to take into account, each of them reducing the time limit. For one thing, they didn't have the whole fifteen miles to work in. He had taken both the transceivers with him. The special sets given to them had a range of two miles – so although the Germans on Anholt wouldn't be tuned in to the same frequency, their monitors would certainly pick up some kind of signal as soon as he was within radio range. After that, whether he was caught or not, the whole show would be blown. Finally, if they did overtake him in the thirteen-miles-minus available to them, it would have to be secretly and above all silently: a single shot would give the game away as much as a radio signal.

Could they pull it off in less than thirteen miles when their quarry had probably covered six or more already? Webster thought they could; at any rate they'd have a damned good try!

Luckily each dinghy was equipped with its own built-in reinflator, for the chemical release automatically filling them with compressed air on contact with the sea water worked only once. Within ten minutes the bulbous grey craft was afloat and they were hastily stowing explosives, weapons and what other supplies remained to them in the bow and stern. Reilly – presumably for reasons of lightness and because he knew his pursuers would have eaten nothing since their tins of emergency rations at noon – had only made off with the waterproof cartons of provisions. But he would still have his pistol and grenades.

"Pull her up to this rock," Webster ordered in a low voice. "Then try to climb in without wetting your bloody feet. If you

127

start out with cold, wet feet on this show, you could freeze before we're halfway there."

"Oi reckon Oi got cold feet already, never mind the bloomin' sea!" Hewitt jested.

"Pack it in, that man," Hawkins rapped at once. "Don't let me hear that kind of crap, even as a bleedin' joke. Now come on, you fuckers. Move!"

The dinghy was low in the water and sluggish to move by the time they had all crammed themselves between its bulging sides. Webster settled himself in the bow with the powerful Hewitt beside him. Next came Hunter and McTavish, and then Zygmund with Sergeant Hawkins. Constantine, still concussed from the savage blow he had received, was propped up in the stern, the only man without a paddle. "Now you take the time from me," Webster said, "and you put every ounce of strength you have into every damned stroke. You've got to paddle as if your lives depended on it . . . and I wouldn't be lying if I told you they did. It's a little different from stroking a varsity eight, but here goes . . . *ONE*-and-two-and-three-and-four . . . *ONE*-and-two-and-three-and-four . . ."

Wet blades gleaming dully in the dark as they stabbed in and out of the water, they moved slowly away from the rocky shore. The sea was choppy at first, with short, steep waves crumbling into foam, which made it hard to estimate how deep the paddles could be plunged. Before they were a hundred yards out, Webster's wet feet warning proved superfluous: sea water was swashing about below the duckboards on the rubber floor of the tiny craft and their proofed battledress was dripping. As soon as they drew out from behind the promontory, however, the surface relapsed into a long, easy-paced ocean swell, the dinghy rising and falling eight or ten feet every half-dozen strokes.

The lights of the Swedish base, which had swum into view as soon as they left the shelter of the headland, rose and fell, rose and fell too, then gradually vanished into the dark. The sky was scattered with cloud, but stars shone brightly against the blackness between.

Webster steered them due west, lungs labouring and muscles crying out for relief as they strove to keep up with the manic power of his strokes. They had been paddling for over an hour

128

when he paused in mid-stroke, lifted his blade from the water and muttered a command for them to stop. His keen ears had detected an alien sound somewhere ahead among the splash of paddles, the gasping of breath and the hiss and gurgle of water past the stern. Heads bowed over their knees, the others gulped in lungfuls of sea air and relaxed their tortured sinews, thankful for the respite.

Webster rose to his knees, scanning the heaving horizon each time the dinghy lifted to a swell. Dammit, he had been right! The slap of a crest against curved wood; a creaking boom.

A couple of hundred yards off their starboard quarter, a fishing smack was hove to under the dark sky.

The sails were reefed, but he could dimly make out her silhouette against a pale bank of clouds above the horizon in the north-west. He glanced at the luminous dial of his Rolex. If they were going to make it, he should be able to distinguish some sign of the Anholt coastline by now. He stared ahead, straining his eyes through the night.

Nothing but the endless crests and troughs of the swell, racing relentlessly towards the south-east.

Webster made up his mind. "Joe," he whispered, "you OK?"

"I . . . I guess so," Constantine murmured from the stern. "My head's better but I feel sick as a bloody dog."

"Forget it. You speak Swedish, don't you?"

"Some. I was an exchange student at Uppsala University in '33, and once at the Embassy in Ottawa, I was liaison—"

"Fine, fine. There's a fishing boat ahead. We're going to take her over. I want you to board her with your Buntline and hold up the crew. Talk to them in Swedish – with a German accent if you can – and tell 'em no harm will come to them if they pile into this bathroom toy and head for home. We're well outside Swedish territorial waters now, but I'd rather the Jerries were blamed for the hijack. Try and kid them you're a Nazi officer on some kind of bloody exercise. Zygmund, you go with him and keep spouting away in German while we transfer the gear."

Silently, crouching as low as they could and dipping their paddles deep, they spun the dinghy around and manoeuvred it nearer the unsuspecting smack. They were only three

129

crests away when there was a shout from the fishing vessel. Constantine yelled something back in Swedish. Then, as they drew closer and closer, he rose shakily upright with the long-barrelled pistol in his hand.

The inflated rubber side of the dinghy scraped the gunwale of the larger boat. Constantine scrambled aboard, closely followed by his leader and Zygmund. There were four fishermen – weatherbeaten sailors in sea-boots, oilskins and peaked caps. They fell back, astonished and outraged, before the menacing Canadian.

Constantine barked an order in heavily accented Swedish. Zygmund added a phrase in German. The fishermen protested, gesticulated. Constantine shouted, waving his gun. The sailors muttered sullenly – but they crowded together near the stern, waiting for the members of Webster's group to heave their equipment and supplies aboard while Zygmund rasped out convincing Nazi commands.

When everything had been transferred and the dinghy was empty, the four Swedes clambered in, urged roughly on by Constantine, and paddled reluctantly away towards the east. "Wacko!" said Webster with a satisfied grin.

"They're going to complain, aren't they?" Constantine said. "There'll be one hell of a fuss."

"An international incident already!" Zygmund added.

"See if I care," Webster said. "If anybody's going to be accused of violating Swedish neutrality now, it's going to be the Boche and not us!"

He looked around his prize. The smack was about twenty feet long, half-decked for'ard of the mast, with a wide, duckboarded well in the centre of which rose a doghouse covering the engine. It was probably a slow old tub, wide in the beam and clumsy to manoeuvre, but it would be a damned sight quicker than a rubber dinghy with six paddles! "Right," Webster said crisply, "now I want a 360-degree watch kept for Reilly. He should show in about fifteen minutes if this craft makes the kind of speed I expect. Hunter – you take the wheel. Approach the island in a series of wide sweeps."

Hunter was short and sinewy, with the kind of pale blue seaman's eyes that crinkle up through a lifetime of squinting at obstacles obscured by fog or sleet or salt spray. Or through a lifetime of cigarettes drooping from the corner of the mouth. He lit up now without asking permission, shielding the match flame with a cupped hand as he reached for the wheel. Webster bent down and cranked the handle projecting from the rear of the engine housing. At his third attempt the motor fired. Hunter shoved the gear lever into the forward position, spun the wheel and the boat started forging steadily through the swell towards Anholt.

"Where did those chaps come from?" Webster asked the Canadian.

"They were Swedish all right," Constantine replied. "They come from Falkenberg. It's quite a way – thirty or forty miles, I should say. I guess they weren't exactly enthusiastic about the idea of paddling all that distance. Quite apart from the loss of their boat."

"Poor sods. I'm sorry, but there was nothing else we could do – not if we want to be sure of overtaking Reilly. Let's hope they think of making for Karlsö. They even lost their bloody catch!" He nodded towards the stem, where fish scales glinted phosphorescently beneath the thwarts.

"Hey, we could use some of that catch – after we've caught Reilly! Be useful to supplement the iron rations, don't you think, boss?"

"If we catch him. It's not going to be easy, spotting a dinghy low on this swell," Webster said. "You fellows spread out around the boat, keep down . . . and for God's sake keep your eyes skinned."

Hawkins went to the stem, Constantine to the stern once more. Hewitt and McTavish lay prone on the foredeck, and Zygmund stayed with Webster himself, crouched down by the gunwale, one on either side of Hunter. The fishing smack chugged west in widening circles.

Twenty minutes later, they could make out the long, low bulk of Anholt as a darker mass against the horizon each time the craft lifted to the swell. The rectangular oulines of the fortifications were still between four and five miles away, Webster estimated. They had a couple of miles to spare before the traitor would be within radio range of the base. Hunter altered course a few points to bring them parallel to the island's north-east – south-west shore.

131

The wind was fresher here and the waves steeper. They had been sailing a further fifteen minutes, listening to the even beat of the engine, the creak of rigging and the slap of sea-water against the planks, when Hawkins suddenly whispered from the starboard bow: "Major Webster! Major Webster, sir – I think I saw the treacherous cunt. Over there . . . below one of those pale messenger clouds, sir . . . Lie down here by me and you'll see."

Webster climbed up onto the half-deck and wormed his way for'ard. He followed the direction of the big sergeant's pointing finger as the bows lifted and sank. Straining his eyes to separate darkness from darkness, he saw – he thought he saw – yes, by Jove, he did see! Hawkins was right. A squat shape bearing a single frenziedly working silhouette was outlined momentarily against the sky. He waited while the fishing boat rode another swell, sank into a trough, lifted again, to make sure – then clapped Hawkins on the shoulder and crawled back to the well to whisper instructions to Hunter.

Reilly's dinghy was only two or three hundred yards away. He must have heard the pulse of their engine. But he would reckon he was in no danger from fishermen; he would simply press on and hope they didn't notice him among the waste of waters, or hail him to offer help.

Hunter slammed open the throttle and took the boat surging between the dinghy and the shore, as though he was making for the island. The timbers shuddered to the thrumming of the motor. Foam hissed past the gunwale as the unwieldy craft heeled over . . . and then, at the last moment, when the dinghy was only fifty yards away on the port beam, he put the helm hard up and ran straight for the smaller vessel.

Webster was up on the decking again. "Right," he murmured to Hawkins and Hewitt, "whichever side he comes, get him, make sure you do – but for Chrissake keep it quiet!"

Still hoping that he might be unobserved, Reilly had stopped paddling, crouching as low as he could between the inflated sides of the dinghy until the fishing vessel had passed by. Now he rose hastily upright, swaying with the motion of the sea, his Buntline in one hand, a grenade in the other. When it was evident that they intended to run him down, he shouted something unintelligible and pulled the pin of the grenade with his teeth.

The blunt prow of the fishing boat drove hard into the dinghy, canting it up out of the water and then capsizing it. The pistol spun from the Irishman's hand as he catapulted into the waves; the grenade splashed beneath the surface.

There was a muffled thump underwater . . . a geyser of white foam imprinted for an instant against the dark . . . and then a seething circle of bubbles, widening slowly as it drifted past the smack.

Hewitt's huge body leaned outboard, the arms outstretched. He uttered an exclamation of satisfaction, jack-knifing himself back into the well as he hefted the sodden, struggling form of Reilly on deck in a single powerful heave. Webster hauled the runaway to his feet by the collar of his waterlogged tunic. "You stinking little rat," he grated in a rare burst of rage. "You filthy, fucking, traitorous bastard!" His fist crashed into the scowling Irishman's face. Reilly's head snapped back and he gave a choked cry.

"Traitor to who?" he spat. "I owe nothing to your rotten, class-ridden country and the murderous scum who occupied my—"

The tirade was cut off as Webster struck him twice again – a short, jabbing, stiff-arm blow to the heart, and a straight left that whistled through the air to crack against the point of the fugitive's jaw. Reilly shuddered. His knees buckled and he folded forward from the waist. Then, as the boat tilted to a swell, he collapsed in a heap on the duckboards.

"Hey, boss!" Constantine called urgently. "There's a light flashing from the fort on the island there – look: they're signalling!"

Webster spun around, licking his bruised knuckles, to stare at the winking point of illumination above the faint outline of the Anholt coast. "My God, that's torn it; they must have picked up this old tub on their radar screens. They're asking us to identify ourselves."

He glanced hastily around the dark cockpit. There was an Aldiss lamp beside the engine housing, but he had no idea of the code or the form of answer required. "Quick – pile back in that dinghy and load all the gear into it," he rapped. "They'll blow this boat out of the water if they don't get a reply."

Hunter put the smack about and drew near the upturned

133

craft. Reilly's helmet and sidearms, along with the entire stock of their provisions, had gone overboard when the dinghy capsized. But there were still three paddles trapped between the surface of the water and its rubber floor. They righted it and drew it alongside, hurriedly transferring the stuff they had already offloaded from their own dinghy, together with some of the catch from the fishing boat's well.

The signal lamp on the island was flashing again. "That's it," Webster said. "Get in there, all of you. Hunter – lash the wheel of this hulk, set her half ahead and point her at the island."

"What about Reilly?" someone asked.

"The hell with him. Leave him here. After what he tried to do to us, he can take his chance. In any case," Webster said, "we've neither the time nor the space to take prisoners on this show. Strip off his battledress, webbing and boots, and chuck 'em in the sea. There's an old pair of seaboots and an oilskin aft, stuff him into those. And look sharp."

While Hawkins and Hewitt tore off the unconscious man's outer clothing, the rest of them piled into the dinghy and held it close to the larger vessel's painter as Hunter sent it ploughing back through the swell towards the Nazi stronghold. Before they had finished, a livid orange flash erupted from the coastline ahead. A fountain of sea-water shot into the air with a dull roar a hundred yards off their port beam. Seconds later they heard the reverberating rumble of the gun that had fired. "Warning shot," Webster said tersely. "The next one will be on target. Come on, me hearties – *move!*"

Propping Reilly up in the stern, Hawkins and Hewitt transferred to the dinghy. Hunter was the last to leave. As his wiry, compact figure stepped aboard and sank down in the inflated boat, Webster and Hawkins shoved hard against the fishing vessel's hull.

The dinghy floated free, rapidly falling astern as the threshing screw of the other craft carried it away into the dark.

Webster took one of the paddles, handing the other two to Hewitt and the big sergeant. "Start working . . . and go like hell," he ordered. "You take the port side, Hewitt, and use all your strength. Hawkins and I will balance you on the starboard."

They had completed less than a dozen strokes when flame

belched again from the tip of the island, flickering redly on a bank of low cloud. Six shells this time burst with ear-shattering detonations a quarter of a mile behind them. The white towers of water thrown up had scarcely subsided into the sea when the distant battery fired another salvo.

For a heart-stopping moment, Zygmund and Constantine, facing the dinghy's stern, saw the fishing boat outlined against one of the pale fountains of steam and spray. Her mast had snapped and she was down by the head, her rudder and screw tilted up clear of the swell. Then an overshoot burst deafeningly only a hundred yards away, sending the lightweight dinghy bobbing wildly over the sea as angry waves creamed outwards from the explosion.

With their third salvo, the coastal gunners got it right. At least one shell made a direct hit on the stricken vessel. The night split apart in a fiery thunderclap. Beyond the blinding carmine core of the shellburst, splintered planks went spinning into the dark, trailing spirals of flame. A single mushroom of smoke marbled with tongues of fire boiled skywards. Then there was silence, broken only by the patter of debris splashing back into the sea.

"That's no perishing buckshot they're firing," Hunter observed after a moment. "That's heavy-calibre stuff all right – 360 mm, I shouldn't wonder! D'you think this ruddy dinghy'll show up on their radar screens, sir?"

"No way," said Webster. "We're too low in the water for radar, and there's no metal in the hull for their sonar to bounce off. But that doesn't mean we can relax – even with Reilly out of the way, even if he wasn't close enough to radio a warning. We must move on in until we're a couple of miles offshore – and then circle the whole southern end of the blasted island."

"There's a port down there, isn't there?" Constantine asked.

"A small one, yes. Mostly fishing craft. It's at the south-western tip. And, according to the map, the safest place for us to make landfall is on the north bloody coast! We have exactly one hour and forty minutes to make it before the moon comes up . . ."

He dug in his paddle with renewed energy, and the dinghy rode steadily over the swell towards the shore.

Chapter Thirteen

The creek penetrated an area of flat land covered with clumps of grass and stunted shrubs. At its seaward end, slabs of rock worn smooth by the pounding of waves sloped down to a wrack-strewn beach of gravelly sand. It was here that Webster decided to make their shelter.

In the pale light of the moon, Hawkins, Hewitt and McTavish roofed over a cleft between two boulders with flat stones and then spread driftwood, seaweed and flotsam over these and the neighbouring outcrops as though washed up there by an extra-high tide. When it was finished, there was just enough space for all of them to cram in between the damp and sulphur-smelling walls, and it was virtually undetectable from anywhere except the water's edge immediately in front of the entrance. A small niche nearby was similarly camouflaged to house the deflated dinghy and the bulk of their supplies. Finally Hewitt excavated a foxhole for a lookout in the soft, sandy earth beneath an alder bush at the head of the creek.

Shortly before dawn they made a tiny fire in front of their hideout and cooked some of the fish they had salvaged from the hijacked boat. They ate ravenously, drank a little of their limited supply of water and then warmed themselves with swallows of Hawkins's akvavit. Webster posted Zygmund to guard the entrance to the artificial cave, ordered the others to try and snatch a little sleep and went to take the first watch at the creek-head himself.

Just before the sun rose, he stood upright behind the alder and risked a quick look around. Two hundred yards away, a dirt road ran along the spine of the island. It was bordered by cultivated fields. He saw scattered cottages and smallholdings shrouded by the mist still lying in the hollows, and he could make out the roofs of the little port beyond a gentle rise in the land to his right, at the southern tip of the triangle's base. Away to the left, where Anholt narrowed to a point, the Nazi fortress stood against the vanishing night – a massive complex of pillboxes topped by the three two-gun turrets they had come to destroy.

From where he stood, he could look out over the sea on the far side of the island. While he watched, the leaden surface of the water brightened. The high cloudbank blazed a bright crimson, and then suddenly all the colour drained from the sky over the eastern horizon and the incandescent rim of the sun appeared, blinding him with its white light. Still dazzled, he was observing the sun hoist itself slowly into the sky, throwing the flat grey outlines of the landscape into sharp relief, when he heard the whine of gears from the direction of the port.

Webster lowered himself once more into the foxhole. A cloud of dust appeared over the tops of the grasses. Cautiously, he raised his head. Two armoured Bussing-NAG half-track personnel carriers were rattling along the dirt road towards the fortress. As they came closer, he could see that they were loaded with steel-helmeted troops in field-grey greatcoats. Two hundred yards behind, a Mercedes-Benz staff car bounced along the rutted track.

Webster whistled soundlessly to himself. It looked as though this must be a morning shift on its way to relieve the garrison on the base. If it was, this meant that the German units guarding the guns were quartered in the village and not at the fortress itself – which would make the planning of his formidable task that much easier.

Raising his field glasses, he watched the small convoy halt at the entrance to the fortifications. There were two sentries by a striped barrier pole. A sandbagged machine-gun emplacement stood at one side. Kid stuff, really, Webster reflected; if the Germans were fearful of intrusions from the sea, they were certainly not expecting a land attack so far inside occupied territory! Passes were not even inspected, he noted.

The sentries saluted, the barrier rose and the convoy swept past to disappear from sight around one of the pillboxes. Ten minutes later, the same three vehicles reappeared and returned to the port. As far as he could see, there were eight men in each carrier – four fewer than on the outward jouney. This suggested that the base worked with a reduced staff during the night. If so it would be greatly to his advantage: seven men against sixteen was a much more plausible equation than seven against two dozen. But there were two more questions to be answered before he could even think of starting to plan an assault . . . well, three really, for he must certainly get a closer look at the place, and the layout of the buildings, before he acted.

First though he had to know whether the men he had seen were guards only – or whether, apart from the two or three officers who might be expected to have been in the staff car, they represented the total strength of the garrison, including gunners and radar operatives. Webster feared that they were probably extra to these specialists. But the second question was even more vital: were they working eight-hour or twelve-hour shifts?

On this one point hinged the lengths of the odds stacked against him.

Time was pitifully short if they were to put this stronghold out of action and then make the forty-five mile trip to Laeso and repeat the dose by midnight tomorrow. Most commanders would have dismissed the idea as impossible, but to Webster nothing was impossible: there were merely varying degrees of difficulty to be overcome.

In this case, the degree of difficulty was high. There was little cover on Anholt, so in practice any attack must be confined to the hours of darkness. Moreover it would have to be completed long before dawn to allow them time to regain the dinghy and be out of sight of land before daybreak. Making the hazardous sea crossing would be less of a problem once the guns were out of action; it would depend on what kind of air support the garrison could call up. Even so – given that their intentions remained secret – it gave them less than six hours to plan and carry out the entire Laeso show . . . and it had been Fortune's lot who were briefed on that one!

This, however, was a problem that could – that would have to – wait. They would need more time for the Anholt operation because there was more to do. The imperative was to destroy the radar and sonar installations. The batteries were less important: they could hardly be called a danger if they didn't know there was anything to fire at. Even if Webster's

138

commando succeeded only in that first objective, even if the garrison was alerted, the submarine carrying the observation unit might well run the gauntlet of the guns, depth charges and whatever else the Boche had to throw at it, providing there no longer existed the means to locate and direct accurately. The unit might even get through entirely undetected.

But this was where the importance of the shift system came in. It was now just after six o'clock in the morning. If the garrison was on eight-hour tours, reliefs should arrive at 1400 and 2200 hours. Presumably the first of these would still be at day strength, that is twenty-four men. And, because of those odds, this would mean that the attack must be delayed until after the smaller shift arrived at 2200. Which would simply not allow enough time . . .

If on the other hand it was a twelve-hour tour of duty, they would switch over to the smaller squad at 1800 hours – and Webster could go in any time after dark with four additional hours to play with.

The hell of it was that he would have wait, doing nothing, until two o'clock in the afternoon, checking whether or not there was a changeover at that time, before he knew which way the wind blew.

Meanwhile anything and everything he saw would be useful. Turning the problems over in his mind, he watched the flat countryside. The sun was well over the horizon now, and soon a faint, wintry warmth dispersed the mist and began to penetrate his chilled bones. Groups of workers from the cottages emerged to labour in the fields. A motorcycle dispatch rider rode out to the base and then returned to the port. Webster logged it all down.

At eight o'clock, Hewitt crawled along below the bank of the creek to relieve him. Webster passed on the results of his vigil and asked if everything was under control back at the cave. "Constantine be runnin' a temperature," the huge West Country man replied. "Oi reckon the noight air musta chilled un. Settin' up there after bein' coshed an' all . . . then not paddlin' to keep the blood circulatun."

"Did you use the medicine chest?"

Hewitt nodded. Hunter had given the sick man a shot and a couple of the special pills with which they had been provided.

He was now sleeping. Apart from that, everything was fine –
"'Ceptin' it be cold enough down there to freeze off a man's
bollocks!" Hewitt said.

"'Into each life a little rain must fall'," Webster quoted with
an unsympathetic grin. He handed over the binoculars and a
small notepad with a waterproof pencil clipped to it. "Put down
everything you see," he said. "Every damned thing. Note the
exact times. Only use the glasses if you're sighting between
the branches of this bush: you let the sun hit those lenses,
and you might as well heliograph our arrival or run up a
Union Jack!"

"Yes, sir."

"I'm going back into that cave to try and grab a spot
of shut-eye. McTavish will relieve you at noon. If there's
anything . . . wake me up, fast."

"Very good, sir."

After the leader of the unit had crawled away, Hewitt settled
himself into the shallow hole he had dug, his heavy head
cocked to one side and his large countryman's eyes squinted
against the low sun's glare. His breath steamed in the cold air
as he chewed on a stick of gum he had saved from the previous
day's emergency rations.

He had been there less than an hour when he tensed suddenly
and raised the field glasses to his eyes. A five-man patrol led
by an NCO had marched out from the base. Instead of taking
the dirt road which led to the port, they cut through the fields
and headed for the shore, pausing by each group of workers
they passed.

Hewitt cursed, raising himself slightly and adjusting the
focus wheel of the binoculars. Evidently it was a regular
patrol: the NCO was scrutinising papers. The squad left the
last line of labourers and began to walk slowly along the low,
grassy bluff above the beach, scanning the rough terrain as
they advanced. They would be at the creek in less than half
an hour. Hewitt swung around, refocused the glasses and raked
the coastline rising towards the port. At first he saw nothing.
Then, filing between two clumps of osiers, he caught sight
of a similar patrol approaching from the other direction. The
creek was about halfway along the northern coast of Anholt. It
could well be the point where the two patrols met. Presumably

they would then cross the island, separate and then return along the other shore to their two bases (thought Hewitt, who had been in the army for twelve years and knew something of the military mind).

Five minutes later, he was shaking Webster by the shoulder in the cave. Webster was awake in an instant. "Bugger," he said when Hewitt had made his breathless report. "Does it look like a special patrol or a routine operation?"

"Routine, sir, Oi reckon. Leastways they bain't headin' over here direct. They're checking the passes of them coves workin' that dratted sugar-beet."

"Are they actually on the beach?"

Hewitt shook his head. "On the lip of the bluff, sir. But lookin' down."

"Probably a regular duty," Webster said. "It's hardly worth building an Atlantic Wall up here, or staking out barbed wire, even if they had the men. But they take a look – just in case, maybe a couple of times a day. If they come down to the shore we could be for the high-jump. If not . . . well, we'll see just how good the sergeants' camouflage efforts were, eh?"

He looked around the circle of attentive faces in the gloom of the bivouac, all of them relying on him, waiting for him to make decisions, his responsibility. Or were they? Glancing quickly back again, he thought he saw McTavish turn away to mutter something under his breath. It sounded suspiciously like "Playboy!"

Although he had several times before noticed the little Scot favouring him with a hard stare, Webster nevertheless felt that momentary drop in the morale experienced by anyone hearing an unflattering comment expressed by someone they thought had no reason to dislike them.

"Did you have something to say, Sergeant McTavish?" he asked sharply.

The Scot shook his head. "Naethin' . . ."

In a cloak-and-dagger show of this kind, rank could customarily and conveniently be forgotten, but McTavish's omission of the word 'sir' was so marked and so obvious that the gap almost made a word in itself. And it wasn't a word that was respectful.

For the moment, though, this wasn't the time to pursue

141

the matter. Webster motioned them all to silence and settled down to wait. Huddled back as far between the rocks as they could squeeze, each man could hear the thudding of his own heart over the crash of waves and the stealthy drip of water somewhere behind.

Time passed.

Then, faintly at first, the tramp of feet, an occasional crisp command and – barely evident – a distant clink that could be . . . what? Buckles on the slings of carbines? Breech blocks against metal belt clips? Magazines? No, the guns would already be loaded. Webster put his lips close to Hewitt's ear and whispered: "The foxhole?"

"Covered her with branches. Then leaves. Marked the earth at one side – scratched un with me nails, like maybe a dog had been diggin' there. Oi reckoned there better be a reason, loike, in case the Krauts noticed somethin'. Best Oi cud do in the toime."

"Good man. Spot on."

The footsteps had stopped somewhere above and behind their shelter. It was impossible to guess where.

For an eternity they crouched there, scarcely daring to breathe, staring at the bright wedge of sand and sea and sky revealed in the artificial cave mouth. The waves advancing on the shore looked larger now, and there was a breeze blowing the foam from their crests as they broke. A cloudbank lay stormy and dark along the horizon.

Constantine shifted his position and began to mutter in his sleep. Webster clamped a hand over the Canadian's mouth and raised a warning finger when the man's eyes opened.

The cave mouth darkened; a shadow fell across the entrance. Expecting the polished leather of jackboots, Webster caught his breath and eased off the safety catch of his pistol . . . then visibly relaxed, realising it was only a cloud which had dimmed the pale sunshine outside. There was sweat on his forehead, and his hawk face was as grey as the rising sea.

Terrifyingly close, a harsh voice barked something in German. The seven commandos tensed. A reply came from further away. Then again the tramp of booted feet approaching, an order, a parade-ground halt. As Hewitt had thought, the creek was the rendezvous for the two patrols.

142

For several minutes, the two NCOs exchanged gossip. Webster couldn't quite make out the words. And then, crisply:

"Heil Hitler!"

"Heil Hitler!"

The clump of boots as the squads came to attention. The rhythmic tread of many feet marching away into the distance. A silence broken only by the breaking of waves, the swash of retreating water.

"By Jove!" Webster expelled his breath in a long sigh of relief and wiped a sleeve across his brow. "You were nearest the entrance, Ziggie. Could you hear what they were saying?"

"Routine material," Zygmund reported. "The lousy Danes, they should pull their weight in the fields. One of them had found a broad in the port, she puts out. The batteries had sunk a fishing boat last night that refused to identify itself. They figured it for Swedish and the brass were scared of repercussions, but they were only carrying out orders. Wasn't it a bastard about the cigarette ration, and like that."

"Nothing more about the boat?"

"I don't think so . . . Oh, yeah: they'd only salvaged one body and that was unrecognisable. So a single Swedish sailor, why the fuck would he risk death sailing into occupied waters?"

Webster frowned. The seamen whose boat they had hijacked would be talking their heads off. Their story of seven men who'd forced them into a dinghy at gunpoint would make headlines in the Swedish press. There would be outraged editorials, perhaps a diplomatic protest. The story would be too late for today's editions but it would surely be splashed tomorrow. That made the time element more vital than ever. For if the neutrals believed with the fishermen that the takeover was Nazi-inspired – the dinghy had been stencilled with Luftwaffe markings for just such an eventuality – the Germans themselves would certainly know that it wasn't.

As soon as the story broke they would know that there were at least six men, armed and desperate men, unaccounted for in the sector.

The Anholt base must be taken before that happened.

For a full half-hour, Webster kept them silent in the shelter.

Then, after Hunter had made a cautious reconnaissance, he posted Hawkins as lookout, allowed Hewitt to prowl along the shore, searching for edible shellfish among the rock pools, and went back to the foxhole himself. The sky was overcast now, and the breeze had freshened. The flat countryside was as grey and desolate as the sea surrounding it, the temperature lower than ever. The returning patrols were specks above the further coastline.

At noon, an ancient lorry groaned along the track from the village distributing what looked like soup and bread to the workers in the fields. By one o'clock it had returned. Half an hour later two larger trucks, each accompanied by two Wehrmacht men, pulled up on the dirt road a mile apart while the labourers loaded into them the produce they had been stacking all morning.

The hands of Webster's Rolex crawled on towards 1400 hours. If there should be a personnel convoy heading for the base at the time . . . God, he didn't even want to think about it!

Ears strained for the tell-tale whine and clatter of half-tracks, he held the glasses to his eyes with numbed hands, ceaselessly watching the road from the port. So ferocious was his concentration that he forgot to check his watch. Next time he looked, it was five past two.

Scarcely daring to believe it, he kept looking. Fourteen hours ten . . . a quarter past . . . 1420 . . . By Christ, they'd hit the jackpot!

Well, relatively. The bastards were on twelve-hour shifts. They could go in at dusk.

His sigh of satisfaction was from the heart. At last, the action he craved. At last the chance to do rather than just think. That was fine – but was it going to be that easy? Do what, for a start? Go in at dusk. Splendid. But go in precisely where? And to what? And how . . . above all, how?

There was one hell of a lot to find out before he could answer those questions. And hardly any time in which to do it.

Did the patrols make a second tour of the island before dark? If so, how was he ever going to get near enough to the base to check the layout of the fortifications? A frontal attack with guns blazing was out of the question. Even an idiot would

144

hesitate to storm fortress walls if he had no idea what lay on the far side – and, foolhardy though he might be, daredevil though he was, Webster was no idiot. Especially when the lives of six companions were in his hands. In any case the garrison commander would have reinforcements up from the port in ten minutes.

No, it had to be infiltration by stealth. But whoever heard of that kind of show without prior intelligence? Somehow or other he had to get close to that goddam base within the next couple of hours. Close enough to see exactly how it worked. Gritting his teeth, he swung the glasses back over the road until they were trained on the sentries at the entrance.

"If you are wanting some information, maybe you better can ask," a voice said quietly in English just behind him.

With a stifled exclamation, Webster rolled over, his hand flying to the gun butt in his shoulder harness.

A girl wearing a fur coat and laced boots was standing by the alder bush, looking down at him.

Chapter Fourteen

She was tall and blonde and slender. Her nose was straight
and her eyes were a clear blue. Beneath the wide brow
and flat, Nordic cheekbones, the face sloped in to a small,
determined chin. She wore no make-up and her cheeks were
flushed with the wind. Webster thought she was very nearly
the most beautiful sight he had ever seen.

"What the hell are you doing here?" he muttered huskily.
It was the only thing he could think of to say.

The smile curving the girl's delectable mouth widened,
revealing small, even teeth. "I came to see you," she said.
"Or whoever is the leader of you."

"But how on earth . . . ?"

"You are not the only one watching the Germans. We did not
see your landing, but some friends of mine witness you making
your shelter after the moon is up. It is very well done."

"We?"

"There are Danish patriots everywhere," the girl said.
"Because our country is overrun, this does not mean that we
lie down and do nothing. There was a group of people – a cell,
you call it – further to the south. Near Bagenkop, on the island
with the name Langeland, and again near Marstal, on Aerö. We
did feed these people with information, but the Germans caught
them, all, three weeks ago – no, it was more nearly four. Some
they killed and some they took away. So now we continue to
watch and gather information, waiting for somebody who will
be able to use it, to send it away perhaps on a radio."

"Well, damn me!" said Webster. He was staring up at her
legs, long and tapered above the boots. They were beautiful
too. Feeling suddenly at a disadvantage, he scrambled into
a sitting position. If the Danes had some clandestine underground operatives on the island, why hadn't O'Kelly and the

War Office types had more explicit information to give them on the layout of the base? It was unlike the Captain to send people out inadequately briefed. "Tell me about it," he said.

Her name was Irmgaard Kraul. Her father had been mayor of a small town in the southern part of Odense; her mother had died when she was twelve. Not long after the occupation, her father had been shot by the Germans, along with five other hostages, after a Wehrmacht patrol had been ambushed and decimated near the town. Determined to seek revenge, she had left the area and at first gone underground. "But how the devil did you end up here in the back of the beyond?" Webster asked.

Irmgaard flushed. "I am not proud of this part," she said. "It is a disgusting thing. I became the . . . friend of a German officer."

"Christ Almighty! Why, in God's name?"

"You do not understand," the girl said. "People were starving. It was one way to obtain food, small luxuries, cigarettes and give them to those whose needs were greater than mine – so maybe they could feel human again. Also, I told myself, I could have my revenge by gathering information and passing it on to people who could use it. But I see now that it was not a good thing. You are right to be angry. Many people of my country are angry too: they spit when I pass in the street."

"I'm not angry, honey," Webster said gently. "Just trying to work out why you had to do it, that's all."

"Honey. That is a strange thing to call a girl. Are you American?"

"English. So how did you happen to find yourself up here on Anholt?"

"My German master receives a promotion: he becomes the commander of the Nazi radar base and the batteries here. He is not so bad – one of the more civilised, in the army, not the Gestapo or the SS. But he is transferred and a pig, a gunnery specialist, takes his place."

"And the pig?" Webster said. "You have not been forced to become his—"

"The Herr Colonel Heinz Ulrich Bosendorff, of the 176th Flakregiment" – she pronounced the name with distaste. "No, he wish me to become his . . . his mistress . . . but I always refuse."

"You said *Flak*regiment? But I thought . . . ?"

"Seconded for special duties in the Baltic after training at a secret gunnery research establishment near Stettin. The men who operate the batteries have special training also. It is a new technique."

Webster's pulses were racing. The ex-mistress of the ex-base commander tumbling into his lap like a ripe apple. And an ex-mistress harbouring a grudge at that. It was too good to be true! She could probably answer half the questions bothering him on the spot; she could give him the complete rundown on the garrison routine, its strength, its dispositions, the whole bang-shoot!

But could he trust her? Wasn't it perhaps a little too good to be really true? Could the apple be overripe?

And if she did know all these things – again the disturbing thought crossed his mind – why hadn't this absolutely vital information been passed along with the other intelligence to London?

"And you?" Irmgaard was saying. "What kind of special duties have seconded *you* to the Baltic?" She gazed approvingly at the lines of experience graved on Webster's wintry face. It was the kind of face, rakish in its way, that looked as though its owner had a hangover even when he was sober. It was a face, nevertheless, that she thought she could trust.

"Well," Webster answered guardedly, choosing his words with care. "I guess it's fairly obvious that we're not here to take holiday snaps of your sunny coast." Could she be a Nazi plant? Surely not. If the Germans had found out they had unexpected visitors, and wished to discover the secret of their mission, they'd have no need to set a honey-trap: they could simply blast in and take them, then hand them over to the Gestapo. In any case, if they had decided to bait a trap with a blonde, she would certainly have posed as a member of the Danish underground – but surely the last thing she would admit was a relationship with a German base commander? On an impulse, he backed his own hunch. He would take her story at its face value. If his trust was misplaced, it meant they were finished anyway, so what could he lose?

He jerked his head in the direction of the base. "We were sent," he said, "to destroy those guns and put the new radar unit out of action." There was no need to tell her more than that. She didn't have to know why.

"That is good," the girl said gravely. "We hoped, my friends and I, that this would be your answer."

He decided to rid himself of his remaining doubts. "Irmgaard," he said, looking into her eyes, "the information on which our briefing was based came from a Danish cell – probably the one you were talking about, the one the Germans destroyed. Perhaps *their* information, about the guns and radar I mean, came originally from you and your friends here?"

"But yes. The others would not have known. It is difficult to move about freely in Denmark now, and Langeland is a long way – more than two hundred kilometres in a straight line, a hundred of your miles."

"Then there is something I do not understand. If you were in a position to know the details of the base – how it worked, how it was guarded, how many men are there, exactly how they are armed and that kind of thing – why was this information not transmitted to London also?"

She caught on at once. "You do not trust me," she said sadly. "I understand. Why should you? And the answer is that others too mistrust an ex-collaborator, the whore of a German officer."

He shook his head. "I still don't understand."

"The cell on Aerö and Langeland was official. It had been – how do you say? cleared?—yes, cleared by London. It was working for the Allied intelligence network; its members were, well, professionals. Like my friends here, I am just what you call an enthusiastic amateur."

Baby, Webster thought to himself, eyeing the curve of her coat where it was thrust out by her breasts, *don't I wish the hell you were!*

"So although they would transmit the fact that radar, sonar and guns existed," the blonde went on, "because you see this could be verified from other sources, any of the details you cite they would not pass on – even though we gave them."

"Why not, for God's sake?"

"That is their orders. Only send what can be checked.

149

Rumours and guesses and hearsay are worse than no information, because they can be planted or deliberately misleading. Therefore dangerous to people like you." She shrugged. "Alas, in my position, the details I give are regarded in this way."

He grinned at her. "Not to worry. In general, I suppose those orders make sense."

"Also the routine have changed since the cell was destroyed, and I have learn much more since, so it *would* have been misleading. But, until you come, we have nobody to pass this new information on to."

"Right." Satisfied, Webster dismissed the subject at once. No point wasting any more time on it. "Did anyone see you come this way?" he asked. "Are you allowed to go where you want on the island?"

"But yes. I go where I wish. Often I walk along the shore here. Nobody will find it unusual."

"Good. Now I'd like you to walk on down to our shelter. Sit on a rock and look out over the sea. Make sure you are hidden by the bluff. I'll crawl back along the creek, post a man to relieve me here and join you there. I have a stack of questions I'd like answered."

Ten minutes later, having told the astonished commandos of the new development and sent Hunter up to the foxhole, Webster dropped down beside the girl on a flat slab of rock and started his catechism. The sea, receding towards low water, looked angrier than ever, the sky was now dark with hurrying clouds and a clinging dampness had been added to the bitter cold. It seemed as though they might be in for a dirty night.

"They work twelve-hour shifts, changing at 0600 and 1800 hours, right?" he began.

She nodded, shivering suddenly and wrapping the fur coat more closely around her slender body.

"Sixteen on the night trick, twenty-four on the day?"

"Twenty-six actually. Plus the officers."

"Twenty-six, then. Why the difference, and how many officers?"

"Sixteen men and two officers work the radar and guns," she said, ticking the numbers off on her fingers. "The commandant and his adjutant in Central Control. Ten extra men during the

150

day for guard duties – two details of five men like you see on patrol."

"Isn't the place guarded at night?"

"Oh, yes. Of course. By the regular sentries from the guard-room. But they are quartered on the base. They do not have to be transported in and about."

"How many of them are there?" Webster asked.

"Four on duty, four on call and four resting," Irmgaard said. "At any time. With two under-officers. They are from a special MP unit."

"Do they patrol the whole time?"

"It is not thought necessary. There are two on the gate and two with the machine-gun at all times. The four on call remain in the guard-room, making a . . . a tour? . . . yes, a tour of the perimeter every half-hour."

"So there are no sentries, no regular sentries at the back of the fortress?"

"No, except at the hour and half-hour, when they make this tour."

"Right. Now, these ten extra men who come in for the day patrols – how do they work?"

"Outside mainly. They are ordinary Wehrmacht; they police the country-side. They make one patrol of the northern half of Anholt before noon, checking papers and—"

"Yes, I saw that. They meet up with the southern patrol from the port."

"Exactly. And another patrol just before dusk – to remind islanders there is a curfew – before they return with the convoy which has bring the night shift."

"Well, that's clear enough," Webster said. "The layout of the place now, the plan – I guess you know it pretty well? Could you explain it to me?"

"Of course. I draw it for you. It is very simple. Look . . ." Irmgaard leaned forward, picked up a piece of driftwood and traced two broken circles in the coarse sand, one inside the other. The openings were 180 degrees apart, the outer one at the southern extremity, the inner at the northern. "The outer ring is stores, clerical offices, quarters, signals and the guard-room – just to the right of the entrance – all built continuously into the fortifications. The inner ring is administration: the headquarters block, the commandant's office and quarters for the clerical staff."

"How many of them are there?"

"About ten. They are all girls from the Helferinnen – uniformed communications auxiliaries. They are taken into town on Saturdays. Otherwise they do not leave the camp."

"Let me get this right. If you want to get inside the inner ring, starting from the main entrance in the south, you have to make a complete half-circle, between the two sets of fortifications, before you come to the second entrance?"

"Yes, that is correct." She dropped a pebble into the centre of the smaller circle. "And here is what you call the works – the operations bunker, with the gun turrets above and the magazine below."

"I suppose you wouldn't know anything about the specifications?" Webster asked hopefully.

The blonde Danish girl smiled. "Naturally I do. Above the bunker there are six 380 mm naval guns arranged in three turrets rotating on a common axis. Apart from surface-to-surface shells they also fire anti-submarine missiles, fused by the radar computer to explode at any depth. I do not know the details. There is a wide-beam Freya radar, and two five-metre Würzburg bowls modified in some way to work with the sonar and pick up undersea craft. That is the new secret." She had been speaking rapidly and tonelessly. Now she stopped.

"I can see why they sent us," Webster said. "You certainly got all that off pat!"

"It has been photographed from a German document and then made into English by a friend – and after this I have learned it by heart so that I can pass the information on . . . when there is people to pass it to."

He nodded. That made sense. A lingering doubt that the details might in some way have been a plant, designed to deceive, vanished from his mind. "How do the crews break down?" he asked.

"Break down? Oh, I see . . . Well, inside the bunker, the two Würzburgs and the Freya each have a plotter, with two officers in front of the radarscopes. There are three men and an NCO in each turret – sixteen men and two officers in all, like I tell you."

"And the other two officers?"

"In the headquarters block."

"So, apart from the twelve permanent guards, everyone on the night shift except those last two officers is on duty either in the bunker or one of the turrets? Every man, that is."

"I suppose so, yes."

"One final question," Webster said. "Where the hell are the antennae – the radar aerials – located? Inside the compound? I'm damned if I could see a sign of them from here."

"No. There is a small cliff on the far side of the compound and they are below that, the Würzburg bowls on the shore and the Freya on a hillock a small distance away. There is a Heinkel seaplane too, on the other shore. It can be directed to a target by radar and drop depth charges." She erased a segment of the outer circle with one neat, booted foot.

"There is one more thing I should tell you," she went on. "This outer ring does not completely surround the fort. Here, where I have rubbed out, the cliff serves instead."

"You mean the fortified wall stops, each side, at the edge of the bluff?" Webster asked with quickened interest.

"Yes. This bluff is only about twenty feet, but it is an overhang in sand, not possible to climb."

"And the gap, the place where there is no wall because of this, is almost opposite the entrance to the inner circle?" He gestured at the diagram in the sand.

Irmgaard nodded. "There are some small trees below the bluff," she said, "and – all the children here know this but the Germans do not – beneath the trees an animal have made a tunnel, which the young ones enlarged many years ago, before the war, for their games."

"An animal?"

"Quite big, yes. What do you call him? He is wide and flat behind, with stripes . . . so . . . over his head."

"A badger?"

"Perhaps. Anyway, this tunnel still comes up beneath some bushes inside the compound, near the bunker. It is quite hidden."

Webster was staring at her. "My dear old girl! Are you telling me," he demanded slowly, "that there is an old badger's earth leading into the base? That long ago the kids enlarged it?

That maybe a man, a small man, could get in and out of the place without being seen? Is that what you are saying?"

The blue eyes opened wide. "But of course."

"Irmgaard," Webster said fervently, and at that moment he almost meant it. "Irmgaard, I love you!"

Chapter Fifteen

By profession, Nils Bergg was a schoolmaster. But an inability to agree with the Nazi criteria of what was a suitable education for the children of the New Europe had led him to abandon the academic life and work as a farmhand for his friend Olafsson. At least under the high, wide skies of Jutland, with the flat land stretching away limitlessly on either side, he had the illusion of physical freedom. Besides, the tough open-air work kept him physically fit . . . and being employed in a sadly undermanned sector of the Danish economy reduced the risk of being drafted to Germany for forced labour in a munitions factory.

There were additional advantages. Farming is no nine-to-five job. Produce must be harvested and delivered; at certain times, work has to continue after dark or begin before dawn. Bergg therefore enjoyed a certain mobility, a lack of the requirement that he must be in a certain place at a specified time, which was a great help in his work as liaison between Olafsson's unit and other underground cells in the region. Even the Nazis were not going to insist that farmers must work by the clock rather than the weather.

He lay now beside a stack of peat in an area of marsh and lagoon north of Aalborg, scanning the long, straight road through field glasses for the German motor-cycle patrol that was due to pass. The wind, which had backed around towards the west, hissed through the reeds at the edge of the lagoon, occasionally pitting the dark surface of the water with a scatter of raindrops.

They had come more than two-thirds of the way from Aarhus to Frederikshavn; now they had less than thirty miles to go. So far, Bergg's personal blueprint for illegal travel under the eyes of the occupiers had worked well. The system was based on

155

the fact that, to the uninitiated, one wagon loaded with turnips or sugar-beet looks much like another . . . and the supposition that, to a non-fighting German soldier, one blond, bearded Dane of medium height also looks much like another. Provided that he has papers to match his face.

When Bergg wished to travel beyond the confines of the area in which he was permitted to move, therefore, the plan went into action. He would hitch up Olafsson's horse to a loaded wagon and drive it to some secluded place on the fringe of his own area. Then, leaving the wagon in a field producing the same crop as his load, he would walk a short distance to a bar or café and take a drink. In the café would be a bearded man of similar description who had left an identical wagon loaded with the same crop on the fringe of the adjacent area. The two men would then simply exchange ID papers. The second man would take Bergg's place and return the wagon to the Olafsson farm; Bergg himself would take over the other's load, together with his identity, and continue to the limit of the next sector, where the process would be repeated. In this way Bergg became Aaronsen, Aaronsen became Claus, Claus was transformed into Svensson and so on. And at any given time each link in the chain would have a valid reason for being where he was, with genuine papers to identify himself.

Each journey of course had to be well organised and minutely planned: the timing must be exact and the movement of wagons should coincide with farming practice in the region. The toughest part had been finding half a dozen reliable men sufficiently alike for their passport photos to be interchangeable. And even when this had been done there was the loyalty of their families to be considered, for sometimes the members of the chain were required to maintain their aliases, away from their homes and perhaps in other people's houses, for several days at a time. Fortunately this was not such a problem as it might have been in some of the other occupied countries: there were few collaborators in Denmark; betrayals were rare and the Danish police were celebrated for the blindness of their official eye.

Sometimes, if there were fugitives to be moved or arms to be transported, it was thought to be safer for the members of the chain to swap identities but retain the original wagon. In

156

this way a single load, handled discreetly, could accompany Bergg across half the country.

This was what was happening now. On the far side of the lagoon, beyond the stacks of turf that would warm the local population in winter, sugar-beet stretched away to the horizon. The wagon was standing on a muddy track beside a heap of newly dug beet. The horse was grazing some way off. Peters was leaning on a shovel, ready to begin the pretence of flinging the crop from the heap to the already loaded wagon the moment Bergg signalled that the patrol was on the way. And beneath the load, the clandestine merchandise – Charles G. Fortune and the Canadian Renard – were concealed.

Olafsson and his daughter were cycling to Frederikshavn openly: they had permission to go to the port to arrange for the importation of fertiliser from Sweden.

Bergg lowered the binoculars and tilted his head to one side. He was exhausted. He hadn't slept for three nights – and the last had been the worst. Organising the getaway from the island, disposing of the arms they had won in the raid on the exchange, contacting friends who would supply them with a fresh set of bicycles, forcing the others to ride hell-for-leather across the country so that they made the wagon before daybeak – all this, plus the loss of Bramming and Svenderup, had brought him almost to the end of his resources. Still, the operation had been a success, even if it had alerted every Nazi in Jutland to watch out for 'the dastardly murderers and saboteurs' who had so wantonly destroyed and slain! And of course there was still more to do. There always was.

He inclined his head more steeply. Yes, over the moan of wind he could hear a distant mechanical throbbing. It grew louder. Bergg thrust two fingers in his mouth and whistled shrilly. By the wagon, Peters jerked into activity, shovelling beet from the stack over the tailboard.

Far down the road, two motor-cycle combinations came into sight. By the time they bumped over the track and wheeled to a halt beside the wagon, Bergg was standing shouting at Peters as he worked. "Get a move on, man, for God's sake!" he stormed. "We'll never make the depot at Sulsted before dark unless you put your back into it!" He glanced once at the Germans and continued his harangue.

A *feldwebel* and two soldiers strode across to the wagon, leaving the fourth man behind the Spandau machine-gun in one of the sidecars. The NCO brusquely demanded papers, scrutinised them and then nodded to the two privates. Methodically, they begun thrusting their bayonets in among the loaded beet. Bergg didn't even look. He made the customary complaint about damage to the crop in a time of shortage – which was as usual ignored – and waited impatiently for them to finish. The sloping plank floor of the wagon had a false bottom just deep enough for two men lying flat on their faces to be hidden.

The German faith in routine was one of the things that helped Bergg more than anything else in his undercover work. The recognised way of checking that there were no stowaways in a load of hay or a wagon full of vegetables was to run bayonets through it from every angle. No angle would be left unpierced; thoroughness was all. If the bayonets drew no blood, the necessary concomitant was that nobody was concealed in the load. It saved time and effort, wasted if a wagon had to be unloaded and reloaded.

The same mentality was applied at the cooperative agricultural depot. If each individual wagon load of beet was checked when it came in – and if there were the correct numbers of carters and workers in the sheds at the end of the shift – then it followed there was no need to recheck when twenty wagon loads were taken from the depot to the docks in a single articulated eight-wheel truck. There couldn't be anybody concealed in that because nobody was missing and the cargo had already been searched. That was logical, wasn't it? Efficient, too, and practical, since it saved manpower and avoided unnecessary work.

The only thing wrong with the theory – Bergg thought thankfully not long before midnight that evening – was that it didn't actually work.

By that time he was staring down through a grimy glass window at the dockside twenty feet below (the last in his chain of bearded men was a crane driver at Frederikshavn). The rain had turned to a fine drizzle, and now the cold night air was condensing into a mist that clung to clothes and hair and eyebrows, dewing the metal walls of the crane cabin with moisture, blurring the figures of dockers and sentries beneath

158

the masked lights along the quay. The loading of the old Swedish tramp steamer was almost completed. She was due to clear the harbour boom at midnight; only the last truck load of beet remained to be transferred to her after hold. And somewhere in that load the two men who had escaped from the Mitchell were concealed . . .

Bergg was uneasy. He had wanted that particular artic to be unloaded first. But Olafsson had been against it: the stowaways might be smothered in a load from a subsequent lorry before their accomplices aboard could spirit them out of the hold. The Nazis were jumpy that night; there was a nationwide alert for the saboteurs who had wrecked the telephone exchange, and in addition there had been some scare story about a fishing boat in the Kattegat the night before. Apart from that, they had been late leaving the depot and the truck was in fact last in the line waiting to crawl through the dock gates. There was no chance of switching anything around or bending the regulations with the military in their present mood, Olafsson said. It had to be accepted: it was just one of those nights.

A longshoreman materialised out of the murk below, signalling up to the cabin. Bergg manipulated levers and twirled wheels. The chuffing of the donkey engine deepened; the crane and its cabin rolled crabwise along the railed gantry in front of the customs shed. When it was immediately above the tail of the truck, Bergg released the brake acting on the grab cable. The cabin quivered slightly as the steel hawser ran out over its pulley and lowered the toothed iron jaws of the grab until they were just over the piled sugar beet.

The longshoreman crossed his arms above his head and then flung them wide. Bergg hauled on the lever and halted the grab. He spun a wheel and the jaws inclined, opening wide, ready to bite into the load.

This was the crunch moment, waiting for the go-ahead from the Nazi *gauleiter* controlling the dock. A Wehrmacht officer in a peaked cap and an ankle-length greatcoat strode along the quay with two helmeted soldiers.

The officer was carrying a clipboard with papers attached. He walked around the truck, officiously demanding the driver's documents, checking bills of lading, verifying the licence plates. The longshoreman had folded his arms and was leaning

159

against a bollard; two dock labourers, standing on the roof of the truck's cab ready to help with the loading, lit cigarettes and waited patiently.

Bergg was sweating. He stared along the length of the dock. There was another Nazi section halted by the gangway that ran up to an open port in the tramp's rusty hull. Further along, he could see the other crane driver and his mate climbing down the steel ladder from their cabin; the ship's crew were already battening down the for'ard hatches in the well deck. The next berth was empty: a German freighter bound for Oslo had pulled out an hour earlier. Above the oily dark of the water in the basin, boxcars stood on rails shining in the misty light. The stink of diesel from the donkey engine had for the moment drowned the dockside smell of fish and tar and wet soot.

Peters leaned over Bergg's shoulder and peered through the fogged glass. "What in Christ's name is the bastard up to?" he demanded. "If he doesn't let them get on with it, they'll miss the bloody tide!"

Bergg shrugged. There was nothing he could do. Getting hot under the collar only wasted precious energy. He was glad to have Peters with him just the same – especially after the loss of Svenderup and Bramming. They would be difficult to replace. But Peters would have been harder still. A statistician by profession, he had turned – in association with Olafsson's daughter – into a remarkable forger . . . and he had a genius for appearing so oafish, such a simpleminded country yokel that half the time the Germans neglected to ask for his own papers at all. Peters had the ability to fade into the background at any time in any place – as a navvy, a plumber's mate, the halfwitted assistant of an electrician, anything. Yet if he was by chance asked for identification, his hand plunged unerringly into the right pocket – of many stitched to his carpenter's overalls – to produce some document suitable to the time, the place and the job he was supposed to be doing. Bergg dreaded to think what would happen if Peters were ever to be searched! Instead, he thought of the two foreigners lying beneath their coverlet of beet in the truck below. They were saboteurs like himself, but so different to look at and so different in character – Renard, the lanky Canadian with the sardonic twist to his mouth; Fortune, the oddly named Englishman whose toughness and

160

steely determination were in such contrast to his ridiculously youthful appearance. It was Fortune, with his funny schoolboy vocabulary, who had been so insistent on carrying on with their crazy mission until the man he had called in London had told him no, take the boat to Göteborg and leave it to the others. They must be sweating at the delay a damned sight more than he was, Bergg thought.

He switched his gaze back to the old steamer. The skipper was leaning over the wing of the bridge, calling down to the German officer and pointing to his watch. A thin plume of steam drifted from the ship's funnel.

At last the officer stepped back and waved his arm. The long-shoreman pushed himself upright and signalled. The labourers on the cab roof trod on their cigarettes, picked up their shovels and moved towards the grab. Bergg caught his lower lip between his teeth and reached for a lever. The iron jaws jerked, opening wider still. It was always a tricky manoeuvre, this. To avoid damaging the crop, dockers helped fill the grab with their shovels on the first bite. After that, once the surface of the cargo had been breached, the jaws could handle it on their own: the stuff would tumble down automatically to fill the grab each time the lower jaw wedged itself into the pile. Any contraband – human or otherwise – must therefore be transferred, with the dockers' help, in that first load. And although the high sides of the articulated truck shielded the surface of the crop from the eyes of anyone standing directly below, some diversion was usually arranged to distract the guards' attention at the crucial moment.

What complicated things tonight – Bergg shivered at the thought – was the fact that Olafsson had insisted that his daughter go with the fugitives. There were in truth three people concealed among the beet in that truck.

And although at a pinch the grab could accommodate two, three at a time was an impossibility. The supercargo would therefore have to be transferred in two separate operations . . . and it was not feasible to organise two diversions: that would be just a trifle too suspicious.

Bergg had been against the whole thing. It was too risky, he had argued: pulling off the same stunt twice on the trot would be tempting providence. It could compromise the foreigners'

161

escape; the girl herself could be caught; the whole network could be blown if anything went wrong. But Olafsson had been adamant. As an ex-public employee, Anya had her fingerprints on record. The Germans were making a lot of noise about the sabotage of their exchange. If they were to find prints on the wrecked automatic dialling equipment and run a check on the files at the public record office . . .

That should have been taken into account before, Bergg said. Then she could have worn gloves. He quite understood a man wishing to save his daughter from arrest and probable execution; he understood a father wanting to know that his child was safe in neutral Sweden. But not at the expense of others, not at the risk of imperilling the operation. Surely they were all in it together, sink or swim, the way they always had been? Would it be right to make an exception now – even for the best reasons?

The reasons overrode everything else, Olafsson said. If Anya was fingered as one of the telephone exchange raiders, he himself would be implicated and the whole cell would be forced to disband. If she was out of the way, he would leave the farm – just vanish underground – and they could carry on as they were.

Bergg thought this special pleading was dishonest, and said so. If that was his attitude, Olafsson should never have permitted his daughter to take part in the operation, in any operation, he said. There had been a bitter argument, but finally Olafsson had had his way: he was after all the boss. Now Bergg was conscientiously carrying out his part of the plan.

Below, lifting the top layer of beet swiftly but carefully, the dockers were beginning to load the grab. The German officer was staring up, one jackboot tapping impatiently. A segment of blue jersey appeared among the mud-coloured roots in the truck. Bergg caught his breath. One of the labourers paused in his shovelling and wiped his sleeve across his brow. It was the signal for the diversion.

It was produced dead on time. The operator of the other crane, mounting his bicycle to leave the dock, skidded on the greasy surface of the quay, somehow mishandled his brakes and cannoned into his mate. The two of them fell together, knocking into the soldiers at the foot of the gangway. There were angry shouts. The officer by the truck, perhaps suspecting an attempt to rush somebody aboard the ship, started towards the mêlée, followed by his men.

So far, so good. Operation proceeding according to plan.

In the moment that the officer's back was turned, the dockers hauled a slight figure out from the load of beet, scrambled it into the grab and hurled a couple more shovelfuls on top before the longshoreman waved to the cabin.

Breathing fast, Bergg wrestled with his levers. It was not easy to manoeuvre the crane with precision, and the man whose place he had taken had been able to give him only a few short lessons. The jaws of the grab almost closed. The coughing of the donkey engine became once again more laboured as the grab rose until it was suspended immediately below the tip of the crane arm. Bergg released a brake and the whole arm jerked gradually down from its near-vertical position in front of the cabin until it was projecting at an angle of 45 degrees – and the tip was directly over the open hold of the tramp.

Very carefully, Bergg paid out the hawser so that the grab was lowered from the crane tip, to sink from sight into the bowels of the ship. One of the deck hands raised an arm.

Bergg spun the wheel that opened the jaws.

Peters blew out his breath in a gasp of relief. "One," he said. "And two to go."

"They moved too fast", Bergg complained. "They should have packed in two the first time, while it was safe. Which one was it? Did you see?"

Peters shook his head. "One of the men, I think. I couldn't really see. They were all kitted out with fishermen's jerseys – and those boys had whoever it was in there like a flash of lightning."

"Well, let's pray that this time lightning does strike twice," Bergg said. He raised the grab and swung the crane back and up, manoeuvring the toothed iron bucket until the open jaws were once again poised over the truck.

The Nazi officer was stamping towards it with his men, having soundly abused the crane driver and his mate for their clumsiness. Bergg lowered the grab until the open jaws touched the beet.

The two dockers positioned themselves on top of the crop so

163

that their backs partially obscured the grab from the Germans' view. They began shovelling.

The officer shouted something and gestured towards the ship and then the crane cabin. Bergg couldn't make out the words over the chuffing of the donkey engine, but the man's meaning was clear: *Time is short: forget the shovels and get on with it. Operate the grab!*

It was then that Olafsson emerged from the truck's cab. Bergg hadn't known that he had taken the driver's place. Perhaps he had hoped to create some further diversion and help his daughter's escape; perhaps the suspense was finally too much for him and he simply lost his nerve. At any rate he jumped down from the running-board and started towards the officer.

The truck rocked slightly on its springs as he took off. One of the dockers lost his balance and fell. In the back of the truck, a portion of the cargo was dislodged and beet cascaded into the space left when the first load was removed.

A shout. One of the soldiers was pointing up between the slatted sides of the truck.

Even then, all might not have been lost if Olafsson hadn't panicked.

His fears for his daughter proved too much for his power of reasoning. Bergg saw his mouth opening, saw the big teeth gleam in the lamplight – was he shouting something? – then the man turned blindly and scrambled back into the cab. The big Bussing-NAG diesel burst into life with a roar. The truck shuddered . . . and surged forward.

As it careered away along the dockside, the heavy grab, already below the level of the truck's high sides, swung back and burst open the tailboard, spewing sugar-beet out over the rain-wet quay.

Horrorstruck, Bergg and Peters stared through the cabin window. The scene was to stay with them the rest of their lives: the empty, open grab, swinging and juddering on its hawser . . . shouting soldiers with raised guns . . . a trail of beet, bouncing and rolling across the cobbles . . . the greatcoated officer leaping aside and the Nazis by the gangway aiming at the windscreen as the truck thundered towards them.

In the back of the truck, two figures stumbling upright,

startled by their exposure – a big-hipped girl with a neat cap of dark hair, and a lanky Canadian wearing a fisherman's jersey.

Gunfire crashed out from the two groups of soldiers. The truck lurched, slewed sideways, then hurtled on to smash head-on into the line of boxcars standing in the siding by the empty berth.

More shouting. The clatter of booted feet. Sharp commands barked. A bleat from the steamer's siren, echoing in the mist.

Faces pressed to the glass, Bergg and Peters stared through the cabin window, desperately trying to make out what was happening at the far end of the dock. But the mist was swirling in from the sea now, thickening the lamplight, wreathing around the grey figures milling beside the wrecked truck. Men crowded around the telescoped cab. An officer waved his arms at a carrier bringing more soldiers from the guard-house at the dock gates. The dockers and the longshoreman had vanished.

The siren sounded its mournful cry again. The gangway was hauled aboard and sailors cast off ropes. A narrow gap appeared between the dockside and the damp, rusty plates of the tramp. The Swedish skipper was going to make that tide, and the hell with the remainder of the cargo!

In the distance, two figures were hustled away by the soldiers. Bergg shook his head as they were swallowed up in the murk. "Handcuffed," he said bitterly. "The girl and the Canadian. Too far away for me to see if they were hurt."

"He will be shot as a spy," Peters said. "He is in civilian clothes and he has no proper papers."

Bergg sighed heavily. "The girl too – or worse. As they were trying to escape it will be assumed that they are guilty of the telephone exchange affair. She will be tortured: the Nazis will want to find out about the rest of us."

"Do you think she will break?"

"What does it matter now?" Bergg said.

The gap between the ship and the dock widened. For the third time the siren boomed. In the misty light at the far end of the quay, the soldiers were levering something out from the mangled wreck of the cab. "They must have got

165

Olafsson with that first burst as he passed the gangway," Peters said.

Bergg was crying. "The fool," he shouted, pounding the steel wall of the cabin with his fist. "The stupid, blind, quixotic, bloody fool!"

Chapter Sixteen

Gnarled roots webbed the undercut face of the sandy bluff, though the leafless tops of the oaks reached no higher than the wall of the compound above. Where the wall ended, the occupiers had positioned a vertical *cheval-de-frise*, a half-circle of iron spikes garlanded with barbed wire, to discourage intruders. A similar barrier linked wall and bluff on the far side of the gap. Beyond this shallow step in the topography, the island stretched away to its low-lying point in the north-east.

On a small prominence a hundred yards away, the intricate metalwork of the Freya antenna turned ceaselessly on its axis like some futuristic windmill. The two big Würzburg bowls stood side by side on the further shore, owl's eyes staring towards Sweden and the seabed. All three of the scanners were on reinforced concrete plinths surrounded by double lines of electrified wire hung with warning notices in red. Webster took no notice of them. There would be no point wasting explosive on dispersed targets when a well-placed charge in the bunker could destroy their screens and render them useless.

The Heinkel seaplane was a different matter. Rocking on its sabot-like floats in the shelter of two curving artificial breakwaters, it represented a constant threat to their escape in the dinghy – and the second phase of the operation. They would have to put it out of action.

The voyage to Laeso was going to be difficult enough in that vulnerable craft without the additional hazards of air attack, Webster thought grimly, looking around him at the sea and the sky. The wind moaned through the Freya aerial and under the low, scudding clouds surf broke with a sullen roar all around the tip of the island.

It was just after four o'clock in the afternoon. He was

crouched with Irmgaard in thick undergrowth at the foot of the bluff. They had made their way separately to the chaos of boulders beyond the base where the sandy shelf overlaid a basalt dyke running out under the sea, and then re-met among the bushes. "They are used to seeing me go for walks," the girl had urged. "If I wander up, and then around the rocks to the point, they will think, 'Oh, there she is again' – and they will look no more. But all the time you can be moving just below me, on the shore, and remain unseen." Realising that she was talking sense, Webster had crawled, scuttled or wormed his way along the shoreline parallel to her route, according to the height of the grassy bank shielding him from view. Now he was going to take a look inside that compound.

He would never have found the old earth if she hadn't shown him exactly where it was. Even the bushes veiling the entrance to the tunnel were themselves hidden behind a thick oak bough which had split off partially, years ago, from its parent trunk and drooped to the ground. It was impossible for a human being to get into the hole until the bough had been pulled aside. Clever bloody badger! Webster thought.

Concealed in the undergrowth, the two of them had watched the guard patrol the gap at four o'clock. When they returned at four thirty, Irmgaard was to be plainly in view, apparently watching the breakers tumble among the rocks at the point. She was then slowly to return and make her way back to the port the way she had come – Webster once more invisibly accompanying her along the shore. During the intervening half-hour, he reckoned, he should be able to negotiate the tunnel twice – once in, once out – and take a look at the interior of the fort which lay beyond its inner end. He had to, otherwise he would never get clear of the area before the Wehrmacht patrol left the base for their second half-circuit of the island.

Leaving all his battle kit except the pistol hidden in the undergrowth, he gave the girl the thumbs-up sign and crawled into the old burrow beneath the bough she was holding aside. It was just wide enough for his broad shoulders.

The sandy tunnel slanted into the bank, twisted sharply and then began climbing.

Webster did not suffer from claustrophobia, but he couldn't

168

avoid a spine-chilling awareness of the hundreds, thousands of tons of earth and rock and sand between him and the open air above as he inched forward on elbows and knees, the pistol grip in one hand, the pencil flashlight in the other. Sometimes the earth widened enough to allow him to crawl quite fast; sometimes it narrowed so much that he had to jam his shoulders against the sand and thrust with his toes, listening to the ticking noise of falling grains over the thudding of his heart and the laboured gasps of his breath. If he provoked a roof-fall blocking his exit . . . or, worse still, onto his own back, leaving him to suffocate in the airless dark, his cries unheard as the cold weight remorselessly blotted out consciousness . . .

He thrust the macabre thoughts from his mind, concentrating on the job in hand as the passage twisted and turned, spiralling upwards on its path to the light and air. Smaller holes burrowed by underground creatures ran off to right and left. We're all in the fucking underground now, mates! Webster thought to himself wryly – and was astonished to find that he had spoken the words aloud.

Once or twice he heard a furtive scurrying around a bend in the tunnel ahead; every now and then, some nameless, glutinous shape shrank away from his hand or contracted into tiny cracks and fissures in the wall. The worst moment – his heart almost stopped – was when his efforts to force his way through a particularly tight section did dislodge a portion of the roof. It fell like the clammy hand of death across the backs of his knees.

But at last the dank, musty stillness surrounding him was sweetened with fresher air. A cool breath played on the hot, sweating skin of his face. He must be nearing the exit: he had to be especially cautious now.

The last few yards were steep and difficult. He could feel the moisture rolling off his back as he hoisted his body up the incline, made one final turn . . . and found himself squinting his eyes against the sudden dazzle of light in the opening ahead.

He was looking out from under a tangle of bushes in an overgrown corner of the compound. He could see concrete walls, the corner of a pillbox, a row of ablutions huts, windows silhouetting the bent heads of girl clerks on the far side of the space. The clacking of typewriters and teletype machines, along with an indeterminate murmur of German voices, came to his ears.

He knew at once. His seasoned campaigner's mind took in all the details, processed them, evaluated the results, came up with the answer.

Negative.

They could never make it. Not the way he had planned. The odds against them would be far to high.

Now that the fortress was around him, something in three dimensions, something he could actually touch, the cold wind of reality swept away the last remnants of wishful thinking.

He had only six men against a dozen specially trained MPs and twelve more soldiers, available at the first whisper of trouble, from the turrets above. With all this cover at the defenders' disposal, with all these angles and corners and flat roofs, and two concentric circles of open ground fifty yards wide separating the entrance from the target . . . No, they'd never, ever make it. Not in a hundred years. Six men in a Sherman tank perhaps, with a squadron of rocket-firing Typhoons flying ground support to soften the place up first! But six men on foot mounting a frontal assault? Don't make me laugh.

Even if they accounted for the entire guard in a surprise assault – which would itself be a miracle – those six men would have to cover half the circumference of the outer circle before they even reached the inner. Then there was another fifty yards of open ground separating them from the bunker. And they'd be sitting ducks for anyone in the turrets the whole damned way.

Webster heaved a sigh of resignation. He stared up at the massive pods of riveted armourplate, each with its two giant barrels canted skywards like the antennae of some evil Martian insect. Three hundred and eighty millimetres, the girl had said. That was fifteen inches. They looked more like sixteen-or eighteen-inchers to him. Impaled on their reinforced concrete podium, the batteries could have been something straight off the *Scharnhorst* or the *Tirpitz* – except that the battleship guns had a limited traverse and these bastards could each turn a full circle independent of the others. It wasn't the guns worrying him now, though: it was the crews manning them. The base of each two-gun turret was surrounded by a narrow, railed platform. Anybody on one of these – or on the steel ladders leading to them – could command all of the open ground between the two circles of fortified buildings. And between the inner circle and the countersunk entrance to the bunker that he could just see beneath the huge gun podium.

Half a dozen commandos trying to make it across those open spaces would be slightly more vulnerable than the celluloid ducks at a fairground shooting stall.

All right. So blasting their way in via the entrance was a non-runner. The way in was out. Use the tunnel, then, the way he had? Webster thought not. One man could be concealed by the bushes he was peering through, maybe two. But not six. By the time the last man was extricated from the burrow, the others would have been spotted and shot down one by one.

What the hell was left then?

As the question formed in his mind, a parade-gound NCO's voice shouted an order. There was a rattle of shouldered arms and a heavy tramp of feet. Webster flicked his gaze down to his watch. Christ – it was four thirty already! The next perimeter patrol was on its way . . .

Shuffle back feet first – or risk a disturbance in the bushes being spotted and emerge, turn around and go back head-downwards so that he could see his way?

The hell with the risk. Positive action pays off! Wasn't that what war was all about anyway? Dragging himself from the hole, he twisted around and plunged in again the other way in a single snakelike movement as the marching feet approached.

To save himself from wasting mental energy on the frustrating and negative results of what he had hoped would be an invaluable reconnaissance, he thought of other things on the uncomfortable journey back to the foot of the bluff. It was a hell of a thing, he reflected – he must be the only man in wartime history to have tunnelled *in* to an enemy camp! It was a far cry from all those Hollywood escape sagas where the exhausted escapee at last bursts through to freedom . . . only to find himself staring at a pair of shiny jackboots. Camera pans slowly up to Gestapo man's face. Sadistic smile. *"Ach, so. Ve haf been vaiting for you, Herr Vebster!"*

It was then that the idea came to him.

171

A lunatic idea, of course – a hare-brained, daredevil, impossible, million-to-one chance of an idea that could never work. He liked it.

He was going to do it, too. It was an idea typical of Webster – as was the conviction that he was damned well going to make it work. Provided certain questions were answered to his satisfaction. And the person who could provide the answers was waiting for him down below.

He found her among the rocks where the dyke ran under the sea, out of sight of the base below the bluff. The wind was tolling her hair like a golden bell. "You made it?" she said with shining eyes. "Did you find what you—?"

"Later," he interrupted. He was still panting. "Irmgaard – tell me; you know the routine. What would happen if they caught us up there, coming out of the burrow, before we had time to sabotage anything? What would they do?"

She frowned. "If they caught you? They did catch someone once, a member of the Danish underground, a partisan. He had rowed all the way across from—"

"What did they *do?* Did they shoot him on the spot?"

"Oh, no." She was still puzzled. Her nose wrinkled when she smiled. "They called my colonel – he was still in command at that time – and he radioed his superiors on the mainland. They do not have the right, or the personnel, to deal with such matters here. The Gestapo wanted to interrogate the prisoner, to torture him, so that they could discover the names of his contacts. You know what they are like."

"What happened then?"

"There is a German naval craft, an MTB, based on Grenaa. It is a small port, the nearest to us on the mainland. They send the MTB with a squad of sailors to pick up the prisoner and take him back there."

"That's just what I thought!" Webster exclaimed exultantly. "Now tell me how far away is Grenaa? How long did the boat take to get here?"

"Ssssshhhh! They will hear you. It is more than seventy kilometres – nearly thirty-five miles. I suppose two hours. Perhaps less. They are very fast ships."

"The faster the better! Two more questions: one, where is

172

the man who took the place of your . . . friend? Where is he now, at this moment?"

"The pig? He will be in his quarters at the port. He comes here on duty at eight." The blonde girl shivered. "I have been summoned to see him at six thirty. For an apéritif, he says."

"Good. I'm sorry – I'll explain later – but that is good. Second question: you said you had friends on the island who know about me and my companions. Would they help us? Perhaps create some kind of diversion somewhere?"

"But of course," Irmgaard said. "Anything at all. Just tell me."

Webster told her.

Afterwards, jumping down from a weed-covered rock – they were hurrying towards the bivouac before the evening perimeter patrol set out – Webster slipped on the slimy surface and fell, cutting his face slightly against the barnacle-covered side of the dyke. As he struggled to his feet, smothering a curse, her hand flew up to touch the injured place. A small trickle of blood ran down his left cheek. "Oh," she whispered. "Your poor face . . ."

The contact of her fingertips with his flesh released some trigger inside Webster. That side of him which had engraved the rakish lines of experience and dissipation around his mouth and eyes submerged the professional warrior on the hunt.

"There's something else I'm going to tell you!" he cried hoarsely.

His arms were inside the fur coat, crushing her to him, feeling the long, soft warmth of her body melt against the hardness of his own. He kissed her on the lips, their mouths smashing together, clinging, opening as the hot wet tongues probed. She was breathing fast, her body trembling. Her hands cradled the back of his head, under the cold rim of his helmet.

Behind them, the layered sand of the bluff had been scooped out by wind and water where it rested on the dyke, making a shallow cave. He drew her savagely down into its shelter. "*No!*" she gasped. "Not now! The patrol—"

"Fuck the patrol!"

Irmgaard was panting. He could still taste the sea salt from

173

her skin on his lips. Suddenly the blue eyes glinted in the half-light of the hollow. "I have a better idea," she said.

For the second time, it was like a length of iron clicking into place over the two ends of a magnet. Their bodies homed on each other, his weight pinning her to the sandy floor. His fingers clawed into the flesh between her shoulderblades and the strap of her brassière. Her hands were trapped between them, clenching on his loins. They kissed again.

Webster leaned his weight on his elbows, tearing open the buttons of the flowered shirt she wore tucked into the waistband of her skirt. There was a clasp linking the taut satin cups of her brassière. He tore that open too, and then his hands were on the warm, softly shifting swell of her breasts, the nipples hard against his palms. His breath hissed in between his teeth as she unzipped his fly and he felt the cool grasp of her fingers wrap around him.

Webster eyed the tenderness of her breasts among flowers, thrust up against his own calloused fingers. Irmgaard altered her position and he slid down between silk-sheathed thighs. Small cries escaped from her throat; there was heat and there was moisture and the graze of hair . . . and then all at once the skirt was up around her waist and as she guided him he was easily, scaldingly, wonderfully inside her.

Forceful and compulsive, his need drove him on with a savage tenderness, softly battering her against the hard sand while her strong young hips arched up to meet his thrusts.

For a timeless moment there was nothing but the hot clasp of flesh and the thundering of the blood. Then the waves burst among the rocks in showers of spray and all his life he would remember the curve of her throat, the pulse hammering wildly under his lips as she clutched him to her fiercely in the throes of her release.

Later she opened her eyes and there was a wetness glistening on her cheeks. "It may be the only time," she said despairingly.

"Absolutely not," said Webster. "I mean no way: it can't be. It mustn't be."

Neither of them saw the short man with the outraged expression who scurried away among the rocks between the bluff and the spume blown back from the waves by the rising wind.

Astonishingly, they still had time to get back to the bivouac before the patrol marched out from the base. Irmgaard stood above him on the bank of the creek as he crouched below – a slender and solitary figure pretending to look out over the white horses rolling in from the west, already parted from him by more than the few feet of space separating their bodies. "Are you sure you've got it all lined up?" Webster said. "There's a hell of a lot to remember, I'm afraid, and timing's everything on this show. Are you certain you can go through with it?"

"More certain than I have ever been in my life."

"You can rely on your friends to play their part – to make a diversion as soon as the ship arrives, and then to cut the lines . . . but not before the squad has set out for the base?"

"Completely. You must not worry. It will be all right."

"Attagirl!" Webster crowed. "Here . . ." He fished a crumpled Gold Flake packet from the breast pocket of his tunic and tossed it, together with a few sticks of American chewing-gum, up onto the grass at her feet. "Tell them to scatter the wrappers of these around and leave the cigarette pack near the break in the wire. If they do that, the Jerries will blame us for that as well. I don't want any reprisals among your friends here."

"That is very thoughtful of you." Stooping to pick them up, Irmgaard stared into his eyes and whispered: "I must go now. The pig will be expecting me. And I do not even know your name!"

"My friends call me Ian, my associates That Bloody Man Webster. Do you think you can handle your end of it? That's the most important part of all."

"It will be – how do you say? – it will be a pleasure."

"And you'll get the paper and the specimen signature to us, through your friends, and drive straight out to the base as soon as you have . . . as soon as it's over?"

"I will remember . . . Ian."

Webster gazed up at her tranquil face beneath the hurrying clouds. There was moisture in the air and the roar of the sea was louder than ever. "Whatever happens," he said, "meeting you will have been the best part of it."

She smiled. An inscrutable female smile. "In any case," she said lightly, "according to your plan we shall be meeting later tonight, no?"

175

He shrugged, sighed, partly in surprise, partly with regret at the contrariness of life. "Damned if I know," he said. "I certainly hope so, old thing. But it's the craziest plan I ever heard of. It's so bloody silly, it might even work!"

"It's no' the fairst time I've said it, and it'll no' be the last," McTavish announced. "Yon feller's naethin' but a playboy, one of them upper-class fools that fancies themsel' a sight too bloody much – and acts with nary a thought for anyone else. I say we shouldnae stand for it."

"What do you mean – not stand for it?" Hunter asked.

"It's our lives at stake, isn't it? I don't mind riskin' mine for a real man, a proper officer knows the way things shud be done. But I'll be damned if I'll fuckin' sacrifice mesel' for thon jumped-up pansy!"

"Are you sayin' we did'n ought to obey orders, then?" Hewitt demanded in astonishment.

"Aye. I am that. This is not like normal regimental sairvice, after all. In this kind o' job we shud be able to choose a leader oursel' – a man we can trust," the Scot said viciously.

From the back of the cave, where he was lying, Joe Constantine spoke weakly. "Do you realise what you are saying, Sergeant?"

"I do, sirr." McTavish spat contemptuously. "An' I say the man's not fit to lead us an' put our lives at risk with his awfu' Hollywood ideas!"

"Well, I dunno . . ." Hewitt began doubtfully.

"He's all right," Zygmund said. "I worked with him before."

"All the same . . ."

Hunter said: "What do you mean, Mac – not fit?"

"Fornicatin'!" McTavish shouted. "Lyin'. Puttin' the rest of us at risk while he dips his bloody wick! You think that's the way—"

"Now just a minute . . ." Constantine interrupted angrily.

"I tell you I saw 'em!" McTavish cried. "In a wee cave. Away up along the shore there."

"You saw what?"

"Poking! With that blonde Danish hoor. He was shaftin' her like a bull with a bluidy coo! It was worse than some back street in the Gorbals or a couple up agin' a wall in an alley

176

behind Green's Playhouse of a Saturday night." McTavish's voice quivered with outrage. "Tellin' us lies! Sayin' he was out there on recce when all the time he was set to stuff some skairt while we shiver here in this perishin' cave!"

Sergeant Hawkins had taken no part in the conversation. He had been squatting down at the entrance to the bivouac, gazing out over the whitecaps at the darkening sky. Now he rose slowly to his feet, turned massively around, reached out a hand and grasped the front of McTavish's battle tunic. Lifting the little man by the bunched-up fabric, he slammed him against the rock wall of the cave. "Just shut your filthy fuckin' mouth, you dirty little Scotch runt," he said quietly. "He's a brave man and a fine bleedin' officer. If I hear one more word out of you, one more soddin' word, you foul-mouthed cunt, so help me I'll smash your face in!"

The entrance to the cave darkened. Webster ducked down and came in. "Everything under control, Sergeant?"

"Everything under control, sir," Hawkins replied woodenly.

Webster repressed a smile. He couldn't resist it. "McTavish," he said sharply, "there's a gleam of brightwork on one of your webbing buckles. Surely a man of your experience should know that all metal must be dulled on a show of this kind? Get out on the beach at once and find some mud to rub on it."

Part Four

The Constant Tin Soldier

Then spoke the Tin Soldier, who stood on a chest of drawers: "It is so sad and lonely here; the day is so long and wearisome and the nights are longer still . . . but it is charming to find that one is not entirely forgotten!"

Chapter Seventeen

"I don't want any shooting," Webster said. "At least, you can fire in the air if you like, to make it look convincing. But don't hit anyone. I don't want Jerry to get cross with you. If you come out of the burrow dead on 1830 hours, the patrol should pick you up right away. You can surrender as soon as you like . . . just so long as the show you put up convinces them."

Constantine and Hunter still looked dubious. In full combat gear, complete with pistols, grenades and four of the water-proofed explosive packs, they stood in the lee of the bluff near the cave where Webster and Irmgaard . . . Resolutely, the commando leader concentrated his mind on the mission. "Something worrying you, Joe?" he asked the Canadian.

"No, not exactly. But it's just that . . . I mean what the hell are we supposed to do when Phase Two starts? If they've locked us in the brig, as they will have—"

"Bugger-all," Webster cut in. "You just sit tight in there until we let you out, that's all. There'll be plenty to do then, I promise you! Plenty. But I'll be there to brief you." He hesitated, looking narrowly at Constantine. The man's temperature was down but he was still occasionally seized by fits of shivering and his lean face was pale and drawn. "I'll go over it once more," Webster said.

"As I've explained, there aren't enough of us to take the place by frontal assault. Even if we blasted our way past the entrance, we'd never get near enough to the bunker to spike the radar and guns. All right? So we have to take it somehow from the inside. With me so far?"

"Yes, sir," Hunter said. "But I don't get the reason for splitting up. United we stand, divided we fall, and all that. Why can't we *all* use this burrow you found, and take it from there?"

181

"Because," Webster explained patiently, "it's too narrow to get the whole bunch of us out in reasonable time, that's why. As it is, you'll have to shove all your stuff ahead of you along the tunnel. And there's cover for two chaps in the bushes, no more. After the first two, they'd lift us out one by one like trout from a bloody tank. We're chucking you two in the deep end, *knowing* you'll be taken, because it'll give us an in. And believe me, you're the lucky ones: you'll be able to rest for a couple of hours in a nice dry cell! That's why I chose you – you, Joe, because you're still a bit under the weather; Hunter because he's the only one that hasn't had any sleep today."

"So we go in and allow ourselves to be taken . . . ?" Hunter began.

"Right. I'm betting on the fact that Jerry, laying his greedy hands on two blokes loaded with explosives *inside the perimeter*, will jump to the conclusion that he's netted the whole works. A two-man sabotage team caught red-handed. Iron Crosses all round! He'll think the way you thought, Hunter: if there were more than than two, why the hell would they have split up?"

Webster paused. He drew a small, leather-covered flask of whisky from his hip pocket and handed it to each man in turn. "They'll ask questions, of course," he said. "But you'll answer them. Tell them there were originally three of you, but the third got written off when a fishing boat you'd pinched got blown out of the water by their guns. That'll account for Reilly's body, if it's been found. You had a rubber dinghy in tow and the two of you completed the trip in that. You can even let the buggers *see* the dinghy and the bivouac if you think it'll make the story more believable. The rest of us will have cleared out long before then, and we'll leave the boat and enough supplies scattered around for the story to hold water."

"But those Swedish sailors," Hunter objected, "won't they be screaming? Won't it be in all the papers . . . I mean like how *seven* men hijacked them? Won't the Krauts read those papers? I mean the only dinghy they saw was the one they themselves paddled away in."

"You shouldn't end a sentence with a preposition, lad," Webster said severely. "Of course it'll be in the papers, and of course Jerry will read them. But not until tomorrow. With what they know about the fishing boat, and what you can tell them about the cave, they'll believe the story all right. Especially when they've sent a squad to the creek to check. After that, it's a matter of routine." Webster took back the flask and stowed it in his pocket.

He said: "They caught saboteurs once before. The Danish lady told me. And the drill is they radio their superiors on the mainland. The superiors want to ask more questions . . . and find out who sent you, and why and so on and so forth. So they whistle across an MTB with a squad of Boche bluejackets to bring the prisoners back to the mainland. And the Gestapo."

"Thank you very much!" said Constantine.

Webster ignored the interruption. "We now have the situation where the guards on the base are *expecting* a squad of Kraut navy men to show up," he said. "So when a squad does appear, complete with passes signed by the commandant – who's due to remain in the port until eight – they're going to let them in, aren't hey? The only thing is, it may not be exactly the kind of squad Jerry expects."

Constantine nodded slowly. "Like you said, it's the craziest idea I ever heard of." He looked up and grinned. "But I kinda like it. The only thing is: what happens if the guys on the base call up the goddam commandant?"

"They will," Webster said. "Naturally. He'll be the one who'll order them to radio the mainland."

"But won't he scoot out to the base himself, the moment he knows what's cooking? I mean, Jesus, captured prisoners . . . You know."

"Of course he will. At least, he would normally." It was Webster's turn to grin. "But tonight, somehow, I don't think he will. That'll all be taken care of. Don't worry." He glanced at his watch in the thickening twilight. "Come on now: it's after six. Time I showed you two fellows your private route into the Giant's Castle!"

Treading warily in the half light, he led the two commandos towards the undergrowth and the fallen tree concealing the old badger's earth.

Heinz Ulrich Bosendorff, Colonel, chosen after special training from the 176th Flakregiment to command the secret base on

Anholt, leaned forward to look into the mirror and clipped a wayward hair from his moustache with a long, thin pair of scissors. The room reflected in the glass was austere but comfortable. The cottage furniture was polished, the gate-leg table set with the remains of a meal and two empty bottles of Rhine wine. Beyond the bed, the curve of Irmgaard Kraul's back threw a graceful shadow on the whitewashed wall.

"You must be aware, Fräulein Kraul," the Commandant said, "that since you were unable to follow my . . . predecessor . . . to his new command, you are technically in breach of regulations, remaining on this island. You should of course be back on Odense, where your papers and your movement permit were issued."

Irmgaard sighed, glancing at the reflection of her slender body as she tried to avoid thinking of the Englishman whose hands had so recently been caressing it. She knew exactly where the conversation was going to lead, precisely why she had been invited – summoned, perhaps, was a better word – to Bosendorff's quarters. But she said simply: "Yes, Colonel, I am of course aware of that." And then, swallowing before she could get the words out: "And I am naturally . . . grateful to you personally for . . . the permission . . . to remain here on Anholt."

"There is no question of a permit," the German said. "So far. Let us just say that certain formalities have been deferred, certain restrictions relaxed. These privileges could of course be rescinded at any time. If I in turn were to be transferred, for example. Or for . . . a number of reasons not unconnected with your behaviour."

The colonel had finished trimming his moustache. After a final glance at the reflection of his heavy features, he turned away from the mirror and tossed the scissors carelessly on to the bedside table. He cleared his throat. "Were there to be . . . personal reasons . . . for your presence here," he resumed, "the situation might be seen in an entirely different light. Indeed, I have it in my power as commanding officer to modify the status of any Danish national whose behaviour in favour of the occupiers merits this."

Irmgaard contrived a smile. The menace in the man's remarks was glaringly evident, even if it wasn't as brutally expressed as she might have expected. Sleep with me or else. She repressed a shudder. She must at least pretend to play along – or allow him to think she was interested – if she was to help the Englishman the way he wanted. Through the room's wide window she stared eastwards toward a bank of angry clouds. The sails of three fishing boats returning to the harbour glowed amber in the light of the setting sun. "I am flattered, Colonel, as well as grateful for your interest," she said. And then, seeking a way of prolonging the interview without becoming too involved: "You did say, I think, that we might have matters to discuss . . . over an apéritif?" She glanced at the empty wine bottles on the table

"What? . . . Oh, yes of course, my dear. A glass of good Rhine wine?"

"That would be very nice," she said demurely. Anything to delay the physical approach she was sure would come.

Bosendorff walked through an open doorway into an ante-room. He was wearing uniform trousers, highly polished boots and a loose jersey. Seconds later he reappeared holding a long-necked brown wine bottle and a flask of schnapps. He splashed wine into a tumbler – already used, she noticed – and handed her the glass. Raising the flask in perfunctory salute, he gulped a mouthful of the liquor from the neck. "To our future association," he said thickly, swallowing again. "You are a very attractive young woman, Fräulein Kraul – strong in the body, blonde, with good, firm breasts. You could almost be German," he conceded.

Irmgaard inclined her head, sipping the delicately perfumed white wine – excellent but a little too sweet for her taste. There was no need, for the moment, to find more words.

"I am obliged to visit the base later," Bosendorff said. "You will excuse me if adopt a more formal attire." The remark was a statement – an order, even – rather than a polite question.

Once again, the Danish girl nodded without saying anything. She sipped again.

He vanished into the ante-room, reappeared with a high-collared, bemedalled officer's tunic on a hanger and draped the garment over the back of a chair. He took a third swig from the flask, set it on the table and pulled the jersey over his head.

He was wearing no under-vest. Again Irmgaard was forced to hide a tremor of repulsion as she looked at his meaty figure. His sandy hair was close-cropped and his pale, freckled skin was covered with a reddish-gold down through which womanish breasts obscenely protruded. She raised her glass, this time to gulp down a much larger mouthful of wine. Bosendorff interpreted the movement as a toast. He picked up the flask and drank again, then poured wine into the girl's glass until it spilled over. "There is no reason, however, why we should not indulge ourselves," he said, "in a foretaste – what the damned Yankees call a trailer – of what could turn out to be a satisfactory relationship." Bending down, he reached towards the armchair in which she was sitting, closed huge hands around her upper arms and dragged her to her feet.

His grip was immensely strong, the spatulate fingers digging in, bruising her tender flesh. It was clear that this was a man for whom violence was a natural means of expression, a man to whom the concept of consent was totally foreign. For the first time she experienced genuine fear as well as disgust.

There had been violence too in the way she had coupled with the stranger she had met on the shore. But that had been the violence of two human beings, two equals drawn irresistibly together by the compulsion of their mutual attraction and their need. There had been tenderness and care underlying the savagery of their lovemaking. What a woman would suffer with Bosendorff, she knew instinctively, would not so much be lovemaking as the rutting of beasts. He would take her as a man might take a tankard of ale on a sweltering summer day.

Forcing her back until she was brought up against the bedstead, he thrust her abruptly down, half sitting, half lying on the mattress.

A telephone on the bedside table was ringing.

"God in Heaven," the German choked, "am I never to be left in peace?" Withdrawing his grasp on her arms, he plunged to the edge of the bed himself and scooped the receiver from its cradle. "Yes? . . . Yes? . . . What is it, then? . . . *What? Good God Almighty!*"

Slowly, he shifted into a sitting position and listened to the voice quacking in the earpiece. "In the compound, you say? Under those bushes? Somebody will pay for that negligence!

186

. . . Nothing less than gross incompetence . . . Yes, yes: you did right. And they did not offer much resistance? What did you find out? . . . No! It's unbelievable! . . . Now listen – send a signal to Früchtnicht at Grenaa immediately. At once. He will order the boat over with a detail to take charge of them. In the meantime, the strictest precautions . . . You are sure there are no more? Good. Keep them under lock and key . . . No, no: I will attend to that here. Yes, as soon as possible.

"That was Lanzmann," he said as he replaced the receiver. "It seems they captured two saboteurs inside the perimeter. Britishers, in uniform! Can you believe that? Apparently they are the remaining members of the crew of that fishing boat we sank last night. It wasn't Swedish at all." He shook his head, picked up the phone again, and dialled a number.

"Major Frodenburg? Bosendorff. Listen – Lanzmann has captured two spies on the base . . . Yes, yes. It's all under control . . . He will call Grenaa on the radio at once. But they have revealed they have a hideout. You are to take a patrol at once and investigate. It is on the north coast, by the creek where the patrols rendezvous. I shall have something to say to those NCOs tomorrow! . . . Take lights with you and shine them inshore from the high-water mark. It is well concealed, apparently . . . A rubber dinghy and other supplies . . . A full report, I insist, with photographs, at once . . . Heil Hitler!"

He turned around to find the girl reclining at full length now. "I must leave immediately," he announced.

Irmgaard shifted her position slightly, so that the woollen skirt she was wearing rode up towards her hips, revealing the white flesh of one thigh above the dark top of a tightly pulled-up silk stocking. She had already undone the top button of the flowered blouse. It was essential, she knew, to keep the base commander in his quarters longer than this if she was to keep her promise to the Englishman. In any case he must on no account leave the port.

Very slightly, she undulated her hips, arching the centre of her body up off the bed. "I thought, Herr Colonel, that we had a little . . . unfinished business . . . to discuss," she said huskily.

As he opened his mouth to deny her, she fingered open the

187

second button of the blouse – enough to show that she wore no brassière, nothing beneath the lightweight garment.

He hesitated. Then, with an inarticulate cry, he launched himself at her, spread-eagling her across the covers with the weight of his body as he ripped open the fly of his trousers.

Savagely, he kneed apart her thighs, clawing with rude hands at the flimsy garment sheathing her loins. With his other hand, he ripped open the flowered blouse and lowered his lips towards the tender swell of naked breasts exposed. She could feel his hardness against the base of her belly. She bit her lip to stifle an anguished sob.

Bosendorff had frozen, his thick lips working beneath the bristly moustache. He was staring at a red patch on her bared throat which bore the unmistakable marks of Webster's teeth.

"Why, you slut!" he shouted. "You dirty little Danish whore: you've been opening your legs to those fishermen! You, the mistress of one German officer and the intended of another! By God, I'll teach you to dishonour our uniform by giving yourself to racial inferiors . . ."

He began slapping her viciously across the face, the stinging blows leaving angry weals on the pallor of her cheeks as he punctuated each delivery with screams of abuse.

Half blinded by tears of pain and humiliation, her face showered with spittle from the man's foaming mouth, Irmgaard groped wildly for the bedside table. Her fingers touched the scissors. Clenching her hand around them, she raised her arm and plunged the needle-sharp blades with all her strength between his nude shoulders.

Bosendorff's whole body stiffened. His eyes opened wide and a choking cry bubbled from his throat. Then, as the seed sprang for the last time in his loins, his mouth opened to vomit blood which splashed hotly over the girl's breasts and he fell inertly forward.

With a moan of horror, she dragged herself out from under his dead weight and ran, fighting down her own nausea, to the shower she knew was on the far side of the ante-room.

Ten minutes later, fully dressed again, she rolled a sheet of official paper into the typewriter on his desk and tapped out

188

three lines. She went quickly through his briefcase until she found an ID document with his signature on it. Then, averting her gaze from the bed, she hurried from the room and locked the door behind her with shaking fingers.

Chapter Eighteen

Otto Bjerke crouched down behind a stack of crab pots, the two pieces of paper that Irmgaard Kraul had given him safely buttoned into the breast pocket of his windcheater. It was eight fifteen – three-quarters of an hour since the girl had driven out to the base in Colonel Bosendorff's Mercedes-Benz staff car, forty minutes since Major Frodenburg had led a squad of men out towards the northern coast in one of the half-tracks.

Bjerke shivered. The wind, raw against his face and smelling of fish, was bitingly cold. But there were other reasons to make his muscles tremble tonight. He was risking his life just being on forbidden ground after curfew; also it would be the first time he had killed a man. He was just nineteen years old.

The boat couldn't arrive before nine at the earliest, especially with the big seas running now, and the Englishman Irmgaard had sent had warned him not to act until the last possible moment. It lessened the margin of risk, the lean, lined soldier with the Errol Flynn moustache and the flinty eyes had said. Bjerke grinned mirthlessly in the dark. Risk was a relative term: to the foreign guerrilla, trained in the arts of combat and sabotage, it was just one factor to be considered in the fulfilment of his mission. To a young, unarmed Danish fisherman under the Nazi occupation, it was a dry-mouthed fear that submerged everything else in his mind.

For the tenth time since Bjerke had taken up his position, the sentry below paced past him towards the end of the jetty. Every twenty minutes, he made rendezvous with the guard patrolling the far side of the port. Bjerke would have to do it the next time the German came by, in order to give himself time to settle with the second man and signal his friends before the boat arrived. After that he would have to change clothes and double up to make appearances on both sides of the harbour in case anyone should be watching. The Germans were quartered on the far side of the town, but there were busybodies everywhere.

His heart thudding in his chest, the boy watched the guard march back and meet his opposite number by the lifeboat-house. They conversed for a few minutes in low tones, stamping their feet and slapping their shoulders through the long greatcoats to minimise the cold. Then, shouldering their rifles, they marched out on their beats again. Neither of them was to know – thought Bjerke, the hairs prickling the nape of his neck – that he was striding out the last few paces on the road to oblivion.

It was very dark and not a glimmer of light showed from the shuttered houses clustered above the quays. For some reason the young Dane recalled Christmases before the war, when the water in the harbour was bright with reflections and you could see gay streamers and tinsel through all the windows. He wondered how long it would be before he could expect to see lights reflected in the water again.

Outside the sea wall, waves roared on the rocks as the swell surged between the piers to jostle the fishing boats moored along the quay. The sentry passed him again.

Now.

Rising to his feet, Bjerke sped silently after the German, the heavy woollen socks he wore over his boots muffling his footsteps on the damp cobbles. At the end of the jetty, the sentry passed momentarily out of sight behind a fish-loft before he faced about to make the return journey. He would do it there.

As soon as the dim blur of the man had merged with the bulk of the building, Bjerke swarmed up the ladder leading to the flat roof supporting the blacked-out harbour light. The steel wire fishing line was noosed and ready in his hand – large enough to slip easily over the coal-scuttle helmet, not so wide that it would give him time to cry out before it tightened. Catlike, the boy stole to the edge of the roof and looked down. He was in luck: the sentry had leaned his gun against the wall to light an illicit cigarette.

Bjerke held the wire noose between his two hands, poised it over the head of the unsuspecting man below and then cast it accurately over the dull gleam of the helmet. In the same swift movement, he reached out, took a turn of the line around his gloved wrist and pulled upward with all his strength.

There was a dreadful smothered gargling sound from underneath as the thin wire bit into the sentry's throat. Boots slithered frantically on the greasy quayside. Bjerke hauled with every ounce of power that he could command, the muscles cording on his forearms and his brow dewed with sweat despite the cold. When the spasmodic jerking of the line turned to a slack weight, he paid it out slowly until the body subsided to the cobbles, then jumped down beside it.

Unbuttoning the dead man's greatcoat with trembling fingers, he stifled a cry of horror as something warm and sticky flowed over the back of his ungloved hand: the wire had almost severed the German's head from his shoulders.

Bjerke shrugged into the voluminous garment, settled the helmet on his own head and stripped the socks from his boots. A moment later, he shouldered the rifle, stamped out the glowing end of the fallen cigarette and began tramping back towards the hard.

It was only as he approached the lifeboat-house that the enormity of what he had done hit him. He had committed murder! He was responsible, moreover, for a crime which could bring death as a retribution to dozens of his own fellow townsmen. The sweatband of the dead man's helmet was warm and yet clammy on his forehead. Bjerke's breath rasped in his throat and his calf muscles twitched uncontrollably.

The dark shape of the other guard was materialising against the night. He murmured something in German. Bjerke grunted noncommittally . . . and then, as the other repeated what was evidently a question in an irritated voice, he unslung the rifle and jammed the barrel with all his strength into the pit of the man's stomach.

Taken completely by surprise, the German folded forward from the waist, the breath exploding from his lungs in an agonised gasp. Bjerke reversed his grip on the weapon, swung it over his shoulder and brought the butt crashing against the winded sentry's neck with manic force. The man uttered a strangled cry and swayed on his feet. Bjerke leaped forward to catch his rifle before it clattered to the ground. He lowered the writhing, moaning German to the wet cobbles and then smashed the butt of his own weapon again and again, with a kind of hysterical fury, into the space below the brim of the man's helmet. It was only when the sound of splintering bone had altered to an obscene pulpy noise that he realised he had killed his second human being in less than ten minutes.

Sobbing with the reaction, he bundled the inert body between a winch and the wall of the lifeboat-house, wiped the brass butt of the gun he carried on the sentry's greatcoat and stamped out noisily along the man's beat. Twice more he marched the length of each jetty, running swiftly and as silently as he could along the dark hard between them each time in the hope that no chance onlooker would notice that a single soldier was now doing the work of two. He looked at the luminous dial of his watch. In five minutes it would be nine o'clock. He put his hands to his mouth.

Eerily in the night, the cry of a kittiwake echoed above the roofs of the silent houses.

Almost at once a sheet of flame leaped skywards from an abandoned fish-loft on the far side of the port. It was followed by the crackle of what sounded like small-arms fire and a couple of deeper explosions. Nils and Sven had started the 'diversion' that was designed to draw what remained of the garrison away from the harbour quays during the crucial minutes when the German MTB was due to surge in between the breakwaters and make fast. Until it was discovered that the 'attack' was no more than an unexplained fire, the Chinese crackers and maroons – a pre-war hoard treasured in secret anticipation of the liberation they hoped for one day – should keep the occupiers busy!

Already Bjerke could hear a confused shouting and the tramp of feet from the military quarters beyond the harbour. The guard was being called out and every available man directed towards the disturbance.

A shadow detached itself from the boathouse wall. "Bloody good show! You did very well, old chap," the lean Englishman in battledress said quietly. "Have you got the papers?"

Bjerke unbuttoned his pocket and handed them over.

"Wizard!" said Webster. "Now get shot of that Kraut uniform, find your friends and push off to cut the telephone cable linked to the base – but not before you hear a truck heading out that way after the ship has docked, okay?" He pressed the young fisherman's arm and added: "We couldn't have done our job without you . . . Don't forget to leave the English cigarette packet and the gum wrappers somewhere around when you cut the wires. That should take the heat off anyone living here and lay the blame for everything, including the sentries, squarely on us."

"And then?" Bjerke asked.

"Then you all get the hell out and hotfoot it for home and beddy-byes. If anybody asks, you heard nothing and saw nothing, right?"

"Right," Bjerke repeated, wildly excited now by his part in the operation. He was about to say more when he paused, cocking his head to one side.

Faint but unmistakable, the beat of powerful twin-screw diesel engines came to their ears over the crashing of the waves.

Chapter Nineteen

Rudi Lanzmann came from Westphalia. With his dark hair and blue eyes, he looked more Irish or French than German. Convinced, as he always had been, that he could make a better job of running the base than the Bavarian pig who was his superior – or even the more civilised officer who preceded him – he sat now in the HQ orderly room with a satisfied smile. He had acted on his own initiative during Bosendorff's absence . . . and now there were two saboteurs safely locked in a cell behind the guard-house. Two saboteurs, moreover, who had quickly reacted to Lanzmann's skilful blend of threats and persuasion to tell him all there was to know about their doomed and pathetic mission. With all their brutality, the Gestapo at Grenaa would be able to find out no more.

Lanzmann had in fact radioed the mainland before he rang the colonel, knowing what his chief's orders would be. There was no harm letting the staff officers know just who was responsible for this minor coup, and Bosendorff was quite capable of taking the credit himself – although not the blame if anything had gone wrong. Nothing could have gone wrong, though, not when Rudi Lanzmann was duty officer. He sighed and shook his handsome head. When were the Anglo-Saxons going to realise that they would never, could never succeed against the military expertise and might of the Reich?

An orderly tapped on the door. "Herr Oberleutnant? There is somebody to see you."

"*Somebody?* Well, who is it, you imbecile? Have you no brains in your thick head?" the duty officer snapped irritably.

"Sir, it is Fräulein Kraul. The colonel's lady . . . that is to say the lady of the previous . . ."

The orderly left the sentence unfinished. Lanzmann had risen hastily to his feet, smoothing down his glossy hair.

The beautiful Danish blonde was the privilege he had envied the young Colonel Breitner most of all. And he was convinced – there had been certain glances, certain nuances of phrase, an occasional, not strictly necessary, touching of hands – that had it not been for Breitner's rank, had the girl been genuinely free to choose, it would have been he himself and not his superior who shared her bed.

And now that Breitner was out of the way, that feeling was stronger still – if only the gross Bavarian who had taken his place did not seem to have the effrontery to imagine that he had the right to inherit the blonde's favours. As it was, Lanzmann knew that the new base commander often enough summoned her imperiously to his quarters to 'share an apéritif' – if not worse, the young man thought furiously.

But what was Fräulein Kraul doing out here now? Bosendorff had said that he would be coming to the fortress immediately: had she in fact come without him?

The question was soon answered. She came into the room breathlessly. "Rudi," she said, "Heinz Ulrich . . . that is, Colonel Bosendorff . . . asked me to drive out here with a message. It seems . . . you captured two spies, didn't you?"

"Saboteurs," Lanzmann said importantly. "Safely under lock and key now."

"That was very clever of you. Well . . . Colonel Bosendorff asked me to tell you that he has gone down to the creek with Major Frodenburg and the patrol to investigate . . . a dinghy, was it? Some kind of hideout? Anyway, he has gone there and he will come out with the naval escort when it arrives to take charge of the prisoners."

Typical, Lanzmann thought bitterly. He has to get in on the act! He has to have a piece of the action somehow . . . to take the credit at least for discovering the enemy's base, when it was Lanzmann's own interrogative skill that was responsible for the existence of that base being known at all. Aloud, he said stiffly: "Thank you, Fräulein. The message is noted."

And then, after a pause: "But why . . . I mean why trouble you to come all the way out here when he could simply have telephoned me from his quarters?"

Webster had warned her this would be the obvious question for a duty officer to ask. She was ready with the answer – and all the more assured because she knew it would soon be true. "He had been informed by a friend," she said, "that partisans could be working with your spies and that his calls here might be intercepted, or even the lines cut."

"Ah, so. It is in any case a great pleasure for me personally to see you here, Fräulein. It seems a long time since we met."

Irmgaard looked at him through half-closed eyes. This handsome, conceited and self-important young officer should be easy meat! She knew very well that he considered himself better, more efficient than his present superior – better as an officer, better as a German, better as a man. Heaven knew, she had often enough been made awkwardly aware of the lustful glances he released in her direction. Such a man should be vulnerable to the grossest forms of flattery. In any case, she had committed herself: she had no position to preserve now. There was (she recalled with a shudder of memory) nobody on the island he could report her to.

"Rudi," she said with apparent impulsiveness, "I have to talk to you. You are the only one who can help . . . It is so difficult: I never get the chance to be alone with you."

"Fräulein?"

"Oh, you must know what I mean. You are a man of sensibility, a man of feeling. We have spoken already, have we not, with our eyes?"

"Of course," Lanzmann said carefully, "anything I can do . . ."

"It's about Heinz Ulrich, naturally." (She must remember at all costs to keep talking about him in the present tense.) "You must have seen; you are intelligent and sensitive and . . . oh, what am I going to do, Rudi? Colonel Breitner was . . . very nice, pleasant enough company . . . but, not to beat about the bush, he had no finesse, no idea. Heinz Ulrich is twice as bad. He wants me to become his mistress, but I simply cannot—He would treat me as an animal corralled for his pleasure, not as a woman at all. He has not the slightest clue what a woman wants and needs."

She contrived a realistic catch of the breath, almost a sob. "I am really coming to the end," she cried. "I can no longer take it. I want a *man*, Rudi – but a man who *understands*. You would understand, wouldn't you? You're different."

She bit her lip, praying that she hadn't overdone it. Could he really swallow all that?

Lanzmann was at a loss for words. Here was a marvellous opportunity for the brotherly, consoling friend routine which he did so well – and which, he knew, could so easily be directed towards a more intimate relationship. But the girl on whom his colonel had set his eye? Could she really mean . . . ?

As he hesitated, Irmgaard slipped out of her fur coat and flung it over the back of a chair. "He says he wants me – but he's totally indifferent. To me as a person. When we are together, I just don't feel I exist as *me* any more!" she sobbed with a stamp of her foot.

The young officer swallowed. The sudden movement had quivered her breasts beneath her blouse. He could swear she was wearing no brassière: he could see the points of her nipples outlined against the flowered silk.

"Fräulein Kraul . . ." he began.

"Irmgaard. Surely we know one another well enough for first names?"

"Irmgaard. Naturally I know what you mean. I have eyes in my head. But . . ."

She moved closer to him. "Would you like to be in his position, Rudi?" she breathed.

Lanzmann threw discretion to the winds. "If only I could! You don't know what it's like, having to stand by and see a beautiful . . . watching someone as wonderful as you, withering through lack of appreciation."

She put up a hand and touched his face. "Rudi, you're sweet. You see – I knew you would understand. Oh, my God, if I don't find some tenderness and understanding soon, I don't know what's going to become of me; I don't know what I'm going to do!" she cried passionately. And, burying her face in her hands, managed to burst into tears.

After a quick glance over his shoulder, Lanzmann put his arms around her, making soothing noises. He was right, too: there was no brassière strap under the sheer silk of the blouse. He had only to undo those three tiny buttons at the front . . .

She withdrew herself gently. "Forgive me. I shouldn't . . . Do you think you could possibly get me a drink?" she asked in a shaky voice.

Once more he hesitated. He knew there was schnapps – but it was in the drawer of the colonel's desk, in Bosendorff's office next door. And he knew that she would know that too.

Brushing the back of one hand across her eyes, Irmgaard absently unfastened the top button of her blouse with the other, as if she was suddenly too warm. And indeed it was very close in the orderly room.

Lanzmann licked his lips. He could see a pulse beating against the smooth slope of flesh at one side of the valley between her breasts. Abruptly, he turned on his heel and opened the door to Bosendorff's room.

He took the stone bottle of Steinhaegger from the drawer – and found to his horror that it was unopened. Never mind: he would simply tell the truth. Fräulein Kraul had asked for a drink when she brought the message, and he had not liked to refuse.

He broke the seal masking the removable cork in the neck of the bottle. His fingers were trembling.

When he turned around with the glasses in his hands, he found that she had followed him and was now standing directly before him.

"N-not here," he stammered nervously. "Colonel Bosendorff—"

"Is being very military with Major Frodenburg somewhere on the north coast," Irmgaard cut in. "Then he is going back to the port to wait for the sailors, so that he can be very naval as well. The boat cannot possibly arrive before nine. You know that very well."

"Yes, but . . . I mean, we cannot very well . . ."

"Do I have to beg you, Rudi? A German officer?"

She was standing against him now. He could feel the resilient warmth of her breasts against his chest. Her hands reached up and gently coaxed his head down towards her face. Her breath played over his lips.

Lanzmann broke free. He placed the glasses carefully on the desk, strode to the door and closed it and then returned to Bosendorff's swivel chair. He leaned forward and flicked the switch of an intercom. "Schultz," he said hoarsely, "I shall be occupied for a half-hour or so. I am putting the lines through to you."

Chapter Twenty

The lean greyhound shadow of the MTB rode between the breakwaters on the back of an extra-large swell and nosed into the jetty with a sudden threshing of screws as the engine-room telegraph rang full-astern. A sailor in oilskins standing at the prow hefted a coil of rope. "Here, you – catch this and make it fast around that bollard," he called to the tall Wehrmacht sentry on the quay. Webster caught the heavy, wet line single-handed and hitched it expertly around the iron pillar. The sailor turned back and moved to a winch. At the stern, a second man jumped ashore and made fast a similar line.

From the flat roof of the fish-loft, Hawkins and McTavish leaped onto his back. The rubbery clatter of his sea boots as he fell was drowned by the sound of exploding fireworks and the shouts of military firefighters on the far side of the village. Before the man could recover from his surprise or cry out, Hawkins's arm was crooked around his neck and the Scot's bony fists were pounding into his belly. Having winded him, they turned him on his face. Hawkins placed a knee in the small of his back and strained the crooked arm towards his own chest. A hamlike hand rose and fell. For a moment there was a subdued and terrible struggle in the dark, then a sudden muffled crack that sounded chillingly loud. As the big sergeant allowed the body to slump to the quay, McTavish stripped off the oilskin, crammed himself into it and jumped aboard to attend to the stern winch. The two donkey engines whined into life, the drums revolved and the MTB eased herself slowly against the jetty.

Webster strained his eyes anxiously at the wheel-house. The boat wasn't really an MTB in the British sense: she was a *Schnellboot* – a fast, scaled-down version of the S-29 E-boat so successfully used against Allied shipping in the English

200

Channel. She would, he knew, be 75 feet long, with two diesel motors against the S-29's three, and a top speed of 35 to 40 knots. She would be armed with a 40 mm cannon, two 20 mm cannons and a couple of tinfish. What was worrying him at the moment, however, was her interior design and the number of her crew. There was no flying bridge, and there would be a helmsman and at least one officer in the wheel-house. Another would be in the chart-room behind. But all the superstructure was well forward on the rakish hull; he was bargaining on the hope that, unless something went wrong astern, all eyes would be fixed on the bow and the quay. So far as he could see, McTavish's substitution for the dead sailor had passed unnoticed. As he watched, Hawkins too cat-footed aboard and hid behind the one ship's boat that was slung athwart the craft amidships.

Everything now depended on their ability to deal with the deck crew silently. Apart from the three in the wheel-house and the sailor manning the bow winch, there would be two looking after the diesels below, and probably a bosun somewhere. None of them was likely to be carrying side-arms. But there would be at least another five men aboard who would have been detailed to collect Constantine and Hunter. They would be ready to disembark and they would certainly be armed. Although the flickering glare of the fire showed no signs of diminishing, the detonations of fireworks were now few and far between: any gunshots in the open air would be sure to bring the military hotfoot to the quayside . . .

Webster swung around and stamped his feet as though trying to combat the cold. With his back to the wheel-house, he eased his pistol from the deep pocket of the greatcoat he had taken from Bjerke. As he fitted a perforated silencer tube over the barrel, he heard a grinding of gears and an army truck, a canvas-covered Opel 3-tonner that Hewitt had miraculously hot-wired and stolen from the island's small motor pool, backed along the jetty and braked opposite the E-boat. The big West Country man remained behind the wheel. This meant that he had failed to swipe a German uniform that would fit him.

"Hey, guard! Where is the officer commanding this unit?" a voice barked from above Webster's head. He turned back to

201

face the ship. A dark figure in a gold-braided cap was leaning over the splash shield beside the wheel-house.

Webster sprang to attention and slapped the butt of his rifle. "Sir. Colonel Bosendorff will be here at any moment. There is a fire on the far side of the village, as the Herr Kapitan will have observed. Doubtless the Herr Colonel will make haste as soon as he sees the ship has docked."

"I should hope so. What kind of reception is—" The clipped voice broke off in mid-sentence. An angry shout had come from the deck just aft of the diesel exhausts: "What the devil do you think you're doing, man?"

Evidently McTavish had made some false move. The bosun?

Feet pounded the steel decking. Hawkins to the rescue?

Webster heard the sound of a struggle, followed by a choked cry and a heavy splash on the far side of the ship.

"God in Heaven!" cried the officer on the bridge. "Guard! What's going on here? . . . What is that you have in your hand?"

"This," Webster said, realising that the charade was over and the cards on the table. He spun on his heel and took aim. Flame spat from the silenced muzzle of the gun, momentarily illuminating the wet armour-plate of the E-boat's hull. The officer was hurled backwards by the impact of the heavy slug. He crashed against the wheel-house and then slid from sight below the screen.

Webster whirled to meet the deck hand, who was leaping at him from his position by the winch. Again the big pistol coughed its message of death. The man's arms flung wide. The shot literally stopped him in midair. He dropped heavily, flipped over the low guard rail and fell between the boat and the jetty just as a swell ground the hull against the masonry. There was a sickening crunch and a fan of blood sprayed over the E-boat's curved steel plates.

A second man had emerged from the wheel-house. Webster swivelled yet again to face him and fired from the hip. Glass shattered somewhere above. The dark figure disappeared. But Webster wasn't certain that he had registered a hit. He couldn't wait to find out now. It was four, possibly five down, and at least eight to go – more than half of whom would be heavily armed.

202

"Let's go," he called urgently in English. "Below decks as much as possible. Hewitt, follow me. Ziggie, stay in the truck and cover the rear." He ran for the low cruiser stern of the E-boat and leaped aboard. Hewitt raced after him from the cab of the lorry. Inside, under the canvas, Zygmund crouched before a bench on which he had spread Colonel Bosendorff's ID papers. In the glow of a shielded pencil flashlight, he was carefully copying the dead man's signature beneath the three lines of typescript on the headed paper Irmgaard had given to Bjerke. When it was completed to his satisfaction, he folded the paper, stowed it in his pocket and then lifted the canvas flaps to climb out over the tailboard. He walked quietly around and stood, waiting, beside the cab on the far side of the truck from the ship.

Aboard the craft, Webster issued whispered instructions. Somewhere below decks he could already hear shouted orders. Speed was everything if they were going to make it.

The four of them dashed up the companionway to the upper deck. They plunged through into the dimly lit, empty deck-house and then separated – Hawkins and McTavish scrambling down a ladder leading to the engine-room, Hewitt and his chief heading for the crew's quarters.

The battle that followed was brief but bloody.

Webster almost ran into a junior officer hurrying from the chart-room to the radio cabin. For the fourth time his silenced gun jerked in his hand. A scarlet flower bloomed horribly in the German's throat. For an instant he teetered against the steel door, clawing at the blood spurting between his fingers. Then he fell through into the cabin, dead before he hit the floor.

So far it had been straight killing, with no opposition. But it wasn't going to be all that easy. As they burst through into a tiny ward-room, a door at the far end banged open. Webster and Hewitt found themselves face to face with another officer and five men carrying Schmeisser machine-pistols. Webster fired one reflex shot and saw a cyclopean eye appear suddenly just off-centre in the officer's forehead before he hurled himself back into the companionway and dropped down behind the armoured bulkhead. At the same time, the explosive scream of the Schmeissers ripped out and a hail of lead streaked down the narrow passage.

203

For a fraction of a second he hesitated. He glanced across at Hewitt, whose vast bulk was crushed upright into the corner on the other side of the door. He raised his eyebrows and shrugged. No point getting hot under the collar about noise now, not after the shattering detonations of those machine-pistols. Every instant wasted would increase the risk of those men running out of the ward-room by the other door, gaining the deck and taking them from the rear. Snatching a grenade from his belt, he pulled the pin.

At that moment two muffled shots cracked out from below. Hawkins and McTavish must have settled the engineers. Drawing back his arm, Webster lobbed the grenade through the open doorway.

The explosion sounded like the slam of a giant iron door, a flat, metallic roar that sent a blast of flame and smoke searing past the two commandos flattened against the curving bulkheads.

Gun in hand, ears still painfully ringing from the concussion, Webster peered warily through the opening.

Brown smoke eddied and swirled in the dim light of a single bulkhead lamp which had escaped the blast. There was a stench of cordite . . . and something else. There were huddled bundles of bloodstained rags on the floor, strewn across a table, and plastered to the benches by what looked like a compote of dark fruit. In the doorway to the galley, a severed leg, still booted and trousered, leaned grotesquely against the buckled jamb.

Webster strode through, kicking aside a mangled machine-pistol, and looked down the passageway beyond. It was empty. Hewitt followed him into the ward-room and wrinkled his nose in disgust at the smell. A portion of raw flesh about the size of a porterhouse steak detached itself from the ceiling and fell at his feet. "Holy Christ!" said Hewitt.

It was almost the last phrase he ever uttered. Immediately afterwards, the E-boat lurched slightly as an extra-powerful swell heaved against the jetty. Hewitt staggered off balance – and the shot aimed at the lower part of his spine caught him high up on the right shoulder, spinning him around to slam against the wall.

Webster had turned to fire before the echoes of the first shot died away. But the dark figure gunning the big man down from the far end of the companionway had already vanished back behind the chart-room door.

As Hewitt slid cursing to the deck, Webster bent low and raced along the passage towards the door. McTavish and Hawkins were at the top of the engine-room ladder. "All quiet down there, sir," Hawkins said, jerking his head below. "What the fuck goes on up 'ere?"

"Under control – except for one of the buggers in there with a gun," Webster said tersely. "Bastard already winged Hewitt. Take one side of the bridge, each of you. I'll stay here. When I give the word, we all rush him at once. Right?"

He flattened himself to the deck and the two men crawled out into the open air and crouched down behind the shields surrounding the bridge wings. "*Now!*" Webster shouted.

Rising swiftly to his feet, he kicked open the door and erupted into the chart-room. The two sergeants burst in from port and starboard at the same time. There was nobody there.

"Shit, he must have flown!" Webster gritted. "We've bloody well *got* to get him before he alerts the army types."

It wasn't necessary. Zygmund didn't see the second officer creep down the companionway from the bridge on the far side of the ship. But he saw him dodge out from behind the for'ard winch and step cautiously onto the quay. The officer looked briefly over his shoulder, then started running towards the lifeboat-house.

Zygmund bit his lip. There was a gun in his hand . . . but the major had said no noise. Certainly there had been one hell of a rumpus aboard a few minutes ago. But orders were orders. Slipping a wide-bladed throwing knife from the strap around his wrist, he held it balanced by the point. He drew back his arm, squinting in the wavering light: the fire still burned on the far side of the port.

He threw.

It was a difficult shot, and he misjudged it slightly. The heavy knife spun through the air and it was the haft and not the point that struck the fleeing German between the shoulders. He stumbled, slipped on the wet cobbles and fell.

Zygmund landed with both feet on his back, knocking the breath from his lungs. The officer gagged, twisting wildly as he reached for the gun that had fallen from his hand. Zygmund stamped on his fingers. A high shriek of pain sounded over the crunch of breaking bone. Locking his good arm around his attacker's legs, the German brought him down and the two of them grappled furiously on the hard stones. They rolled over, clubbing at each other's throats. And suddenly the cobbles were no longer hard beneath them: they fell over the edge of the quay and plummeted, still locked together, into the icy waters of the harbour.

Zygmund splashed to the surface first, groaning for breath as the bitter cold numbed his diaphragm. Striking out for the side, he found an iron ladder stapled into the stone wall. He turned his back to it, hooked his elbows through one of the rungs, and thrust the German underwater with his feet when the man's head emerged.

The German surfaced, gasping, for the second time. Zygmund locked his feet on either side of the man's neck and pushed him under again. The water threshed and swirled. Frantic fingers clawed at the Pole's legs, but he tensed his muscles and kept them stiff, bearing down with all that remained of his strength. Gradually the struggles beneath the surface weakened and died away. When they had ceased altogether, he released his grip. The German sank like a stone.

Webster was waiting on the quayside to help Zygmund out of the water. "Good show, Ziggie," he murmured. "I was afraid he might have been the one that got away."

"He should b-b-be so l-lucky!" Zygmund stammered, trying to still the chattering of his teeth. "How did it g-g-g-go?"

"Noisy. All under control now. But the bugger you just got rid of winged Hewitt. The others are trying to patch him up."

Hewitt was lying on the chart-room table. They had cut away his sleeve and stanched the flow of blood, but he was in considerable pain. There was no exit wound. Webster assumed the slug must be lodged against the shoulder bone. Hawkins found a first-aid kit and dressed the entry wound, then they rolled him over onto his back and strapped his arm to his chest. Finally, white face bathed in sweat, Hewitt swung his legs to the deck and stood groggily upright while the big sergeant slung a Kriegsmarine greatcoat over his shoulders. Webster completed the picture by clapping a naval officer's cap on his head.

206

"Think you can make it if we prop you up on the bridge?" he asked solicitously. "Hate to ask you, laddie, but every man counts on this show; it'll stave off questions if they see a lookout. We should be back in less than an hour."

"Doan' you worry, sir. Long as Oi bain't expected to deliver a right cross, Oi'll be all right," Hewitt croaked with a brave attempt at humour.

"Back in less than an hour, he says! So there is maybe a fifteen-minute bus service on this perishing island?" Zygmund muttered darkly ten minutes later as he climbed into a German uniform. The rest of them were already disguised in whatever they could find that fitted them. Webster was dressed as a petty officer, Hawkins and the Scotsman as ordinary ratings and Zygmund, dried out at last, sported the gold braid of a naval commander because of his perfect German.

Leaving the wounded man leaning against the canvas dodger on the far wing of the bridge, they hurried down to the quay and transferred their supplies to the Opel from the hiding-place they had found behind the fish-loft. Webster took the wheel and started the engine. Zygmund sat beside him and the two sergeants stayed beneath the canvas cover in the back, each with a Schmeisser across his knees. As they rumbled across the cobbles they could see that the fire was still burning. "Thank God for those brave Danish kids," Webster said fervently, changing up into second. "Their fireworks must have covered any – shall we say military? – row we made aboard the ship. Let's just hope to hell there's enough tar in that fish-loft to keep the home fires flaming all bloody night!"

"It's kept the port units busy all right," Zygmund said. "But suppose we meet the others on the way back from their treasure-hunt by the creek?"

"Up the creek," Webster corrected cheerfully. "I fixed a couple of booby-traps around that dinghy. I don't think we'll be seeing them, somehow."

They were grinding up the short, steep hill out of the village when a hooded flashlight waved from the side of the road and two MPs flagged them down. Webster pulled up, one hand on the gun resting beside him. "Treat 'em like dirt; pull out all the stops in your Prussian routine," he murmured.

Zygmund leaned out of the cab window. "Naval escort from

Grenaa to collect prisoners on Colonel Bosendorff's orders," he snapped.

"Yes, sir. Your papers, if you please."

Sighing audibly, Zygmund reached into his inside pocket and produced the document to which he had added the commanding officer's forged signature. One of the MPs scanned it in the light of the torch while the other studied the front of the lorry – which, in a garrison as small as this, he must have known as well as his own uniform.

"Thank you, sir," the first man said, handing back the paper. "And your own identification?"

"Good God, man," Zygmund exploded, "don't you recognise the authority of your own base commander?"

"Sorry, sir. We thought we heard shooting down by the port, and—"

"Shooting? On *my* ship? The solitude here must have addled your brain, you dolt! A few flames from a burning building, a couple of fog maroons set off by the heat and you think you're on the Russian front! Stand out of my way at once. Carry on, driver!"

"Very good, sir. Sorry, sir. Heil Hitler!"

The sentries sprang to attention as Webster engaged the clutch.

"Heil Hitler!" Zygmund replied languidly as the Opel gathered speed.

Leaving the outskirts of the small town, it bumped along the dirt road leading to the base.

Half a mile further on, the track passed a group of farmhands' cottages and dipped through a wooded hollow. As soon as the vehicle had passed, Otto Bjerke and two other young men emerged from the shelter of a clump of alders and ran to a freshly dug hole on the far side of the road. A match flared to show the dull gleam of cables buried in the wet earth.

"Right," Bjerke said. "Just hand me those wire-cutters, would you?"

Chapter Twenty-One

"Double check with me, Ziggie," Webster said as the army lorry crawled with hooded headlamps along the road to the fortress. "The CO should be dead if the girl did her stuff. His number two has been lured to our old bivouac, where we hope he'll win the booby prize. The adjutant and/or duty officer is also being – er – looked after by Irmgaard. And the rest of the port garrison are busy fighting the fire started by our Danish friends. Right?"

"Right," Zygmund said.

"The E-boat is without skipper or crew, waiting for us to take her away, and Hewitt's on the bridge to give the impression that there are still folks aboard, in case anyone has a shufti at the craft."

"Which we hope they won't because after all there are supposed to be two sentries on patrol there, and they're not due to be relieved until midnight."

"He speaketh with tongues of wisdom," said Webster. "The sentries are in fact very definitely *hors* any possible *combat* we may have to face, thanks to the young Fisher King. The lines to the base should have been cut by now, so they can't call up reinforcements or sound any alarms. And the bloody excursions are left to us: out to the base and a clear route back to the boat. All we have to do now is gun down the johnnies out there while they're not looking, then lay the charges in our own good time."

"That's all, he says!" Zygmund observed. "A good time, he says!"

Webster grinned. But he fell silent as they lurched along between the dark fields. He was in truth far less confident than he appeared. It was probable that the fire would have been mastered and the hard bristling with hostile soldiery by the

209

time they got back. If they got back. The sentries could easily be missed: the MPs on the road had heard the shooting on the E-boat; they hadn't been fooled that it was fireworks; others could have done so as well – and come to investigate. As for the attack on the base itself . . . he shook his head. With Reilly dead and Hewitt wounded, he was two men short. Four short until his crazy plan had borne fruit and they released Hunter and Constantine from the glasshouse. Could they possibly get away with a supposed prisoners' escort restricted to a senior officer, an NCO – and only two ratings? When the prisoners were both spies and saboteurs caught red-handed inside an important and top-secret experimental base?

Well, Webster thought, they were damned well going to have a shot at it! At least the duty officer should be temporarily out of the way if the girl's subplot had been successful.

But even if they silenced the guard there would still remain a dozen men on the guns and a further five in the bunker – four if someone had come up to take over from the duty officer.

Speed and total surprise were in fact the most powerful weapons he had. Go in fast – do the job – get out faster: it was the usual Webster formula. It was going to be difficult, though – that was one thing he could be sure of!

Afterwards . . . hell, that too would have to be played by ear. But if they pulled off a successful sabotage act at the base and then got nabbed when they returned to the port, the operation would be marked zero out of ten: unless the batteries on Laeso were silenced as well, the mission would be a total write-off; they might as well have stayed at home.

If there was a second thing he could be sure of, it was that his original plan for a Laeso attack would have to go for a burton, scrapped lock, stock and perishing barrel. They might have managed to lie low for a whole day in a rubber dinghy on the open sea. But now that he had sacrificed the dinghy and proposed to steal a whole E-boat . . .

Webster smiled again. As soon as the sun rose tomorrow, the entire Kattegat would be alive with destroyers and patrol boats, spotter-planes and Stukas; instead of remaining an unexplained mystery, the operation would turn into something that would stir up the complete Baltic defence system like a hornets' nest around their ears. For they couldn't kill every German on Anholt and the news of the raid – and especially the E-boat – would be flashed to the Nazi High Command at once. If not a hell of a sight sooner!

Very well then: they dare not wait until tomorrow midnight to blow up the Laeso batteries. The O'Kelly – Fortescue timetable would have to be amended. As soon as the Anholt show was over, they would have to steam full speed ahead to the other island, silence the guns there *tonight* . . . and get shot of the E-boat before dawn. Instead of having more time to do the two jobs, now they were stuck with less!

Never mind: a 35-knot E-boat equipped with cannons was a handier toy than a rubber dinghy . . . and Fortescue's sub would have to run the risk of surface naval action – operations Webster-oriented – in the area. He changed down into low gear, and the army lorry began climbing the hill that led to the base.

One of the sentries came up to the cab window as Webster braked to a halt. The other stood before the striped barrier pole in the dim light cast by the headlamps, rifle at the ready. "Officer and naval escort for two prisoners, at the request of Colonel Bosendorff," Zygmund barked, handing the forged pass through.

The soldier scrutinised the paper with the aid of a flashlight, handed it back, saluted and waved them on. The pole rose, the second sentry stepped aside. They rolled through the fortified gateway and stopped outside the guard-house. At least they were in!

Webster looked at his watch. The timing was perfect. It was two minutes after ten o'clock: the four men on call would have started their half-hourly patrol, making their way to the far side of the perimeter. With four resting in their quarters, plus the two sentries and two men with the machine-gun outside the gates, that should leave only the two under-officers – and the duty officer? – actually in the guard-house building.

He followed Zygmund from the cab and walked past the blackout shield. Blinking his eyes at the sudden brightness of the interior, he saw a scarred desk, steel filing cabinets, a PBX phone switchboard, orders pinned to a wooden partition . . . and three uniformed men: two tough-looking under-officers with seamed faces, and a fresh-complexioned young *leutnant*.

211

Zygmund handled the dialogue beautifully, with just the right amount of haughtiness, precisely the right touch of senior-service condescension. After the exchange of formalities, he asked for the prisoners to be brought in. One of the under-officers unhooked a bunch of keys from a nail behind the desk, and left the orderly room.

"Little trouble down at the port?" the *leutnant* asked conversationally.

"Trouble?" Zygmund raised a supercilious eyebrow.

"The fire. My opposite number called me. He said they suspected a sabotage there too. We thought we heard shooting a half-hour ago. I was wondering if these prisoners are perhaps not the only—"

"Oh, that," Zygmund interrupted contemptuously. "A few kids' fireworks going off in an abandoned fish-loft! Such a story would never have got about if Colonel Bosendorff had not been away investigating the prisoners' hideout," he said recklessly.

Webster flashed him a warning glance, but it was too late. "The Herr Kapitan seems remarkably well-informed for an officer who has only just disembarked," the under-officer said levelly. "The news about the fireworks was unknown even to the men fighting the blaze."

"Menzel!" the *leutnant* said sharply. "You are speaking to a senior officer. Have a care what you say."

The second under-officer came back into the guard-room. Webster recalled that Irmgaard had told him they came from a specially trained MP unit. This one was shepherding Hunter and Constantine before him. Their wrists were manacled behind their backs, and a third pair of handcuffs linked Hunter's right arm with Constantine's left. They played their part well, shuffling their feet and staring at the floor in a picture of defeat and despair. Webster stared at them incuriously and strode to the door. He barked a command for the escort to dismount at the almost empty lorry.

Hawkins and McTavish climbed over the tailboard and clattered to attention. "Trouble!" Webster hissed. "Deal with the four men on the gate, quick." He turned around and went back inside.

"It would be interesting, also, to learn how the Herr Kapitan

212

happens to have a pass signed by Colonel Bosendorff," the MP under-officer was saying, "when he himself admits that the colonel is not at the port. It is equally strange that he should know exactly where the colonel has gone and what he hopes to find."

"Menzel, I forbid you to—"

"With respect, Herr Leutnant," the MP cut in, "I should like to look over this officer's identification papers."

The young man didn't reply. He was staring with fascination at the left-hand side of the naval greatcoat Zygmund was wearing. Following the direction of his gaze, Webster saw the bullet-hole next to the brass button, the stickily congealed blood around it. Zygmund must have taken the coat from the officer he had shot on the bridge – the first casualty in the port operation.

Three strikes and out, as the Americans say. *Finita la commedia!*

"I have the Herr Kapitan's papers here," Webster snapped. He plunged his hand between the lapels of his own coat. It emerged holding the Buntline he had tweaked from his shoulder rig. Sighting between the two handcuffed men, he shot the MP with the gun at a range of less than five feet. The man was hurled back against the wall and then slid to the floor. In the same fluid movement, Webster swung around and blasted off a second shot at Menzel. The under-officer staggered back, clawing at his shoulder as he tried desperately to draw his revolver from its holster cross-handed. The Buntline roared again, carrying away half the German's face in a cloud of blood and bone splinters before he dropped from sight behind the desk.

From outside there came a flat, ringing detonation followed by a single rifle shot and then the tearing-calico stammer of Schmeissers. The young *leutnant* stood ashen-faced, his lower lip trembling. "Please," he quavered. "Please . . ."

"All right. Hands on the head. Outside. Move," Webster ordered. Snatching the keys from the dead jailer's hand, he followed Zygmund and the terrified youth outside. Constantine and Hunter shambled after them. "Welcome home!" the Canadian said. "We were beginning to be afraid you guys were gonna miss the party."

213

They could hear shouts and pounding feet in the distance. "Achtung! Achtung! Call out the guard," someone shouted.

The two sergeants ran up from the gates. "All done, sir," Hawkins panted. "Grenade for the gunners; Schmeissers for the bleedin' sentries."

"And the machine-gun?"

"Sorry, sir, no dice. Buckled by the grenade."

"Fuck. Never mind. Can't be helped. We've got to get a move on. Up into the lorry, all of you," Webster rapped. "You too," he said to the German. He handed the keys to Hawkins. "Make him release Constantine and Hunter. Shoot him if he doesn't obey."

Before the last of them was over the tailboard, he was in the driving seat, thumbing the starter button. The engine burst into life with a roar. He had let in the clutch and sent the Opel careering around the outer circle separating the two rings of concrete buildings when the perimeter patrol came running into sight.

They scattered as he drove the truck straight at them. One, caught by the offside mudguard, was sent crashing to the ground. The others dropped with parade-ground precision to one knee and started to fire their rifles. Bullets ricocheted off the armour-plate shielding the engine, screaming into the dark. The windscreen starred. Another German slumped to the ground as a Schmeisser spat fire from the back of the lorry. Webster broadsided the vehicle around the final segment of the curve and stalled it just inside the entrance to the inner circle.

From here, their rear would be protected by the corner building, and the truck itself would shelter them from any sharpshooters on the railed galleries around the three huge gun turrets which rose like monolithic modern sculpture exhibits from the podium housing the bunker.

Constantine, freed from his handcuffs, had snatched up a machine-pistol and dropped off the tailboard before the lorry rocked to a stop. Flattening himself against the wall of the building, he inched towards the outer circle as footsteps pounded after them. When the two remaining members of the patrol rounded the bend, he stepped out and let them have the whole magazine – a tall, lean figure limned against the

214

night in the stabbing tongues of flame that belched from the Schmeisser's muzzle. The MPs were cut down without firing a shot.

"Nice work, Joe," Webster panted as they piled out of the vehicle and crouched down below the chassis. "The rest must have sent your bally chill packing! . . . Now listen – this block behind us should be the women's mess hall. Their quarters are beyond. Ziggie, you go in there and keep the little darlings quiet. Fire a burst in the air – tell 'em they'll be all right if they sit quietly like good girls."

The Pole rose to his feet, paused and then kicked open the nearest door. He went in blasting his machine-pistol at the roof, to a chorus of female screams. They could hear his voice shouting in German, and then silence.

An alarm bell was shrilling somewhere on the far side of the compound. All at once, pyloned floodlights flickered, then blazed to life around the inner circle, bathing the open space with brilliance, slicing the façades of buildings out of the dark. Webster swore. He pulled an ordinary service revolver from the holster at his hip and fired a single shot at the nearest light. The glare faded, turned orange, then died as glass tinkled to the ground. Coolly, he shot out a second, leaving the lorry in a pool of shadow and the rest of the area garishly lit.

He thought quickly. Speed was everything now. If his calculations were correct, they were faced with opposition only from the personnel staffing the guns and bunker, and from whoever might be in the headquarters building with Irmgaard. Had he followed his instincts, he would have raced there immediately, to see that the girl was safe, but the success of the operation as a whole must take precedence. No reinforcements could be called up from the port, because the lines were cut. They could on no account, however, afford to allow their assault on this central complex to develop into a siege. Hit them when they're not expecting it, fast – that was the way Webster had always liked to work.

Give the defenders time for second thoughts, to work out strategies, tactics, and they could be faced with grenades, mortars, anything.

He opened his mouth to bark an order . . . and then swung around with a curse. A slight figure had detached itself from the group and was running in frenzied zigzags towards the bunker. The young German officer, profiting from Webster's momentary inattention, was making a break for freedom.

"Shall I let him have it, sir?" Hawkins asked.

Before Webster could answer, three revolver shots cracked out from the gallery surrounding the top turret. The *leutnant* flung up his arms, pitched headlong to the ground, flopped once or twice like a gaffed fish and then lay still. A small cloud of dust settled in the bright light. "Silly young fool," Webster growled. "He might have known they'd be trigger-happy. Shoot first and ask questions afterwards, what!"

He strained his eyes towards the stack of three turrets. The two top ones were above the level of the floodlights and he could see nothing against the glare. The lowest was revolving slowly . . . slowly swivelling on their common axis so that the great gun barrels swung around to point in the direction of the lorry.

"Shit! Don't say they're going to fire those damned things at us!" Hunter exclaimed.

"Not a chance. They couldn't depress 'em this low," Webster reassured. "But if the guns themselves are facing us, they can pump small-arms fire down on us through the slits without leaving the shelter of the turret. And they can leave through the door at the back and get onto that gallery, blast it, without us seeing them."

As he spoke, flame seared from the apertures through which the huge naval guns were thrust. At the same time a withering fire crackled from the top of the steps leading down to the buried bunker. Slugs flattened themselves against the wall behind them, ripped through the Opel's canvas top, clanged off the armour-plate and dug spurts of dust from the ground.

Webster had hoped that only the officers and NCOs in the bunker and turrets would be armed. Evidently he was mistaken. It was a mistake, too, not to have shot up the switchboard in the orderly room: the base might be cut off from communication with the port, but the internal system still worked – and obviously the defence was being coordinated, presumably by the man who was with Irmgaard in the HQ block. He would have to swan over there and put a stop to that!

"McTavish, Hunter, Sergeant Hawkins: crawl under the

lorry and blast off a few rounds at the ladders and turrets," he ordered. "I'm going to try and squash that nonsense from the bunker entrance. That's dead ground there; if I was in possession I might be able to settle whoever's coordinating them from the HQ building. Joe, you follow me and see if you can post a grenade through one of those gun slits."

Machine-pistols and revolvers thundered from beneath the truck as he rose to his feet. He could hear the ricochets screaming off the steel turrets into the night. He couldn't throw a grenade as far as the bunker steps, but at least if he hurled one in that direction it should make the marksmen duck. Stepping out from behind the Opel, he swung his arm.

The grenade fell ten yards short. As the livid flash of the explosion stained the brightly lit compound with brown smoke, he crouched low and began to run. But there were still revolver shots cracking out ahead over the harsh stammer of the Schmeissers. Bullets scuffed the hard earth around his feet. One nicked the heel of his boot to send him sprawling on his face behind the body of the *leutnant*. Frantically, he shuffled closer while the dead man jerked under the impact of slugs thudding into his flesh.

Webster pulled the pin from another grenade, raised his head for a second, swung one arm up and over. The missile spun lazily through the floodlighting to burst with a shattering detonation in the entrance to the redoubt. There was no more firing from the top of the sunken stairway.

Seconds later, he was panting by the sloping wall of the great concrete podium that sheltered the bunker and supported the guns. Dodging wildly through a hail of lead from above, Constantine joined him. Here they were too close under the galleries for the Germans to see them. Warily, they began moving around the circular base of the podium. Webster looked down as they passed the steps. There had been five of them, as far as he could see. Assuming that the *Leutnant* had been called from the bunker to take the duty officer's place when Irmgaard did her stuff, that meant that the entire personnel below ground had been accounted for.

The headquarters building was on the opposite side of the inner circle to the truck, according to the information the Danish girl had given Webster. When they were level with

217

its door, they were immediately behind the three gun turrets above. Webster jerked his head at the spidery steel ladders climbing to the galleries. "Shin up, there's a good chap," he murmured, "and then bend double and toss one through the slit."

Constantine nodded, turned . . . and suddenly swept his machine-pistol upward. A shadowy figure had slipped out of the rear door of the lowest turret. The Schmeisser bucked and blazed in the Canadian's hands. The German folded forward over the low rail and dropped out of sight.

Constantine ran for the ladders; Webster sprinted across to the HQ doorway. He shouldered it open and burst into the brightly lit office beyond. Lanzmann was rising from his seat at the switchboard, the headset still clamped over his ears. His trousers were unbuttoned, his shirt-tails out. Irmgaard, fully dressed, stood white-faced behind him.

Webster's Colt service revolver and the German's P-38 Walther roared at the same time. The bullet from the Colt caught the German full in the chest, but Lanzmann's own slug ploughed harmlessly into the floor: the girl had flung herself forward and hung on to his arm as he fired. It was a dirty war all right. She was never to forget the look of betrayal in the young officer's eyes as he coughed his life blood out over the papers littering the desk.

"Get back in there," Webster rapped, pointing to the inner office. "Take his gun and shoot any Germans you see. And . . . thanks, darling: we'll be back to collect you later."

He hammered the keys of the PBX board with the butt of the Colt, ran to the door – and froze.

Constantine's lean figure was rising into view from the steel gallery floor at the left-hand extremity of the lowest gun turret. Squatting beneath the receding perspective of the giant barrels aimed at the far side of the compound, he lobbed something in through the opening in the armour-plate. Then, still bent double, he hurried towards the ladders on Webster's side of the turret. What he couldn't see – but Webster, through some trick of the light, could – was the kneeling figure with the gun on the top gallery.

Webster shouted desperately, but the sound of his voice was lost in the sporadic bursts of firing from the far side of the redoubt. He raised the Schmeisser and emptied the magazine. But the range was too great. The marksman's gun arm swung inexorably after the racing commando. Constantine halted at the foot of the next ladder to unclip another grenade from his belt. He straightened. The gun arm came up.

He began to climb. Flame blazed from the barrel of the gun.

The whole drama took less than four seconds, but to Webster, watching helplessly from below, it seemed like four hours. The sound of the shots was drowned by the explosion of the first grenade, which sent a blast of fire streaking out through the slit in the turret. Constantine jerked upright and fell backwards off the ladder. He cartwheeled once in the air, crashed on his back against the slanting concrete base of the podium and slid to the ground in a crumpled heap.

Webster had reloaded the machine-pistol and jammed the Colt back into its holster. He ran crazily towards the redoubt, firing as he went, before the Canadian hit the ground. The German on the top gallery withdrew inside the turret and slammed the steel door.

The commando leader dropped to his knees beside the broken body of his number two. Dust smeared Constantine's battered face. Blood had already soaked through most of the front of his battle tunic, and it was clear from the contorted position in which he was lying that his spine was fractured. As Webster bent over him, his eyelids fluttered open. "Joking apart," Webster murmured, "don't try to move. We'll get you out of here, old bean, if it's the last thing we do."

The ghost of a smile creased Constantine's sunken cheeks. "No shit!" he croaked. "Don't try to . . . kid me, boss. The big joke is . . . over." He choked, fighting to speak through the tremors shaking his body. Webster bit his lip, leaning closer to catch the incoherent phrases that were scarcely louder than the dying man's breath.

". . . worry about me. Good bunch of guys. It'll be . . . I'll be . . . Been a real pleasure, Major . . . Good luck, and . . . sink one for me . . . Göteborg . . ."

The Canadian's eyes filmed over. Scarlet froth bubbled from a mouth that was suddenly slack. The head twisted sideways and the rigidity of the body subsided. Cursing,

Webster thumbed lids over the lifeless eyes and stumbled to his feet.

Hawkins and Hunter came running around the far side of the redoubt as there was a renewed burst of firing from below the truck. "Mac's making the buggers keep their soddin' heads down, sir," the sergeant said. "I thought maybe we should try a bleedin' close-up."

"Good. The lower turret's out," Webster said. "Take one of the others each. I'll cover you from this side." He gestured upwards. The two top turrets had revolved so that their rear doors were hidden both from the three men below and from McTavish beneath the lorry on the far side of the compound. The gun muzzles now pointed at a spot halfway between the HQ block and the entrance to the inner circle. As soon as the two commandos started to swarm up the ladder, Webster raced around the plinth, away from the gun barrels, to keep those exit doors under observation.

The top turret turned with him, so that this door remained hidden. But they'd have to stop soon or the door would once again be within the Scot's field of fire. Nevertheless, Webster was on dead ground so far as the crews peering through the slits were concerned: if the top turret knew he was circling the podium, they must have a man outside directing them. He ran wider into the compound, to give himself a better sight-line.

Yes – a dark blur lying along the gallery floor, just distinguishable in the gloom above the floods. He brought up the Schmeisser.

Over the pounding, staccato detonations of the weapon in his hands, he heard a high-pitched scream. Something dropped and clanged metallically on the gallery below. Probably the watcher's gun.

Hunter had reached the gallery around the central turret. He sidled along with his back to the curving armour-plate, then turned and thrust the muzzle of his machine-pistol in through the slit from the side, raking the gun from left to right as the flames from the volley flickered redly in the gap. The top turret had stopped moving. Light rayed into the night as the rear door opened a crack. Webster blasted off a dozen shots at it. The light vanished and the door banged shut.

Hawkins was on the gallery now, approaching the gun

barrels with his Schmeisser at the ready, but there was no more firing from either turret . . . and suddenly the coughing of McTavish's Buntline also stopped.

Hawkins's voice floated down from above. "Sir, there's a white cloth hangin' out between the gun barrels up here."

"Tell 'em to come out with their hands up," Webster called. "Tell 'em there's a whole company waiting out here! I'll cover the door. Hunter, you take the middle and cover the ladders."

There was still a fair proportion of the garrison alive, he saw when the prisoners had been marshalled in the compound under the lights: the ten Helferinnen marched out by Zygmund, half a dozen unarmed cooks and orderlies who had been flushed out of the canteen and the clerical quarters, the three surviving members of the top turret crew and four wounded – a sentry, two men from the centre turret and the MP he had run down with the lorry.

"Take them to the guard-room and lock them in the cell where they kept you," Webster said to Hunter. You go with him, Ziggie. The girlfriends should have got used to you by now. Sergeant Hawkins – take charge of the party. And don't hesitate to shoot if anyone tries anything off."

"Very good, Major."

"McTavish, you're supposed to be an explosives expert. You come with me and we'll attend to the charges."

McTavish nodded, wiped a sleeve across his sweating brow and walked back towards the Opel without a word. Webster didn't know what to make of the wiry little Scot. He had played his part in the attack; he carried out orders to the letter; but his animosity towards his commanding officer was still an almost tangible thing. Webster tried not to let personal feelings influence his judgement, but he had to admit that the invective he had overheard in the bivouac had left him smarting. Was the little sergeant's disapproval, and the vilification it engendered, provoked by some Calvinist Puritan streak unable to support the idea of joyous sex? Was it a class thing? The ancestral Scottish hatred of the English occupier? Or did McTavish belong to that old bullshit-and-red-tape army school that couldn't stomach anything that wasn't done by the book? There was no way of knowing; perhaps he was a suppressed voyeur . . . or simply envious?

Webster tried to put the problem out of his mind as they unloaded the waterproof sacks of explosive from beneath the riddled canvas top of the truck. "It's a shame aboot puir Lieutenant Constantine," McTavish offered after they had worked a few minutes in silence.

Webster looked at him. "Quite," he said shortly. "But he should have kept his eyes open. How many times in training have I drummed it into you people . . . ?" He shook his head and said no more.

"What'll we be doin' with the body?"

"Doing? What *can* we do? Take him back in the lorry, I suppose. If the balloon doesn't go up at the port, take him aboard and bury him at sea. If it does, or if they suspect anything, we may have to leave him. No choice."

"Aye. It'd be a sad thing if a mon died for his country got no decent Christian burial."

"Naturally we shall do everything possible," Webster said.

The explosives were already separated into small and easily manageable packages wrapped in oiled silk. Some of the charges were gelignite, some plastic, some the compound known as C3 and a few a new colloidal substance developed by backroom experimenters working for the American Office of Strategic Services. Webster rationed them out. "You take the top two turrets," he said. "I'll handle the bunker and the third. Use the colloid for the breech-blocks, jelly for the radio and radar chassis, plastic for the ammo lifts, switch gear and levers. You can fuck up the big ball-races and the turntables the turrets are mounted on with C3. Is that clear?"

"Aye."

McTavish collected primacord, firing pins, detonators and the delicate wrist-watch mechanisms they would use for the delayed-action timing. All the fuses were small and exceptionally neat. "What time would ye be wantin' her to go up then?"

Webster looked at his own watch. It was just ten thirty. "My God," he said, "that was quite a half-hour! Set them for one hour and fifteen minutes from now. I want us to be well clear of this damned island before she blows."

While McTavish made his way aloft, he stepped carefully over the bloody shambles on the steps leading to the bunker. Down below in the air-conditioned gloom, a faint electrical humming stirred the silence. The sterile air was acrid with a hint of stale cigarette smoke.

Webster scanned the layout. Red, green and blue pilot lights glowed among the complexity of equipment lining the walls. Dials, levers, switches, transformers and junction boxes gleamed above the myriad multicoloured wires webbing the looms of computer banks in the pale greenish light diffused from the hooded radarscope screens.

Webster smashed the ground-glass plotters' tables and put the butt of his revolver through radar screens. Then he set to work methodically laying charges in the most vulnerable places, where the least explosive would do the most damage – wiring boxes, transformers, input and communications channels, cathode tubes and, above all, the memory banks and programme acceptors of the computers.

Fifteen minutes later he taped the last two phials of the OSS colloid, already fused and timed, to the breech-blocks of the 380 mm guns in the noisome, blood-spattered lower turret. Finally he packed plastic around the ammunition hoist and went back to the headquarters block to rescue Irmgaard.

"We're through now, honey," he began – and then folded his arms around her as she fell sobbing against his chest. Freeing one hand, he lifted the Steinhaegger bottle from the desk behind her. "I reckon you need a drink," he said gently. "Nothing can ever repay what you have done . . . but I do have some idea of what it must have cost you."

She shook her head wordlessly, but he insisted, filling one of the glasses on the desk and thrusting it into her hand. Irmgaard took a sip of the fiery liquor, almost choked, and then realised it was the glass Lanzmann had been drinking from. "I'm sorry," she whispered. "Only a few minutes ago, his lips . . ." Shuddering, she set the glass back on the desk. "He was a pompous and conceited man," she said. "A true Nazi. Even so . . ." She gestured at the body face down among the bloodstained papers strewn over the desk.

"I know, sweetie. I know," Webster sympathised. "It's not

exactly the way I'd choose to spend a Wednesday night either."

Soon afterwards they walked around the outer circle to the guard-house, Webster with the schnapps bottle tucked under one arm. The truck was waiting by the gate. "It's a bloody miracle, sir, but the tyres are OK," Hunter reported as he emerged from the cab. "Be a bit draughty in the back, though, I should think! We put the rest of the stuff in there."

"And Lieutenant Constantine?"

"Wrapped in tarpaulin. It was the best we could do."

"Right," Webster said. "I'm afraid we may have to use him anyway. I'm one prisoner short now. And I can't substitute one of you people: who the hell would believe in an escort of an officer, a petty officer and one rating! We'll carry him aboard openly, say one of the saboteurs was shot trying to escape if anyone gets inquisitive. What about our own prisoners?"

"In the brig," Hunter said. "And not too happy about it either."

"Super. I'll go and give them a farewell message."

The twenty-three Germans were jammed into a 12 foot by 12 foot cell with an iron grille door of the type seen in a sheriff's office in a Western. "You will hear a number of explosions in about one hour," Webster announced. "There will be no cause for alarm: none of them will endanger you. I imagine the military will come out from the port to investigate before long. Then you will be released." He turned and strode back to the lorry.

Zygmund looked through the bars with a smile. "Just like the Seventh Avenue subway in New York on a Friday rush hour," he said. "All that proximity already! I hope you guys and dolls are racially pure."

One of the Helferinnen – a thin blonde girl with big breasts – spat at him through the grille. The spittle landed in the centre of the swastika on the armband of his Nazi uniform. He looked down at it and shook his head. "You took it right out of my mouth, baby," he said.

As they were climbing aboard the Opel, Sergeant Hawkins said: "Excuse me, sir. You did say something earlier about a Heinkel seaplane? Didn't we ought to blow that fucker too?"

"No time now," Webster replied. "She'd have been a danger

if we were going to spend the whole of tomorrow afloat in a dinghy. But since we're trying now to wrap up the whole show tonight, I don't think we need lose any sleep over some blasted seaplane."

It was a decision he was to regret.

Outside the concrete ramparts of the base, wind howled across the flat country-side, buffeting the tattered canvas top of the lorry. They had gone about a mile along the dirt road when a figure in civilian clothes appeared out of the dark, violently signalling them to stop. Webster pulled up with a squeal of brakes. It was Bjerke, the young fisherman who had helped them at the port. "Take me with you," he pleaded. "Please."

Webster thought quickly. They had brought a spare uniform from the E-boat. One extra man might make all the difference to the credibility of the escort. On the other hand . . .

"I could use you," he said carefully, "as an extra member of the squad. Only I don't want you to find . . . I wouldn't want to make trouble for you or your folks. There could be reprisals on your family if—"

"I have no family," the boy interrupted. "My parents were killed in Flensburg. Besides, if I am missing, my companions will not be suspected for the cutting of the wires. I want to come with you . . . all the way."

A sudden idea came to Webster. "You're a fisherman. Do you know Laeso?" he asked. "I mean how the place is laid out and all that."

"But of course. Often we put in there in bad weather."

Webster trod on the clutch pedal and banged the lever into first. "Wacko!" he enthused. "Jump aboard, boy – you're on!"

Chapter Twenty-Two

The faint glow of the fire to the south-west faded and died as the army lorry carrying Webster and the remnants of his team approached the port. The leader of the commandos had been silent for several minutes, his brow creased in a frown. "Hawkins," he said to the big sergeant sitting beside him in the cab, "it seems to me that we've got our sums wrong."

"Sir?"

"You and Zygmund – you flushed out the whole shoot while McTavish and I were laying the charges, didn't you?"

"Yes, sir."

"And all the Jerries you found were in that cell?"

Hawkins nodded and Webster said slowly: "Then we're four Germans short. The guards, I mean, the MPs: there should have been a dozen of them. Four on guard, four on call and four resting, right?"

"That's what you said, Major."

"The four on guard we accounted for – two sentries and a couple of machine-gunners. The four on call were patrolling when we arrived. We ran down one, killed another firing from this truck, and Lieutenant Constantine finished off the other two. The four who were resting – we got two in the guardroom. *But where the devil are the other two?*"

"Well, they weren't in that bleedin' camp, sir, that I can tell you," Hawkins said. "We searched every nook and fuckin' cranny. And they weren't with the prisoners neither, now you come to mention it. You think maybe they got cold feet and ran out?"

Webster shook his head. "Not on your life. Those johnnies were from an MP detachment. Specially trained for guard duties. And whatever else you say about the Krauts, you can't say they're yellow. No, my guess is that they weren't

226

frightened at all . . . but they ran out all right. I'll give you one guess where they ran to."

"Fuckin' 'ell!" Hawkins said piously. "You mean to alert the bods at the port? They could've done too: we left the soddin' gates open wide. Cunts! How much lead you think they have, sir?"

"Enough," Webster said grimly. He glanced at his watch and gave the accelerator more boot. The Opel bounced and lurched, gathering speed along the rutted track.

They caught the two men up on the outskirts of town – twin shadows melting into the scrub at the roadside as they approached. "Should we stop and smash the buggers?" Hawkins asked.

"No. Shooting would alert the port garrison as much as they could themselves. We'll just have to shift a bit more and see if we can get aboard before they raise the alarm."

The lorry thundered through the narrow streets of the town and careered down the hill leading to the harbour. As they pulled up and leaped to the quay, Webster saw a group of soldiers off to the north of the lifeboat-house. They were milling around while an officer shouted orders: probably re-forming, he thought, before they marched back to camp after quelling the fire. There was nobody on the jetty by the E-boat.

Zygmund started barking commands in German. Hawkins, McTavish, young Bjerke and Webster himself slammed to attention behind the truck. Hunter, with handcuffs on his wrists, climbed over the tailboard and manoeuvred out the slack-limbed, doll-like body of the Canadian lieutenant. He stood supporting the dead man with manacled arms at his waist. The four commandos in German uniform moved in close and Hawkins lifted a hand to help prop up Constantine's lifeless torso. Zygmund gave the order to move off.

"Where the hell's the girl?" Webster whispered to Bjerke.

"She dropped off when you slowed down at the foot of the slope," the boy murmured. "She said you would understand."

Webster sighed. If Irmgaard hated goodbyes as much as he did, he supposed he did understand. Maybe she wanted to get back indoors while there was still time, to be in bed before they started house-to-house searches? All the same, he wouldn't give much for her chances, poor kid, when they discovered Bosendorff was dead. It was probable that someone knew she would have been the last person to see him alive; she'd had a rendezvous, she said. How had she killed him anyway? He would never know now.

Stifling his regrets, he goose-stepped forward with the others, marching the thirty yards to the E-boat, with Hawkins and Hunter now holding up Constantine's body under the armpits. Thank Christ, Webster thought, that there was a blackout and the jetty was unlit. But over the rhythmic clump of their feet they could hear a clatter of speeding footsteps from somewhere behind.

Men were running frantically down the hill. Voices shouted urgently in the night.

Zygmund brought them to a halt alongside the boat as answering cries came from the soldiers beyond the lifeboat-house. Hewitt's great bulk was visible, hunched against the port side of the bridge. "For Chrissake get a move on!" he hissed. "They bastards be comin' this way!"

Webster sprinted from one bollard to the other, casting off, while Hawkins raced for the engine-room and Hunter swarmed up the companionway to the bridge with Bjerke. The others, abandoning all military pretence, scrambled aboard any way they could, lowering their gruesome burden to the deck.

The gap between the ship's hull and the jetty widened from one foot to two feet . . . three feet . . .

"Hey, Major," Zygmund called anxiously. "The supplies, the supplies! Everything we have, explosives and all, is in that truck."

"Forget it," Wester shouted. "Plans have changed now we've swiped this buggy. Stand by to repel boarders!"

The German soldiers were running along the jetty towards the E-boat. The engine-room telegraph clanged. More voices shouted. A searchlight beam lanced the dark and threw every plate and rivet on the craft into blinding relief. And suddenly rifles and pistols were spitting fire at them from all around the harbour. "Please God we're out of this before they bring up the mortars," Webster said to Zygmund.

They stood behind the for'ard winch, crouched over their Schmeissers, blazing away at the nearest Germans, who were about to leap the widening gap between ship and shore. As the soldiers fell, the gap increased to five feet . . . and a powerful throbbing manifested itself from below. Hawkins had coaxed the two 2000 hp diesels to life. The twin screws threshed the dark water; the steel decks vibrated; and slowly the E-boat forged astern towards the opening separating the two jetties embracing the port.

In the wheel-house, Hunter moved a brass lever to full astern and spun spokes through his hands. Bullets were splatting against the armour-plate all over the ship. A machine-gun on the far quay chattered. A pane of glass in the windshield starred; another exploded inwards, strewing the chart-room floor with razor shards. Prone on the deck Zygmund and his leader inched their way back and then dodged their way through a hatch beneath the bridge into safety.

The E-boat's rakish bows swung once against the wooden breakwater at the outer end of the jetty, shuddering the ship from stem to stern, and then they were through – backing out into the heavy swell in the lee of the island as the searchlight and the twinkling points of gunfire dwindled in the dark.

A quarter of a mile offshore, Hunter completed a reverse half-circle and then rang through full ahead. The E-boat began ploughing north-east in the shelter of the low coastline. Webster went up to the wheel-house to take stock.

Hewitt had lost a lot of blood and he was suffering from exposure to the bitter cold. They made him as comfortable as they could in one of the tiny cabins. Constantine's body, and the remains of the naval crew-members, were consigned to the deep – under McTavish's disapproving eye – with the briefest of prayers dredged up from memory by Webster.

With the loss of one man and severe damage to another, they had succeeded, against all the odds, in a desperate gamble: the first part of the mission was accomplished. Crazy though it was, Webster's plan had paid off. But what about Part Two, which could be even more difficult and on which Webster himself hadn't even been briefed?

He took Bjerke into the chart-room. Bracing his legs against the roll of the ship, he went across to a large-scale chart of the area that was laid out on the table. "You know this place," he said, pointing to the outline of Laeso. "There are naval batteries there too, although the radar installation isn't completed. Those guns must be silenced tonight."

The Dane pursed his lips. "It would not be possible," he said. "Not the way you have acted on Anholt."

"Why not?"

"The conditions are very different. The guns are in an old fort near Byrum, the biggest town on the island. The emplacements rise straight out of deep water – and behind there are hundreds of Todt Organisation men building the radar base. They are in bivouacs among the concrete walls and the cement mixers and the earth-moving machines, with guards everywhere. You would need a whole battalion, with artillery and mortars and tanks and maybe air support, to destroy that installation."

"I'm not worried about the installation," Webster said. "That may be for another time. Tonight we just have to put the guns out of action – not even destroy them completely if that is too difficult."

"I do not see how. You could never get near them. Not with – how many men? Seven, one of which is already wounded and sick?" Bjerke shook his head. "Also, I thought you had left your explosives behind, in the truck on the quayside?"

"We did too," Webster said genially. "But I'm hoping we won't need them now. Or any men. You already told me what I needed to know."

Bjerke looked puzzled. Webster shouldered open the door and took him out onto the bridge. They clung to the dodger as the E-boat pitched and rolled in the swell, the wind moaning around her upperworks and shrilling through the aerials. She was built for speed, lightly armoured and lightly armed – as he had guessed, a couple of torpedo tubes, a bow chaser, two stern chasers and two batteries of Oerlikons between the latter and the ship's boat. But she had the one advantage Webster required for the final stage of his absurd gamble against time.

"I'll need your help," he yelled when he had explained it to the boy. "But with those . . ." He gestured towards the bow. "Well, I think we might be able to make it, what?"

Bjerke nodded. "It is a good plan," he shouted back. "If we can get close enough."

230

"Whatsat?"

"I said it was a good—" Bjerke paused, eyes screwed up against the battering of wind and spray. They were level with the fortress, near the tip of the island. Light was flickering redly on the underside of racing clouds. As they watched, tongues of fire shot skywards from the flat-topped silhouette of the compound in a series of small explosions. Seconds later the rumble of multiple detonations rolled across the swell . . . and then suddenly the night itself split open in a gigantic holocaust of flame. Blazing fireballs arrowed away to right and left or rocketed upwards through the clouds. The thunderclap of sound, when it came, cracked their ears.

"By Jove, by Jove!" Webster exulted as the reverberations died away across the sea. "That bloody plastic in the hoists must have touched off the whole damned magazine! Tough for those poor bloody Jerries: I told 'em they'd come to no harm. But what a super stroke of luck, eh?" Shepherding Bjerke before him, he lurched back into the chart-room.

The E-boat lurched too, burying her nose in a huge wave to send spray splatting against the windshield. Now they were clear of the point, the full force of the gale was hitting them. Atlantic rollers crowding into the Skagerrak had broken up into short, steep combers crossing and recrossing the ocean surface as they veered south into the Kattegat and the wind whipped spume from their crests above the shoaling seabed. The ship's slender bows canted upwards as another big wave swept past, its towering crest crumbling into foam, and then smashed down into the next to explode white water all over the foredeck. They dropped sickeningly into the trough, rose like a lift and then smacked for the third time into an advancing wall of water.

Webster staggered up to Hunter, who was wrestling with the wheel to keep them head-on to the seas. The ship was groaning at every seam, reverberating metallically at the impact of each great wave. "Any idea of the weather ahead?" Webster bawled.

"Dirty," Hunter shouted back. "Ziggie's been listening to the ship's radio. Force Eight, freshening to Force Nine."

"Bugger. How long's it going to take to get us there?"

"In seas like this? Two and a half hours. Maybe three. Three

231

and a quarter if it gets any worse. I've got to reduce speed, so that we can ride 'em instead of crashing through. It'll be a rough ride, but it's better than being on a level seabed!"

The bell clanged as Hunter jerked the telegraph lever back to half ahead. "Okay," Webster said. "You do whatever you think best, laddie. Actually I'm going to turn in and try for half an hour's shut-eye. Wake me if anything breaks, eh? Bjerke – you know these waters. You stay here and lend Hunter a hand." He nodded to the two men, clawed his way to the door and went below.

He stumbled into the tiny skipper's cabin that he had appropriated for himself, slamming the door behind him with one foot. The ship was pitching and rolling enough to make him reel about like a drunken man. He took the bottle of Steinhaegger from the pocket of the German greatcoat that he had draped over the cabin's one chair and laid it, with some difficulty, on its side on a shelf. Then he turned thankfully towards the bunk.

Webster's jaw dropped. "Well, I'll be damned!" he said blankly.

Sprawled naked on the narrow mattress, Irmgaard Kraul stared up at him with bright blue eyes.

Chapter Twenty-Three

They made love fiercely, hungrily, lips clinging and loins thrusting, as each strove to obliterate and drown the horrors of that night in the surging tide of desire that engulfed them.

Webster was lost for the moment in a world of the senses – he remembered nothing else, knew nothing else, thought of nothing else. He heard the creak of bulkheads, the hollow boom of waves thundering against the hull and the girl's breath rasping in his ear; he smelled diesel oil and sweat and the intimate odour of woman; he tasted the saltness of her body as he felt the bunk rise and sway and plunge just as he himself rose and plunged within her clasping softness. They came together in a blinding explosion of sensation that left them spent and exhausted, grasping one another savagely close while the catharsis of release sent the blood pounding through their veins.

Later, when the girl's small cries had died away and their breathing had quietened, Webster asked gently: "Sweetheart, why did you do it?"

"I had to," Irmgaard whispered. "It was not . . . just that I was afraid . . . afraid to stay, afraid of what might happen. I had to see you again. It had to be . . . the way it was before. But I was afraid too that you would say no, too dangerous for me, if I asked. So I decided to hide and come secretly."

"My darling," said Webster, "neither of us may see another dawn, but thank Christ you jolly well did!"

Cupping the softness of her breasts in his hands, he laid his head between them and slept. An eternity afterwards, wakened perhaps by the insistent throbbing of the engines or the vibrating hull, he rolled over on his back and pushed her blonde head down between his thighs.

*   *   *

Zygmund sat scowling at the chart-room table, his normally bland face drawn and dewed with sweat. Hewitt, incredibly, was sleeping. Hawkins had come up from the engine-room for a breath of fresh air and a cigarette. In the wheel-house, they could see Hunter and Bjerke silhouetted against the pale green light from the binnacle as they wrenched at the wheel in the heavy seas.

"Fuck me," Hawkins said, "but it's hot down there. You wouldn't think, would you, that a bloke could be too hot in a climate like this? But let me tell you: that soddin' dungeon's hotter than hell! It's a relief to feel the bloody cold. Anyways, hot or cold, I suppose we're better-fucking-off here than we would be in a perishin' rubber dinghy, right?"

"No," Zygmund said hollowly, "that is not right. By you, maybe, that is right, but not by me. By me that is not right at all. My dear father, God rest his soul, did not put me through college at the University of Breslau so that I should spent the last hours of my life bouncing up and down like a volleyball in some Deutsche battleship."

Hawkins grinned. "Why, what's up, Ziggie?"

"I will tell you," the Pole said. "Very nearly everything inside me is up. By me, you see, a rubber dinghy is all right. Maybe it is cold; maybe it rises and falls a little, but it is all right. Why? Because you are working so goddam hard at those paddles you don't have time to notice any rise and fall, that's why."

"You could use a solid bloody meal, that's what," Hawkins needled. "We ain't had a bite all day but that mess Hewitt cooked up at noon. Why don't you piss off to the fuckin' galley and do yourself a favour? There's some slices of würst in there, and a side of fat bacon that—"

"Sergeant, Sergeant, *you* do me the favour, would you?" Zygmund implored. "Just don't mention food – any food – again, that's all. Will you do that?"

But Hawkins was no longer listening to the seasick man. His head was cocked to one side and his eyes were screwed up in concentration. "Tell me, Ziggie," he said. "Do you hear anything?"

"Hear anything? You got engine oil in your ears, Sergeant. I hear wind and I hear waves, a great deal too much of both.

But this is something to make a song and dance about? So we should knock on the major's door, maybe, and give him the news?"

"We might even do that," Hawkins said. He rose from the table and fought his way out onto the bridge. Turning his broad back on the icy sting of the spray, he listened again.

No, he had not been mistaken. Over the howl of the wind and the roar of waves thumping the E-boat there was another sound, faint but unmistakable – a regular pulsing drone that came and went, somewhere above, with the raging of the storm. Hawkins ran back through the chart-room, hurried below, and rapped on the captain's cabin door. "Excuse me, sir," he called. "I think there's an aircraft circling us to the south."

Webster was with him in a moment, buttoning his trousers as he ran up the companionway. "Bloody hell," he shouted after listening in his turn. "You're absolutely right, Hawkins. It must be that blasted seaplane! Why on earth didn't I listen to you and . . . ? Never mind. But how in hell could the thing have taken off in this foul weather?"

"A stretch of slack water in the lee of that point?" the sergeant suggested.

"I suppose so. You'd better get back to the factory and help McTavish with the engines . . . Hey! Zygmund, Bjerke – stir your stumps and man those pompoms at the stern. Wake up Hewitt and take him with you. I'm afraid we may need him. I think we're going to be strafed."

The Heinkel seaplane made its first run before the tarpaulin covers were off the Oerlikons. Webster knew they'd be an easy target the moment he looked at the sea. Despite the whitecaps creaming over the wilderness of dark water, the E-boat was leaving a phosphorescent wake – a broad fan of lacy foam that would show up from the air, even when there was no moon, as clearly as an arrow painted on the night.

The pilot, nevertheless, was making sure before he dropped his . . . what? Depth charges, Webster guessed. The clumsy pontoons fixed to the undercart would rule out any possibility of bombs or bomb-bay doors. Depth charges, then. Fused for contact this time. Two, or at the most four. But it would take him only a few minutes to fly back and reload.

The plane banked and passed over them again. They could

see it as a dark blur against the clouds. Four hundred, maybe five hundred feet. Webster manned one of the pompoms with the wounded Hewitt at his side. Zygmund and the young Dane were on the other. They held their fire as the Heinkel came in for the third time. "Let the bugger think he has it all his own way," Webster shouted.

Hunter had started to zigzag, swinging the vessel in tight arcs that had her smashing her bows into the steep waves one moment, careening over the next until she wallowed broadside-on and her decks were awash. Pinpoints of fire twinkled from the leading edges of the seaplane's wings. Tracer and cannon shells splatted against the armoured shields of the guns and exploded among the upperworks. A blinding flash and a shattering roar a hundred yards off their starboard quarter. "One," Webster muttered to himself. And still he held their fire.

The pilot misjudged his fourth pass, pressing the firing button just after Hunter changed course, so that the shells passed harmlessly across their beam and the depth charge exploded half a mile away. He came in much lower on the next, raking the hull from stem to stern with his guns. The sea quivered and then heaved itself up into a monstrous tower of steam and foam a cable's length ahead of them. The E-boat appeared almost to stagger, then heeled over to steam through the descending cascade of hundreds of tons of icy water hammering her decks. Over the sound of the explosion they could hear the deepening note of the Heinkel's engine as the pilot banked and climbed away.

On the sixth run, the aircraft was lower still. It approached them from ahead in a shallow dive, with all guns blazing. This time Webster yelled: "All right, chaps: let him have it!"

The appalling clamour of the Oerlikons nearly deafened them. They could see the underside of the Heinkel in the stabbing glare each time the multiple barrels flamed and recoiled, flamed and recoiled. They could see the shells ripping into the belly of the plane as it swept overhead with a diminishing roar. And then suddenly the racket ceased and there was only the sound of the storm.

The seaplane continued in the same flat dive until it hit the sea a mile astern with a brilliant orange flash that tinted the whitecaps and sent a dull reverberation rumbling across the waves.

Bjerke was jubilant. "We did it, we did it!" he crowed. "We brought the filthy Boche down!"

Webster was less exuberant. "Don't be too hasty, handing the bouquets around," he advised. "We haven't run up against the real opposition yet, you know."

Twenty minutes later, as the E-boat rose on an extra large swell, they saw the dim bulk of Laeso against the night.

Chapter Twenty-Four

The attack on the second island passed in a whirl of activity. It was going to be an operation right out of Webster's book: straight in, do the job and straight out, win or lose. And of course the hell with the consequences.

The straight out bit might be a trifle dubious, but in any case he had no choice. Bjerke was right: the odds against them were far too long to attempt any kind of landing. The guns would have to be destroyed in a surprise raid from the sea. But shelling would be out of the question, even if they had armaments powerful enough to take out the batteries before they themselves were blown from the water: it was no part of Webster's briefing to decimate the local population. Everything then depended on the accuracy of the young Dane's information . . . and on Webster's own handling of the E-boat's manoeuvres during the next few minutes.

He hurried aft to check the engine of the pint-sized ship's boat and ready the craft for launching. Then he moved Hewitt and the girl to the cabin nearest to it. Bjerke and Hunter stayed in the wheel-house, Hawkins and McTavish were below and Zygmund installed himself in the radio officer's cubby-hole. Two miles off the island, Hunter rang up full ahead. It was 0330 hours.

Webster joined the helmsman and his new recruit at the wheel. "You must be swinging wide and coming in from the east," Bjerke said. "There is an islet at the southern tip of Laeso and dangerous shoal water around him. Look!" He pointed dramatically ahead through the streaming windshield. Black banners raced low across the sky, blotting out stars and hiding the late-risen moon where it hung over the eastern horizon. And ahead, beyond the white-capped crests surging towards the distant shore, they could see an irregular line of breakers creaming against the darker bulk of the land. Hunter spun the wheel to starboard. The lean craft heeled over and rolled along the crests and troughs parallel to the coast.

Ten minutes later they changed course again. And then, on Bjerke's directions, swung west and headed straight for the island. Webster could make out the undulating shape of the coastline, with the serrated roofs of Byrum gnawing the sky towards the southern extremity. Off the starboard quarter he could see a promontory reaching into the sea, a hint of houses crowded on either side of a valley, a rectangular mass standing alone that must be the fort . . . and something else. He strode to the rear of the wheel-house and called: "Ziggie? Did you find your way around that code-book yet? The buggers are signalling us with a lamp."

Excitement over the destruction of the Heinkel seemed effectively to have chased away the Pole's seasickness. "Sure I did," he replied strongly. "They are trying also to raise us on the radio. Some stuff about the local communications system she is all loused up and did we hear from Grenaa. I found the code OK. You want I should answer?"

"Yes. Do it by the book. Radio first in your best Prussian, and then the lamp. Tell 'em we've heard nothing and nobody had phoned with any information by the time we left Grenaa. But it may not do us any good: this tub is supposed to be on escort duty at Anholt – it's not supposed to be in this sector at all. And, let's face it, the whole of the bloody Baltic must know we swiped her by now!"

"The first thing the Boche do," Bjerke said, "they alter the codes, just as a precaution."

"If they know," Zygmund said.

"Of course they know," Webster said. "Even if the phones are out of action, they've got radio, haven't they? You just said so. And where d'you think that bloody seaplane came from?"

They didn't have to wait long to find out that he was right. Zygmund was busy operating the shutter of the Aldiss lamp on the bridge, the radio officer's code-book in his hand, when flame billowed from the upper edge of the dark mass ahead. "That settles it: they know it's us," Webster said tightly. "Zig-zag . . . Bjerke, Zygmund, join the others aft. Get the sergeants up from below. Tell Hawkins to leave her on full ahead."

They heard the scream of the shells passing overhead and then, almost simultaneously, the rumble of the shore batteries and the explosions of the salvo – a cluster of six, five hundred yards astern. "Next time, short . . . and then we're in the shit!" Webster prophesied grimly. The E-boat leaned into the waves, vibrating in every joint.

The second salvo did fall short, as he had predicted . . . but not by much. The seething column of the nearest shellburst was still collapsing into the sea when they steamed through it. The German gunners on Laeso might still be without their new radar installation, but they scored pretty good marks when it came to laying on a visual target in the dark!

Webster grabbed a Very pistol from its clip near the wheel. He was going to make it easier for them still – but he needed the light more than they did. He dashed out onto the bridge wing and fired into the sky. There was very little time left – perhaps only seconds: the time it took to manhandle a shell from the ammunition hoist, slam it into the breech of one of those giant guns and correct elevation and traverse according to orders.

The Very cartridge spiralled up into the blackness, paused and then dropped slowly to burst into a livid green flare that floated down over the island bathing land and sea in its sickly brilliance.

Webster was back in the wheel-house, hauling the rubber-covered handles of the torpedo target-viewing screen this way and that. Everything depended now on what he had noticed when he first saw the ship, the one fact on which his whole insane gamble had been based ever since they left Anholt.

The fact that there were two tinfish in the torpedo tubes ranged on either side of the E-boat's slender prow.

That plus Bjerke's assurance that the gun emplacements were in a fortress that rose sheer from deep water . . .

Yes, by Jove! He could see it all now, could see over the wavetops in the blinding green light the cardboard cut-out shapes of cottage and church, of masts and jetty and rigging – and there, rising massively from the sea to the right, the great wall of masonry topped by three huge pairs of turret guns. *"Right,"* he called, *"hold her steady now . . . Steady ahead! . . . Hold her there."*

He eased the handles a fraction to port. The crossed wires on the screen centred on the line of white frothing along the base of the fortress wall. *"Keep her steady!"* Webster shouted again.

The foam on the viewing screen flickered red as the guns above it flamed into action once more. Webster's hands swept down to the firing controls . . . once, twice. "That's it!" he yelled. "Now get the hell out."

The batteries bellowed.

The two torpedoes leaped from their tubes and arrowed through the water towards the distant fort.

The heaving ocean surface trembled. A spasm convulsed the waves. With a shattering roar, an immense tower of flame and smoke and water erupted into the air just off their bows.

The E-boat lurched. The Very light faded and died.

The night was blasted apart in a hell of heat and noise and screaming metal. A lifetime later, when Webster scrambled to his feet at the bottom of the companionway, the monstrous clangour of the explosion was still torturing his ears.

He peered through choking fumes, saw that the vessel had been hit just above the waterline on her starboard bow. She was already down by the head, wallowing deep in the water and listing so steeply that the guard-rails of her foredeck were submerged and waves broke over the winch and bow chaser. The bridge and wheel-house had disappeared in a tangle of buckled plates and twisted steel. Behind them, an enormous hole had been smashed in the upperworks.

Through the jagged edges of this, Webster now saw the sky to the west burst twice into flame as the two tinfish struck home. His personal eternity had been limited to the time it took a torpedo to cover the distance between ship and shore!

The dual thunderclap was hurting his head again as he reeled aft. Miraculously, they had suffered only one casualty: McTavish had been caught by the blast as he emerged late from the engine-room. He was lying in the wardroom in a pool of blood amidst the splintered remains of the fittings. Webster felt the side of his neck below the bloodied ruin of his face. A pulse still beat faintly there. Draping the injured Scot over his shoulder, he picked up his own greatcoat, which lay among the shattered timbers of the table, and headed for

241

the stern, where the others were already swinging the ship's boat out over the encroaching sea.

On the way, his foot kicked against an obstacle. He looked down and whistled. Lying on the warped decking was a square green bottle, undamaged, which had dropped from a burst-open locker. On the label in red lettering he saw the word Dornkaat. With a smile, he stooped to pick the bottle up.

They had some difficulty passing the wounded sergeant from the steeply listing counter to the waiting boat, but at last they were all packed aboard and Bjerke started the engine. Slowly, they drew away from the stricken E-boat.

Beyond her, vast gouts of crimson veined an oily cloud teased out by the wind above the fort. Webster fired another Very shell. This time the light was pulsating red, red as the flames streaming into the sky from the torpedoed emplacements. With shaking hands, he focused his field glasses . . . over the scarlet waves, past carmined fishing boats and vermilion sea-front buildings to the batteries he had come to destroy.

There had been no more salvoes after the one hit on the E-boat. But he had to know if his last-ditch plan had worked. Or whether the audacious run-in by the stolen E-boat, and everything which had preceded it, had been for nothing. The flare would mean their getaway was witnessed. But he had to know.

Webster caught his breath. The blood leaped in his veins. Anxiously, he refocused, bracing his legs as he stood swaying upright in the rocking boat. And . . . *yes, by God! It had worked!*

A whole section of the massive outer wall had collapsed into the sea under the pulverising effect of the torpedoes, exposing a warren of passages and casemates within the fortress. And into the chasm, one of the gun turrets had plunged in a knot of twisted, crumpled steel. By the light of the flames leaping from the rubble, he could see a second turret, distorted by the force of the twin blasts, teetering on the brink. The third was still in place – but the gun barrels had been deformed as limply as sticks of celery left in the sun by the force of the detonations. They were not totally destroyed, but they certainly wouldn't, couldn't possibly be put back in working order before the British submarine and her vital passengers had safely passed.

Webster's attention was drawn back to the ship they had just abandoned. From inside her hull had come a muffled thump, followed quickly by two more. A single puff of smoke hung above the shattered wheel-house. Then, as inevitably as the return swing of a pendulum, the bows dipped smoothly beneath the surface, the stern with its twin screws rose clear of the water . . . and the vessel slid easily and quietly into the deep. One moment – listing, crippled but still afloat – she was there; the next, there was nothing to see but a mill-race of tumbling foam strewn with crates and casks and eddying planks. An enormous bubble, filmed with oil, broke surface and burst as the flare from the Very pistol faded away.

The ship's boat was heading due east, chugging through the swell in the lee of the island as fast as the underpowered engine could drive her. Webster took the tiller while they attended to McTavish in the light from a flashlamp. "He is not so bad after all," Irmgaard said five minutes later. "The bang has knocked him out and there is much blood – but it has come mainly from cuts with flying glass. When we have clean him up a little, you will see."

"Thank God for that," said Webster. "It's about six miles before we make Swedish coastal waters – but we're going to hit the big seas long before that."

"It should have to be me telling you this," Zygmund interposed, "but I heard the Krauts on the radio before we were hit. And it seems there is a destroyer based on some small port around the other side of the island. They were alerting her before the guns started firing. Five gets you ten she's steaming this way right now: they must have seen us leave the E-boat before she goes down."

"Too right," said Hunter. "Under that damned flare we'd have been as visible as actors on a bloody film set."

"Stop beefing," Webster snapped. "There's nothing we can do about it. That second shell had to be fired to verify that we'd put the guns out of action . . . and we did that, you miserable sods! D'you hear me? We bloody did it! Mission completed and jolly good show all round."

A few minutes later the swell began to break up as they

emerged from the northerly shelter of Laeso. Before they knew what was happening, the boat was tossing in a maelstrom of howling wind and water. Although small compared with an ocean swell, many of the waves were fifteen feet from trough to crest – big enough to dwarf their small craft and threaten to engulf them at any moment. Webster wrestled with the rudder to keep the boat from falling beam-on to the huge seas overtaking them from the west: if they were caught like that, a breaking crest could capsize them in an instant.

Time and again, one of the combers would rear up behind them, its towering peak crumbling into foam, lifting the craft inexorably onward. Then it would go hissing past, dropping them sickeningly into the trough before the next surged up in its turn. But soon the roar and sizzle of waves and the scream of the wind were joined by a more sinister sound: somewhere astern they could hear the steady throb of powerful marine engines. Soon, too, each time they lifted to a particularly large wave, they could see far off to the west the dim grey outline of the destroyer they knew must be pursuing them.

Battered by the furious seas, stung by icy spray, their gunwales almost awash, they crouched down miserably as the boat ploughed on.

"Tell me one thing," Zygmund shouted. "How do we know when we get to these Swedish territorial waters? More to the point, how do the Germans know? They are a different colour, maybe? And even so, the boundary she is nothing but a line on a chart. If they pick us up on their radar, what is to stop the Master Race chasing us over and sinking us there? Excuse us, Herr Swedish Ambassador: it was a dark night and the skipper didn't notice. Most unfortunate."

"He's right," Hunter agreed. "It's not exactly marked by a picket fence and a striped barrier pole."

"Oh, yes, but it is, it is!" Irmgaard cried. "Look, please . . . over there!" She was pointing excitedly ahead. As they rose on a crest they could see, about a mile away to the east, the rakish outlines of two cutters, the white-on-red crosses decorating their hulls clearly visible in the moonlight diffused now between ragged clouds.

"By God, she's right!" Webster's shout was triumphant.

"Those must be Swedish coastguard boats patrolling the territorial limits. The buggers would never dare chase us over the line with those chaps watching." He glanced over his shoulder. "Christ, if we could just make . . ."

The destroyer was much closer now. A searchlight beam stabbed the dark from its upperworks, restlessly sweeping the waves. The gun layers must be seeing them big, centred on the radar screens; now they were trying for a visual, to make it a hundred per cent. Once again the runaways saw the billow of flame from naval guns, the white towers of water rising, falling.

It was just after this first salvo that they saw the power-boat.

It was being carried towards them sideways on the crest of a mountainous wave racing obliquely across the current: a high-speed launch with what looked like two men aboard. The crest hollowed, curled and broke into a flurry of foam with a sound like a shellburst, hiding the launch behind the spray.

Real shellbursts marched towards them across the angry sea, only a couple of cables' length astern.

The launch – friend or foe? Webster stared anxiously over the raging water – reappeared further away. It swung around in a circle, skating crosswise with its bows crashing into the waves, then throttled back and drew level with them as the rapidly closing destroyer fired its third salvo.

A disembodied voice from a loud-hailer battled against the gale:

"Ahoy there! This is the Liberty Boat for Göteborg – special tender for the Hotel Metropole: tickets free, pay at the door; take your seats, sit on the floor! Any more now for the Skylark?"

Unbelievingly, Webster stared through the spume. A slight figure in oilskins was leaning over the power-boat's counter with a grappling hook in its hand.

A boyish figure with blue eyes and an improbable moustache.

"Charles G. Fortune!" Webster bellowed. "For the love of God and all that's holy – that's Charles Goode fucking Fortune!"

It was then that he saw that the man at the wheel was Captain Seamus M'Phee O'Kelly.

Chapter Twenty-Five

O'Kelly shoved the throttle forward and the launch leaped ahead, its stern squatting deep in the water as the bows lifted . . . smashed down on a wave to send a great fan of spray hurtling out on either side . . . lifted again . . . then smacked the sea once more.

It hadn't been easy, transferring the unconscious McTavish and Hewitt (whose wound had reopened with the buffeting they had received and was causing him a lot of pain) but finally they had managed it. Then Irmgaard and the rest of Webster's depleted team had scrambled over the fluctuating gap between the wildly rocking boats. Shells from the German destroyer's small-calibre guns were falling uncomfortably close as they sped away over the storm-tossed sea, but now they had the heels of the Nazi vessel, the coastguard cutters were only half a mile ahead . . . and beyond them lay safety.

"You young bastard!" Webster shouted joyfully at Charles Fortune. "You impossible, ridiculous, conniving bloody bugger! What the *hell* are you doing here, you bastard?" He punched him on the shoulder. "Here was I, thinking you'd be pushing up Jerry daisies, and you . . . How in God's name did you . . . ? Tell me what *happened*, for God's sake!"

Fortune grinned. And then suddenly his youthful face grew serious, seemed to age. "Not dead, old boy," he said soberly. "Dead lucky, though. Those other poor blokes . . ." He shook his head. "When the plane was hit, I think I must have been sucked out through the nose. Believed I was the sole survivor, but met up with Renard and Crisp after I landed, and the local constabulary passed us on to the Danish underground. We – er – we helped them put up rather a good show, but poor old Crisp bought it just before the curtain came down. Then they ferried us up to Frederikshavn. Don't really know what happened there. I happened to be the one they threw back first – being the smallest, I suppose. Anyway, there I was at nought feet, nothing on the clock but the maker's name, and—"

"Hold on, hold on," Webster interrupted. "You're leaving me miles behind. *Where* were you at nought bloody feet?"

"Figure of speech, old man. Makes the story more gripping. Make sure you read next week's instalment of this compelling narrative. Place your order while copies last . . . all right, all right," Fotune said hastily, seeing Webster's face. "I was swung aboard this old tub in the middle of a load of sugar-beet. Before I knew it, there was the devil of a rumpus on the dockside, and we were putting to sea. They told me later that the Jerries had nabbed Renard and the girl."

"The girl?"

"Yes, well, you see, this Danish farmer's daughter . . . Dash it all, I'll have to tell you the whole story later. In the meantime a Nazi patrol boarded us and ordered a search. But by that time our Swedish friends had hidden yours truly in some impenetrable place. So although there was a lot of damage to the sugar-beet, the rotters never did know about the one that got away."

"But how in the world did you come to join forces with the gallant captain?" Webster demanded.

"Oh, that?" Fortune said carelessly. "That was the easiest part of all. We arranged that when I phoned the old boy from Denmark."

"You . . . you *phoned* him? From Denmark?"

"Yes, old lad. Actually it's not as complicated as it sounds. We'd raided this telephone exchange, you see. To help sweeten your Anholt show, we thought. And before she laid the charges, the girl dialled a friend . . . and, well, the outside line was still through, so when we got to the cottage . . ." Fortune sighed. "I think I *had* better wait and clue you up on the whole thing later," he said. "The point is, there was this hook-up through Sweden and I called Archie Lang and he put me through to the captain . . . and the captain told me to meet him in Göteborg last night and . . . well, here we are."

"As soon as I realised you were disobeying orders, and your plane hadn't turned back," O'Kelly shouted at Webster, "I guessed you'd be trying to handle both shows yourself.

Imagined you might need a spot of assistance with the getaway, so we hired this fairground special and decided to stand off Laeso tonight and tomorrow, watching out for you."

"How the hell did you know what to watch for?" Webster shouted back.

O'Kelly handed the wheel over to Fortune and squashed himself down next to Webster in the crowded cockpit. "We were warned about Reilly too late to tip you off," he said. "I was afraid he'd blow the whole show, but when the monitors passed me some stuff about a hijacked fishing smack off Anholt, I guessed you'd kept your eye on the ball. Then some friends of mine in Sweden fielded a raft of frantic Boche signals today and tonight – something about sabotaged telephone lines and *another* hijacked boat. So it wasn't too hard to work out the way you'd think: you couldn't wait around for twenty-four hours in a stolen E-boat, so you'd disobey orders again, put forward the timetable and try for the grand slam tonight. Very well, I said: we'll push off out there right away and see if we can lend a hand. Then, when we saw the fireworks back there— God, that was close!" He had ducked instinctively as a near-miss blasted the waves and showered them with spray. "Anyway, it saves me a second day and night's rent for this marine dodgem car. The accounts department will be chuffed."

Fortune skidded the launch around in a wide curve, jarring every bone in their bodies as the flat-bottomed speedster slammed repeatedly against the crests of the waves. "Wizard show!" he crowed. "Make way for the boy racer there!" A moment later, with the engine roaring, they dashed between the two Swedish coastguard cutters into neutral waters.

A vivid orange flash split the darkness behind them as the German gunners – almost petulantly, it seemed – scored a direct hit on the empty ship's boat before the destroyer put about and headed for home. Hawkins, Hunter, Zygmund, Bjerke and the injured Hewitt raised a ragged cheer. Fortune turned to Webster. "Didn't I tell you on that airfield," he yelled, "that we'd sink one together in Göteborg? We're just a day ahead of schedule, that's all!"

Webster grinned suddenly. "That's right. But no need to wait." He dived his hands into the deep pockets of his stolen greatcoat. "If the captain accepts: permission to report objective gained, sir?" He produced the two bottles of schnapps. "Steinhaegger and Dornkaat, sir: one bottle from each island, as per your esteemed order."

"Well, I'll be damned," O'Kelly exclaimed. He shook the stone Steinhaegger bottle and scowled. "I might have known it," he complained. "Knowing Webster. He couldn't bloody well wait to be asked . . . or get to Göteborg – not even when he's a day early on the blasted timetable. He's jolly well helped himself to a slug of this one already!"

He passed the bottle around. "In the circumstances," he said, "I think it would be in order if we killed this one on the spot." It was the nearest he had ever come to praise.

Feeling the fiery spirit course through him, Webster reached for Irmgaard Kraul's cold hand and squeezed it against his thigh. As the spray showered over them again, the moon sailed out from behind a bank of clouds and silvered the waves. She could see his lean, drawn face crease into a smile in the milky light.

They were chilled and wet and exhausted. Hunger clawed at their bellies. They had suffered death and injury and privation . . . and they still had to face more than thirty miles of stormy sea in an unsuitable open boat. But the true warmth lay within them – in the knowledge that, because of their sacrifice and their efforts, somewhere beneath these dark waters the submarine carrying the observation unit was now free to make its hazardous run.

And for Webster as leader of the expedition there was an extra warmth and an extra reward. As they nosed against a stone jetty at Göteborg in the wintry light of dawn, McTavish opened his eyes. His lips twisted into a smile. "Bluidy good show," he said, "sirr."